TOUCHED BY DANGER

SINCLAIR & RAVEN SERIES

WENDY VELLA

Touched By Danger is a work of fiction. Names, places, and incidents either are products of the author's imagination or are used fictitiously.

Touched By Danger is published by Wendy Vella

Copyright © 2017 Wendy Vella

OTHER BOOKS BY WENDY VELLA

The Raven & Sinclair Series
Sensing Danger
Seeing Danger
Touched By Danger
Scent Of Danger
Vision Of Danger
Tempting Danger
Seductive Danger
Guarding Danger
Courting Danger
Defending Danger
Detecting Danger

The Deville Brothers Series
Seduced By A Devil
Rescued By A Devil
Protected By A Devil
Surrender To A Devil
Unmasked By A Devil

The Langley Sisters Series
Lady In Disguise
Lady In Demand
Lady In Distress
The Lady Plays Her Ace

The Lady Seals Her Fate
The Lady's Dangerous Love
The Lady's Forbidden Love

Regency Rakes Series
Duchess By Chance
Rescued By A Viscount
Tempting Miss Allender

The Lords Of Night Street Series
Lord Gallant
Lord Valiant
Lord Valorous
Lord Noble

Stand-Alone Titles
The Reluctant Countess
Christmas Wishes
Mistletoe And The Marquess
Rescued By A Rake

*I want to thank my SPA girls' friends, Shar, Cher and Trudils.
Friends, critique partners, you are the absolute best buddies a girl could ask for.
You inspire and challenge me constantly, and long may our journey continue.*

*Alone we can do so little; together we can do so much
-Helen Keller*

PROLOGUE

*I*t is said that when lowly Baron Sinclair saved the powerful Duke of Raven from certain death in 1335 by single-handedly killing the three men who attacked his carriage, King Edward III was grateful. Raven was a wise and sage counsel he had no wish to lose, therefore, he rewarded Sinclair with the land that sat at the base of Raven Mountain. Having shown himself capable of the duty, Baron Sinclair was now, in the eye of the King, to be the official protector of the Ravens.

Over the years the tale has changed and grown as many do. There were rumors of strange occurrences when a Sinclair saved a Raven in the years that followed. Unexplained occurrences that caused many to wonder what it was that the Sinclairs were hiding, but one thing that never changed was their unwavering duty in the task King Edward III had bestowed upon them.

To honor and protect the Raven family was the Sinclair family creed.

CHAPTER 1

The sour taste in her mouth was so sudden, Essex Sinclair had no time to brace for the trouble that was about to descend.

"Forgive the inconvenience, madam, but I am about to die in your garden."

Essie leapt to her feet as a large body crashed face-first into her recently planted herbs.

"Cam, Bertie!" she screamed, dropping to her knees beside the man. Pushing her hands beneath his body, she struggled to turn him over. "Come quickly!"

She heard the thud of feet, then several curses rent the air.

"God's blood, Essie, this had better be good!" her brother roared as he approached. "Your scream had me hurling the entire contents of my mug over Myrtle's head. She is not pleased!"

"Help me, Cam!"

He dropped to his knees at her side.

"Christ, is he dead?"

"He fell"—turning, Essie noted a horse now eating the

heads of her carrots—"off his horse." Grunting, she used all her force while Cam pulled from the opposite side. The man rolled and resettled on more of her rosemary, sending a waft of spicy scent into the air.

"He's a big brute," Cam muttered. "And considering the oaks we already have in this family, that is saying a great deal."

He was a big brute, Essie thought, reaching for his head to begin examining. Parting the thick, tawny locks, she searched his scalp for bumps or wounds.

"Miss Essex?"

"I am all right, Bertie, but we have an injured man."

"Myrtle came into the kitchen with such haste, she collided with the wall, so I feared something was not right."

Bertie and his brother Josiah Hemple worked for the Sinclair family. He appeared beside the man's feet, his usually smiling face lined with worry.

"It's his side, Essie."

Cam had opened the man's jacket, and she saw the white of his shirt was stained red to the left of his stomach.

Ripping the shirt open, Essie saw the bullet hole, blood pouring from the wound.

"We have to stop the blood flow, Cam. He'll likely die if not. And that's if the shock doesn't take him. We must get him into the surgery now. Lift under his arms, Bertie and I will take his legs."

They soon had him off the ground.

"Move, Myrtle!" Cam roared at the shaggy dog that barred his way. "I'm sorry for your soaking, but perhaps your glower would be better aimed at my sister, as it was her fault."

Essie shot the animal a look. Her usually fluffy hair was smashed flat on her head, and she did not look pleased.

"We shall clean you soon, Myrtle," Essie said gently, which earned her a tail wag.

It was slow going, and even with three of them they labored with the man's big body. Finally they staggered through the doors of the home she had been born in, and down the hallway where paintings of her family hung in wooden frames, and marks bore proof of the seven children who had lived there.

The treatment room had been set up for her patients and would have everything she needed to help the man. Laying their burden on the table, they all drew in several deep breaths.

"L-lord, I thought your brothers were big men," Bertie rasped.

"He's got a few pounds on us," Cam said.

"I know, look at his feet, they hang over the end," Essie added, looking at the large leather boots. "Go and boil water now please, Bertie, and tell Josiah when he returns to make up Dev's bed. None of the patient beds will be big enough."

"Tell me what to do, sister," Cam said, stepping to the other side of the treatment table as Essie studied the injury. The bullet hole was on the left side under the ribs, and a steady stream of blood still trickled from the wound. Even if the bullet had hit nothing vital, there was still the risk of infection. She would need to clean the area quickly, and if needed remove the bullet.

"Lift him, Cam, and I will see if the bullet has gone through."

Cam did as she asked, and Essie saw no exit wound. However, what she did see made her sick to her stomach.

"Dear Lord."

Lash marks crisscrossed his back from left to right, top to bottom.

"There are so many," Essie whispered in horror.

Her brother studied the marks. "He's either a very bad man, or been sorely mistreated."

"No man has a right to do this to another, Cam. No matter their crimes."

"Some punishments befit the crime."

"Not this." She traced a finger over a welt. "They are old, and it's my guess happened when he was but a child."

"Now that is a crime," Cam said, and she heard the anger in his words. "No child deserves that."

"The bullet will need to be removed."

"Oh joy." Her brother lowered the man back to the table. "Just my luck I was the sibling present when you required a nurse. 'Tis my fondest wish that he stays unconscious until you've finished, because restraining this hulking man will not be easy."

Gathering what she needed from her supplies, Essie was ready when Bertie returned with a pot of steaming water.

"We need to wash the area now, Cam, and remove the blood, then douse the injury in alcohol."

"Must we? It seems such a waste." Cam took the bottle from her hands and took a large, fortifying swig.

Together they set about cleaning the man and stripping off his remaining clothes. Pulling the sheet to his waist, Essie studied the small bullet hole. She would need to make it bigger. She picked up her scalpel and made a small incision. Cam made gagging noises.

"Surely by now you have been exposed to enough blood and various other body fluids to be able to cope with a few more."

"Certain body fluids I am more than happy to share, others I am not."

"I cannot believe you just said that to me," Essie said, concentrating on the incision. "You are a vulgar man."

"I have no idea what you were thinking, sister, and if it is what I think, then shame on you."

Essie snuffled. She and her sibling were not the type to cosset each other, nor hide their feelings. In fact, they spoke exactly what they wanted, when they wanted to.

"Mop up the blood with a clean pad, Cam."

His large hand did so gently.

"If Lord Sinclair was here, he'd bang both your heads together," Bertie said from the foot of the bed.

"Ah, but he is not, therefore we are at liberty to speak as we wish, Bertie," Cam said.

"Now I need to find the bullet."

"Have you done this before, Ess?"

"Yes, four times, and it's never pleasant. Hand me those forceps."

"Yes, doctor."

It was not an easy task digging around for a small piece of lead. It could have gone anywhere, and done considerable damage. Blood started pumping, and Cam staunched it as best he could. Bertie stood in readiness to hand them whatever was required.

"It's like eeling in the pond," Essie muttered.

"You have no idea what's beneath you?"

"Yes." Relief made her knees weak as she located the bullet and eased it from his body, but as it pulled free, the blood started flowing fast.

"I need your strength now, Cam. Hurry! I'm not sure this man will live the night if I do not succeed in staunching the blood flow."

Cam came to her side. His hand slipped beneath her hair and touched the back of her neck. She felt the shiver of power that came when her siblings touched her. They were stronger together, and had proved it many times.

She applied pressure, and several tense minutes later the blood flow eased.

"Thank God," Essie whispered. Now the imminent danger had passed, she felt fear grip her, as it always did when a patient's life was in her hands.

"I'm proud to have you as my sister, Essex Sinclair."

"Thank you," she whispered, and the hand on her neck squeezed gently. He softly kissed her head.

She cleaned the wound and doused it in spirits once more.

"Such a small thing to cause so much pain and heartache." Essie inspected the bullet.

"A necessary evil I'm afraid, sister dear."

Essie quickly closed the hole with seven neat stitches, and then placed a clean pad over it while she got what she needed to bandage it.

"I always get a jolt when I see you doing things like this," Cam said. She glanced up at him. The Sinclair green eyes were studying her intently.

Like all seven siblings, he had dark hair. Tall, he was not as large as their eldest brother, Dev, but still a considerable height and weight.

"You're the gentle sister. The one we go to when we need an 'awww, there there, everything is all right,' so when I see you extracting a bullet from an unconscious man, it throws me."

"Awww, there there, brother, everything will be all right."

Cam snorted. "But seriously, you're amazing, Essie. I just wanted you to know."

"I'll take that compliment, and I love you too, brother."

Now she needed to check for further injuries. Taking her first real look at him, Essie studied the still face. A thick mane of tawny hair would reach his shoulders when upright. His skin was tanned, suggesting hours spent in the sun. The sharp edges and lines of his cheekbones were more exposed with him lying down, and could have been carved from stone. His nose was crooked and large, dark lashes were thick. His chest was broad and defined with muscle; bending for a closer look, Essie noted several old scars on his torso. Some crisscrossed, others were straight. This man had lived a hard life, was her guess.

"A seaman, perhaps?" Cam said. He turned over the man's hands and saw they had calluses. "Some form of manual labor is my guess. The marks to his body suggest this man has seen some tough times in his life."

"Do you recognize him at all, Cam?"

"No, never seen him before. But one thing I do know is that if he lives, it is solely due to you."

Had he deserved his fate? Shaking her head, Essie pushed that thought aside. No one deserved to be shot and die as a result. Or maybe some did. She thought back to one man who had deserved that and more.

"Maybe you could get him something to wear, Cam?"

"It's not enough that I must help patch him up, I must now clothe him also?" he tutted. She watched him turn, then stop.

"I said I was sorry, Myrtle. Have mercy and forgive me, sweetheart."

"Is she looking at you?"

"With eyes that suggest I have taken her last bone," Cam muttered. "I have to say her hair like that reminds me of Squire Fudge. You know he has it carefully arranged to cover the bald patches."

Essie rolled her eyes as her brother left the room, and returned to the man. She started with his head and then worked slowly down his body. He was a handsome devil, and for the first time in many months, a flutter in her pulse made her aware of just how handsome. But she no longer cared for that. Her first and only experience with a man had ended in disaster. He had been handsome, and she'd thought kind. Words had flowed from his mouth and hypnotized her.

"And I will never again allow that to happen," she whispered. "No man will make a fool of me a second time."

When she was sure the bullet wound was the only injury, she took a small bowl and began to walk down her rows of jars, selecting the ingredients for the tisane she would try and pour down his throat. She mixed them with a small amount of hot water, then set it on the rack to stay warm. Next she prepared something for the pain he was sure to wake with... if he woke.

"Christ!"

Essie hurried back to her patient at his gruff curse. His eyes were open, the tawny brown depths filled with pain. She'd seen eyes like that before, in a painting of a lion. The sun was lowering in the sky, but there was still enough light from the windows to pick up the flecks of amber in the iris. Essie was used to the unusual, being from a family that stood outside what was termed normal, yet she had never seen eyes like this on a human. In fact, this man was surely a lion in every way, big and strong. She could feel the power beneath her fingers as she touched the cords of muscle in his arms to soothe him.

"I will give you something for the pain. Rest now," Essie said in the gentle voice she reserved for her patients.

"Who are you?" His fingers wrapped around her wrist and held her as she would have turned away. The grip was surprisingly strong, considering his injury.

"Miss Sinclair, sir. Now do not move, as you will start the wound bleeding again. Release me please."

He did, and she placed an arm beneath his shoulders and helped him upright.

"A few mouthfuls will help with the pain."

He drank and then wrinkled his nose.

"More."

"It is foul."

"And yet good for you, so you will drink every drop." Essie had three brothers and three sisters, and she had coaxed even the most reluctant of her siblings to take medicine when required.

His eyes looked at her over the rim as he did what she asked. The tawny depths were intent as he studied her. Ignoring the flutter in her pulse, she lay him back on the bed.

"Rest now," Essie soothed, brushing the hair from his forehead in a gesture as natural as breathing to her.

"Where am I?"

"Oak's Knoll is my home, and sits at the foot of Raven Mountain."

"Someone tried to kill me," he rasped, pain filling his incredible eyes as he attempted to move. "I must leave here now."

"I have just removed a bullet from your side, sir; to move now would be foolish indeed. Therefore, please lie still while I finish dressing your wound."

Essie felt his eyes on her as she walked back to her supplies to get the jar of her special paste. Returning once again, she said, "This may cause you some discomfort when I apply it, but I fear without it the risk of infection is greater."

He nodded but remained silent, and she began to apply the paste to the wound. He winced, but otherwise remained still until she had finished, not an easy task for anyone. Her siblings usually moaned and made a lot of fuss when she applied it to their cuts. This man, however, understood pain; his back had shown her that. Their eyes met and held, and something passed between them. Attraction? Awareness? Essie didn't know what it was, but it was unsettling. She was relieved Cam chose that moment to walk back into the room.

"I have a nightshirt of Dev's that should fit. No point in using mine when I don't have to."

"This is my brother, Mr. Sinclair," Essie said.

"Hello." Cam leaned over him.

The man studied him for several seconds before nodding.

"Can you give me your name?"

"Max."

"And I am Cam, and this is Essex."

It was natural for Cam to give their first names here in Oak's Knoll. In London, they were Mr. and Miss Sinclair, but not here.

"Lift him up so I can bandage the wound, Cam."

Max flinched as she touched his back, but Essie kept her expression calm, giving no indication she had seen the welts. He grunted as she eased her hand beneath his waist, but did not move as she finished bandaging him.

"I must leave here tonight."

"If you leave you will make it no further than the gate, sir, and will probably undo all the work I have done."

"Be a silly move, old man, to leave now when you're in this state. Best to listen to my sister's advice, as she has just fished out a bullet and stitched you up. In all likelihood she has just saved your life."

"Yet I must try," he said, starting to rise.

"Is there danger here for you and us?" Cam asked.

"No." Max shook his head. "But still I must go."

Essie watched the blanket slip, and reached to help him, but her hand touched his side and he yelped and fell back on the bed, his breathing harsh.

"Y-you did that on p-purpose."

"I would never willingly hurt someone!" Essie gasped. He

glared at her, and then his eyes rolled up in his head as he once again slumped into unconsciousness.

"Well," Cam said, "at least he's out, so we can move him to the bed now."

"He accused me of hurting him." Essie looked down at the man. "As if I would do such a thing."

"Ungrateful is what he is. Now here is Bertie, we shall carry him to Dev's room."

Between them they soon had him dressed and settled in their brother's bed.

"And now you will both come away and eat something, especially you, Miss Essex, as I'm sure it will be a long night."

"Lord yes, I've been smelling whatever you have cooking for the last few hours," Cam said.

Nodding to Bertie, she gave the patient one last look, and left the room behind her brother.

Josiah and Bertie Hemple had lived with the Sinclair family for as long as Essie could remember. Both widowed, they had come because Essie's uncle wanted someone looking after his nieces and nephews that he trusted. Especially as their own father could not be relied upon to provide for his children. Now that they only resided here for a few months of the year, and then only she and Cam, and sometimes their little siblings, the brothers had the house to themselves for most of the year.

Her brother had also insisted that for propriety's sake she bring her maid, Grace, with her from London. So often when she was here alone, there were three servants watching over her. Ridiculous, as she had pointed out, but Devon, her eldest brother, would not yield in this. He was extremely protective of his family.

"Do you think the fever will take hold?" Josiah asked as he placed a bowl filled with the enticing aromas of beef stew in front of Essie. He was a replica of his brother; both men were of average height and of stout build, with gray hair.

They sat at a sturdy wooden table near the fire in the dining room. The table still bore the marks of their childhood, and she felt the usual pang of longing for the rest of her siblings as she looked at it, remembering a time when they had been seated like peas in a pod.

"I hope not, but in truth there is no way of knowing."

"Eat the bread too," Josiah said, nudging it closer to her plate.

"There is no equal to you in this, Josiah," Cam said, spooning in a large mouthful. "I have found nothing in London to match this stew."

"And believe me, he has tried," Essie said. She took a mouthful and let her senses adjust to the taste as she identified each ingredient. Like her siblings, Essie had a heightened sense, and hers was taste. Anything too sweet or sour, anything off, would taste twice, three times as strong as it would for other people. She was always careful to take a small bite of anything new to ensure her senses would not be overwhelmed with what she was eating.

"It's a simple stew, Miss Essex, have no fear."

"I never fear when you are cooking, Josiah."

Cam sniffed the air and sighed. His heightened sense was smell; he was like a bloodhound when walking the streets of London. Woman who wore too much scent made him shudder, and food that was off made him turn green.

"We are to leave for London soon, Essie."

"I will need to ensure he has recovered fully, Cam. Surely you can see that?"

"We shall discuss this tomorrow evening, and remember Aunt has her ball coming up; and needs our help with preparations."

"No, she doesn't," Essie said. "Aunt has been organizing

balls since before we were born. She just said she wanted our help to lure us back to London to attend."

Her brother smiled, flashing his white teeth. It softened his face and removed the cynical edge he often wore. Life had played its hand on the Sinclairs, but none more so than Cam.

"Likely you're right, but as I wish to attend I have no problem with that."

"I know you have a particular liking for Miss Priscilla Partridge, which is why you wish to return to London, and I would not want to stand in the way of true love," Essie teased her brother.

"Indeed, she is a lovely young woman," Cam mused as he used a large chunk of bread to clean his bowl. "However, there is that small matter of her perfume, which is off-putting."

"It's perfume, Cam, not body odor."

"True," he mused. "And she does have nice... eyes."

Essie snorted, knowing full well that Miss Priscilla Partridge had large breasts.

"I pity the poor woman who eventually ends up with you as her husband."

"She will be a woman envied by many. I am considered something of a catch, you know."

His black hair needed a trim and hung over his eyes, his shirt was open at the neck, and he wore no waistcoat. They were always like that here, and never stood on ceremony. He looked handsome and healthy, and as the latter was not something he had always been, her heart was happy to see it.

"Really? I wonder when that happened, as on my last visit to London I heard nothing to indicate it was the case."

"Heartless wretch, you know very well I am in high regard."

"And so humble."

Cam smiled, and she understood what set young ladies giggling. There was a wicked glint in his green eyes that could not quite be trusted. Of course she would trust him with her life, but she was not a silly young lady, just his sister.

"Myrtle adores me, anyway. I just fed her some stew, and all is forgiven."

"You'll not be feeding that hairy beast from my table." Josiah scowled.

"That is no way to talk about your brother, Josiah." Cam winked at Bertie as he got to his feet. "Now, if my nursing duties are over, I shall retire and get an early night. I must look my best for our return to London."

"I can't leave him if he is not well, Cam."

He kissed her head. "I know, love, but he may be stable in a day or two, and then Josiah and Bertie can watch over him. Make sure you get some sleep."

"I will." Essie squeezed the hand he held out to her. They had grown closer since Dev and Eden, their siblings, had both wed. Their younger siblings were still in the schoolroom.

She watched his tall form leave the room as her thoughts returned to her aunt and uncle's ball. She knew they were hosting the event in hopes of finding her a husband. Of course she'd told them she had no wish to marry, but her aunt did not believe her.

It was all right for Cam to be still unwed, as he was a man and therefore it did not matter when he chose to marry, as time was on his side. She, however, was fast approaching spinsterhood, which pleased her, but no one else. Ignoring the pang of disappointment that she would never have a family of her own, she too got to her feet. She would have her siblings' children to spoil, and that would be enough.

"That was a wonderful meal, thank you, and now I will check the patient."

"And no doubt we will find you there in the morning," Josiah said.

"I shall try to find my bed, I promise," Essie lied. "Tell Grace not to wait for me," she added, knowing that otherwise her maid would have a long wait.

She carried a candle down the hall to Dev's room. Heading straight to the bed, she found the patient sleeping. Laying a hand on his forehead, she felt the heat. Not too hot, and yet hotter than he should be. She hoped this did not mean a fever was coming. She checked the bandage, and found it was still clean.

Expelling a breath she had not known she was holding, Essie decided to read for a while, and then she would wake him to take more medicine. She reached for a medical treatise, and sank into the deep chair that her brother had often sat in while reading to his younger siblings. Soon she was lost in the world of medicine, one of her favorite places to be.

CHAPTER 2

Something woke Essie. Stretching, she knew instantly where she was, as she had spent many nights sitting with her patients. Stoking the fire back to life, she then lit the branch of candles she had put beside her chair and carried it with her to check on the patient.

The noise had come from him. He was thrashing about on the bed.

"Damn!"

He was shivering; fever had taken hold. Checking the wound, she found it seeping, and quickly got her supplies. She took off the bandages, cleaned the wound, and applied a fresh pad with salve on it.

"You must stay calm." She talked to him as she worked. Once finished, she bandaged it again, although this time it was not as easy, as the man was now shivering violently.

His pulse was rapid and he was rolling his head from side to side. Gathering all the blankets she could, Essie piled them on top of him and then found two bricks to heat. She ran into her surgery and grabbed more herbs to bring down the fever.

She spent the next hour forcing liquid down his throat and placing bricks around his body, but nothing seemed to be warming him up. She feared for his heart if he did not stop shaking, but could think of little else to do. She felt helpless in the face of his obvious distress. Had her siblings been here they would have helped. She could wake Cam, his strength added to hers—

"H-help m-me."

"I am trying." She took the hand he held out to her and squeezed it in reassurance. "You must try and hold still, or you will tear your stitches."

"S-s-so c-cold."

Not giving herself time to think, Essie stripped off her dress, shoes, and stockings. Clad only in a thin chemise, she pulled aside the covers and climbed beneath. Making her way to where he lay beneath the mound of blankets, she took a deep breath, and careful to avoid his bullet wound, she lay along his good side and wrapped her arms around him. Placing her leg over his, she tried to warm him.

"Try to calm your breathing," she whispered as she lay her head on his chest. "Let me warm you."

His body was shuddering so hard Essie thought it was only a matter of time until his heart stopped beating.

"T-talk t-to me."

He could barely speak. His teeth banged together hard.

"I'm one of seven," Essie began. She told him of her family and the others that had joined it, James and Lilly, and how the additions had only strengthened what they already had.

"We're different," she said softly. "The seven of us are not like other people. And I'm not as strong as them." Essie wasn't sure why she had said those words. Perhaps because for so long they had rolled around inside her head, gaining momentum. Or perhaps because she knew that the man would remember nothing of what she had told him in the morning. Whatever the reason, it felt good to finally speak her thoughts.

She was the weak Sinclair. The one who was just so much less than the others. Looks, personality, and even her heightened sense. She knew, and was sure her siblings did too, although they were too nice to say anything on the matter. But the truth was, she did sometimes feel unworthy.

And you're pathetic for thinking it.

"It's like I'm the pale version of them," she whispered. Looking at the man, she saw his eyes were closed. He hadn't heard her, which she knew was a good thing. People would never understand about the Sinclairs and their senses. Even she sometimes struggled with what they could do.

His shivers were easing, and soon she would get off the bed. As soon as he was completely still. Yawning, Essie thought she would wait a few more minutes and then find her own bed.

Max was warm to his toes. His left side burned from the bullet hole he had received yesterday, but his right felt warm in a nice way. Opening his eyes, he looked to see what was pressed to it.

Curls the color of midnight lay across his chest, and then he remembered Essex Sinclair, the beautiful healer who had saved his life. The memory of her climbing onto the bed and warming him flashed through his head. She had heated him with her body and soothed him with her gentle words, telling him stories of her family and the hopes and dreams she had for her little home, and he had heard every one. She'd said she was different, as was her family, and he wondered what she'd meant.

She'd also told him she was not as strong as her siblings, and he wanted to know what she meant by that too.

Max remembered the first blissful contact of her body. The heat had been instant, almost magical, as if something had flowed from her into him, a healing warmth had banished the wracking shudders from his body.

One leg was draped over his thighs, and a hand on his chest, as if she was keeping him in place. A lover, determined her man stay exactly where she wanted him. Max almost wished that he had not slept, so he could have enjoyed every second of her lush body pressed to his.

He studied the long, elegant fingers with her short, clean nails, and something moved inside him. An uneasy feeling swept over him that this woman was in some way important to him. He pushed it aside. Max didn't collect people in his life, and no one had ever found a special place inside him, nor would they. He felt gratitude and nothing more. It was simply because he was weak at the moment; the feeling would pass.

He picked up her hand. Such strength flowed from those fingers, and she had used them to heal him; it was a humbling thought. She had never met him before yesterday, yet had taken him into her home and cared for him with her body and her mind.

He remembered male voices, and knew there was a brother. Was there also a husband, perhaps? The thought was not a pleasing one, which confused him more. Max didn't care about people, especially not women. If she had ten husbands, and as many lovers, it was no concern of his.

She had forced vile concoctions down his throat last night until finally he had begged her to help him rid his body of the ice that coursed through his veins. Seconds later he had felt the blessed heat of her lying on top of him.

Taking care not to wake her, Max pushed a tangle of curls from her face. She slumbered deeply, and her exhaustion was evident in the dark smudges beneath her eyes. Her skin was tinged with gold, no doubt from many hours spent outside tending the garden he had fallen in. He followed the sweet tilt of her nose and full lips. She was a beautiful woman, this Essex Sinclair. His eyes studied the delicate curve of one ear then continued down to the tip of her chin and below. One of her breasts was pushed high, the creamy swell rising above the edge of her chemise, and Max's fingers itched to touch the flesh. In fact, his body was suddenly very aware of the fact that he had a near naked woman in his arms. Clenching his fingers briefly, he fought the urge to touch.

He'd never experienced such a need before, to possess a woman. An urgency to know her better.

Perhaps he had taken a knock to the head also, Max thought, and it had muddled his thinking.

He touched a soft cheek, and she woke slowly, like a petal unfurling to the sun's rays. Her lashes fluttered, her fingers curled into his chest, and then she stretched slowly, inch by delectable inch of her body moving sensually against his, and it was like an erotic form of torture. He realized the exact instant she became aware of her surroundings because all the softness fled, replaced by tension. Tipping her head back, she looked up at him, and the impact of her gaze travelled through his body like a bolt of lightning.

He had travelled miles over waters, and their depths had held the color of those eyes. Blue-green and rimmed with darker blue, they held his for several seconds. Her mouth opened, and before she could speak he had dragged her up his body and kissed her. *Soft*, Max thought, and incredibly sweet.

Christ!

Just a brush of his lips over hers left his head spinning. Blood pounded through him, and he wanted more of her. Needed more.

"Open for me," he rasped against her lips. She yielded, and

he deepened the contact. Cupping her head, he explored her thoroughly.

"No." She wrenched her mouth free.

Breathless, they stared at each other for long seconds.

"Dear Lord," she whispered, and then she tore herself from his arms and began to scramble backward, burrowing through the covers like a frantic mole searching for the edge. Max guessed she found it, as seconds later there was a thump.

"Are you all right?" he questioned, moving gingerly to the edge. His side burned with the effort, just as his body still burned for her. Looking down, he found her on her bottom. Her chemise had ridden up, showing him the delicious curves of her thighs, and he looked his fill before she slapped down the hem and quickly climbed to her feet.

"Please avert your eyes, sir."

"Not if you handed me ten gold pieces," he said, watching the flush travel up her neck.

She wouldn't meet his eyes, and Max guessed that was because she had woken pressed to his side and he had just kissed her. And hell, what a kiss. His body was still painfully aroused. The woman had set him on fire.

"You, sir, are no gentleman to watch a lady dress when she has asked you not to. Th-then there is the m-matter of that kiss."

"I am indeed no gentleman, Miss Essex, but I would ask you to try and stop any man from looking, considering the beauty you wear so effortlessly." Max said the words as she dropped to her knees, appearing to search under the bed he lay in. Seconds later she was standing once again with a piece of gray wool in one hand. He watched as she efficiently bundled all that wonderful dark hair into a knot and tied the ends with two sharp tugs. "And that kiss was the inevitable result of waking with you in my arms. I defy you to state you did not enjoy it."

She made a scoffing sound and came back to his side. Max ignored the kick his pulse gave as she stepped closer. The woman was dressed in rumpled clothes, her hair a mess, and had him more off-balance than all who had come before her. The beauty, Max realized, was in her bones. Hers was a powerful attraction to any unsuspecting—or injured —man.

"Don't flatter me, sir. I neither want nor need it, and for your information, I-I did not enjoy that kiss."

"Your stutter would suggest you lie, and I will state again that you are beautiful."

She laid a cool palm on his forehead, and he felt the same jolt of awareness at her touch, almost as if he had been stung by something.

"You doubt my words, Miss Sinclair?"

She ignored him, instead reaching for his bandage. Easing her hands beneath, she removed it gently.

"I will make you something to take for the pain, and redress the wound, but I fear you will need to stay in bed for several days."

"You did not answer my question."

"I have no time for Banbury tales, sir."

"My name is Max."

"I know, you gave it to me last night. Do you have a last name?"

"Just Max, Essex."

"I am Miss Sinclair."

"You were Essie to me last night when you talked of your family, and your hopes and dreams."

Her eyes went to his briefly and then away. He knew she wondered why he had no wish to share his last name, and in truth he was unsure. Very probably she had never heard of him. But right here and now, he simply wanted to be Max to this woman.

"I-I…. You heard everything?"

She wasn't happy about that.

"Every word."

Her fingers clenched briefly.

"Are you sure I cannot address you by your last name, sir? It is highly inappropriate of me to call you Max, as it is for you to call me Essex."

"There is no name other than Max that I wish you to use, and I think we can dispense with proprieties between us, considering what has transpired, don't you, Essex?"

"Is there anyone I can send word to come for you?"

He shook his head, having no wish for anyone to know his location and bring danger to her household. "I have no one." After all, someone had tried to kill him, and as yet he had no idea who.

He saw the sadness in her eyes.

"I'm sorry that you are alone."

"I have family in France, but we are estranged, and I like it that way," Max said in a gruff tone. He'd always thought so, anyway.

"Possessions and wealth mean little in life, Max. Do not be ashamed if you have neither. But people, now they are important. Perhaps if you wrote to your family?"

She thought he was penniless. The irony would have made him laugh, were he the type to do so.

"I do not need people, nor do I wish to contact my family."

Her smile was gentle. "Everyone needs someone."

Max could lose himself in that smile. With very little effort on her part, the woman had captured and held his attention. Not an easy feat, considering the man he had become.

"Not I."

His words had been harsher than need be, and the smile dropped from her lovely lips.

"Well, I have people I do need, sir, and I would be grateful if you did not mention again any of what happened last night. I did what needed to be done to warm you, as I feared for both your wound and your heart. I have no wish for that to reach the ears of my family."

Her cheeks were flushed, and she looked so sweet, Max clenched his fists to keep from reaching for her.

"I will tell no one, you have my word."

She nodded, but he could tell she was not entirely convinced, and Max wondered who had broken her trust.

"I have taken out the bullet, but there is always a risk of infection, so please have a care, sir."

She saw my back. The uncomfortable thought came to him suddenly. Max never let people see his scars. Even women he bedded, he did so in the dark. He neither wanted sympathy nor needed it. That was part of Max's life that he kept locked away deep inside him, in that dark dungeon that couldn't hurt or make him weak anymore.

"Do you suffer at all from the welts on your back?"

"No." How had she known what he was thinking? How was it he felt a closeness to this woman after less than a day in her company, and most of that time out of his head with pain?

"If you do, I may have something that will help you."

"I need nothing for them and have no wish to discuss the matter further."

"There is no shame in what you have suffered. The shame lay with those who hurt you."

"How do you know I did not deserve them, Miss Sinclair?"

She studied him through those stunning green eyes, and

Max felt the urge to throw the blanket over his head. He felt exposed before her, something he had not felt for many years.

"No child deserves to be punished in such a manner."

He hadn't deserved it, and had made his tormentor pay when he was strong enough to do so.

"I have never met a woman called Essex before." Desperate to change the subject, yet wanting her to stay in the room, he latched on to his first thought.

"My family all have unusual names." A small smile tilted her lips again.

"Names of places. How did that come about?"

"My parents travelled a great deal."

"So they named you after the places they visited?"

She nodded. He had feeling there was more to the names than that but she did not elaborate.

"Devonshire, Essex, Cambridge, Eden, Somerset, Dorset, and Warwickshire."

"You have an excellent memory, considering you were in pain and had a fever."

"I rarely forget anything."

"Both a curse and a blessing, I should imagine, sir."

"You told me last night that you are different. Will you tell me in what way?"

"I shall make you something for the pain now," she said, ignoring his question. Her words were brisk and nothing like the gentle tone she had used with him last night.

"Why do you not believe you are beautiful?" Max asked, instead of pursing the matter of her difference and why she believed herself to be the weakest member of her family.

She turned away from him, but he heard her words.

"I know what I am, sir, therefore this conversation needs no further airing."

Max watched her walk away, and his eyes were drawn to

the sensual sway of her hips; the woman had no notion of her appeal. She was a bloody walking siren, he thought, adjusting the covers around his hips.

Glancing out the window, he looked at the mountain that loomed above the house. Not unlike when Essex Sinclair had touched him, he felt a jolt of awareness.

"That is Raven Mountain."

He couldn't drag his eyes away from it. Why had the name sent a shiver down his spine?

"It is impressive, is it not, sir?"

Max gave the mountain one last look before he made himself look at Essex Sinclair.

"It would take more than a mound of earth to impress me, Miss Sinclair."

CHAPTER 3

*E*ssie made herself finish caring for Max instead of following through with her first impulse, which was to flee. She cleaned away her things, and tried to ignore the fact that he was watching her every move. She felt his eyes on her as she bent to stoke the fire to life. They followed her across the room.

She had slept with a man who was neither family nor her husband. *Good Lord, how did I allow that to happen?*

"You warmed me with your body when nothing else worked, Essex. I beg of you not to be too hard on yourself... or me."

How had he known her thoughts? She did not turn to face him. Instead, picking up the dirty bandages, she prepared to leave the room.

"Essex, you have my undying gratitude, and my pledge that should you need it, my help is there for you in any form."

She had to look at him after those words. He lay against her brother's pillows like some Greek god, large and tanned. The awareness that shimmered between them was entirely too disturbing.

He should look weak, and yes, he did have pain lines etched in his face, but for all that, he looked strong and healthy. Big, and she wanted to say formidable, but as she knew nothing about him, she could not form such an opinion... yet.

"I want nothing from you, sir. Tending you is no different from caring for my other patients. You have no need to say such things."

"In my world, there is every need. I would have died had I not chanced upon you, therefore I am indebted to you, and I always pay my debts."

Essie shook her head before turning away. "You owe me nothing. Now please excuse me. I will have someone come to you with water to wash, and something to eat."

"But not you?"

"No. I will be back later to check on you. Before I go, however, there is one thing I must ask." She turned at the door to look at him.

"Anything."

"The person who shot you, do you think that danger will follow you here?" She needed to know, had to ask, as she could not put others in danger by caring for him.

"No. After I was shot I rode hard, and then hid in some trees. No one followed. But if you wish it, I will leave now."

"That will not be necessary, if you have said we are safe."

His lion eyes were suddenly intent.

"You would take the word of a stranger?"

Essie nodded. She didn't know why she trusted him. Indeed, she had no reason to, and yet did.

"I would."

She had surprised him into silence. As she left the room, Essie wondered what his story was. Who was he? Where had he come from? Had he no one that cared for him? No possessions or home? He had not stated otherwise when she questioned him. Did he simply find work where he could? Had he nothing binding him to a place? The thought made her feel sad.

"How is the patient this morning?"

Cam was walking down the stairs as she reached them.

"He's better." Essie had no wish to discuss the patient, or where she had spent the night.

"Your wrinkled clothing would suggest you spent the night in that bloody chair in Dev's room, Essex. Tell me that is not the case, and that Grace just failed to press it?"

Looking her brother up and down, she took in his immaculate breeches and polished black hessians. His jacket was deep green, and his necktie immaculately folded.

"Yes, well, some of us care more for people than the way we are turned out," Essie said, brushing her hands down her hopelessly creased skirts. "Are you going somewhere?"

"It is unavoidable, but I am going to the Mullinses to view a horse for Uncle, and you look like the bottom end of a mop."

"I do not!"

"And your hair is tied with string. Tsk tsk, sister, you have let yourself go since leaving London."

She looked up at his eyes and saw the wicked glint. Cam loved nothing better than getting a rise out of his siblings. Essie was tired, so today it was easier to accomplish than normal.

"I have no wish to be considered a dandy!"

Cam snorted. "Come now, dandy? Surely you can do better than that, especially as that term applies to men only. Forgive me if I have no wish to look"—he waved a hand up and down her body—"rumpled and unkempt."

"You smell like a woman!" Essie stormed, because she could think of nothing better.

"That is untrue and you know it. I smell like a handsome, well-turned-out man who is irresistible to all females."

Myrtle chose that moment to appear. She brushed passed Essie and stopped to sniff Cam's boots. She then sneezed loudly and walked away.

"And there is the proof." Essie found herself laughing. "Even the dog cannot stomach that stench."

Cam sniffed the air and wrinkled his nose. "I had thought it pleasant when I purchased it in London, but perhaps...."

"Go." She wrapped her arms around him and hugged him hard.

"You know, of course," he said, wrapping his large arms around her and hugging her back, "that you are creasing my clothes."

"It is a sister's right to do so," she mumbled, enjoying being held.

He sighed. "Very well, I shall endure it then."

He took her face in his hands when she released him.

"Now, you have Josiah and Bertie, and Grace is here. But I think word should be sent to have Mrs. Beadle from the village come in while I am gone."

"Why? You will return by nightfall, surely?"

"Yes, but there is a man here who I do not know."

"He has a bullet wound and can barely leave his bed, Cam." Essie pushed aside the fact that the man had looked far from invalided just moments before.

"I don't care, what I care about is you."

"Lovely though that sentiment is, there really is no need for Mrs. Beadle to come. So go and look at horses, and be sure to check it is not too short in the patterns."

Cam snorted. "I love you for trying, darling, but I think you mean pastern."

Essie was the Sinclair who did not like horses, unlike her

siblings. She had been bitten by one as a child, and after that had declared they were large, smelly beasts she wanted no part of.

"Damn, I was sure I had that right."

Cam snorted once more. "I shall now check on the patient and then be on my way."

"He is sleeping, Cam, and I have no wish for you to wake him."

He studied her, and she kept her face calm. No one could see through you quite like a sibling.

"Do remember not to sniff the air when you reach the Mullinses, it makes you look like one of the hounds."

"I don't sniff the air."

"Not all the time, no," Essie added.

He sighed. "I shall try, but as you can imagine it is hard when every smell is heightened to ten times that of what others smell."

"Nose plugs," Essie said, smiling. "We should really see about getting you some."

"Yes, that would create something of a stir," he drawled. "And on that note, I shall away. Be safe, darling, and I have spoken to the Hemples about one of them being with you from now on when you tend that man."

"Oh, Cam—"

"He was shot, Essie. We have no idea why, or if he is a good or bad man, so you will take care, and not tend him unless a brother is with you. Promise me."

He could go from silly to serious in seconds.

"Very well, I promise, but you will be gone but a few hours."

"Good girl." He kissed her nose and left. Essie closed the door behind him.

"How is the patient?"

"Better, thank you, Bertie, and in need of a wash and some breakfast. Keep the food soft and light if you please. Eggs and a little broth. Tea, not ale."

"I will see to it."

Essie ran to the stairs to her room. Once inside, she shut the door and moved to sit on her bed.

She closed her eyes and remembered waking, pressed to all that wonderful, warm, muscled flesh. Was that how married people who actually cared for each other woke most days? Did her siblings wake with their beloveds' bodies close? The thought made her warm all over. Surely it would be a wonderful thing to wake in the arms of the man you loved. Not that she loved Max… or he her.

"He is a stranger, you fool!"

Disgusted with her thoughts because she had long ago given up on love, she began to pull off her clothes. *He is nothing but a patient to you*, she reminded herself.

The problem was awareness. Something sizzled in the air between them, and she could not deny that fact, even considering he was injured.

"I have brought you warm water for washing, Miss Essex."

"Wonderful, thank you, Grace," Essie said to her maid.

Grace had been with Essie for many years now, and she was a wonderful, sturdy soul who was rarely flustered, which was an asset in this family.

Essie hurried to wash, reminding herself she had no time in her life for foolish thoughts or fancies. She had given those up along with her hopes of everlasting love.

Changing into a clean dress, she let Grace braid her hair. Once she was presentable, Essie headed down to take her morning meal, determined to put all her silly thoughts behind her. She was a healer, and people relied upon her. She would help Max heal, and then see him off her property and never think of him and his lion eyes again.

Making her way back downstairs, she took tea with Bertie and made herself eat porridge with a dab of honey and milk. Josiah came back in when she was nearly finished.

"He's not happy with the meal I placed before him. In fact, he said it wasn't enough to keep a small boy alive, let alone a full-grown man. He then asked for ale."

"There will be no ale," Essie said slowly. "He will eat what is put before him or go hungry."

"He's not a child, Miss Essex."

"I understand that, but he does have a bullet hole in him, and as I am the one who took it out and stitched him up, it is I who am responsible for him. If he has no wish to abide by the rules I set, then he can leave."

"Perhaps you would like to inform him of that," Bertie said, looking rueful.

"I shall. I shall also inform him if he is to stay here, then it must be under our rules."

"Even on such short acquaintance I can see he is not a biddable man, Miss Essex. In fact, he reminds me a great deal of your brothers."

"Lord save us all." Essie sighed as she regained her feet. "Did he ask you to inform anyone of his whereabouts, Josiah?"

"No, he said there was no one who would miss him."

Essie refused to feel sad about the fact that Max had no one to worry about him. Instead she marched back to the room he occupied. When she entered, he was reading one of her books on herbal remedies.

"I hope you do not mind me reading your book, Essex."

"I do not mind."

His smile suggested he knew she did. It mocked her, and made her toes curl inside her boots.

"Now I wish to address the matter of your meals, sir."

"Max."

"I am caring for you, therefore you will eat what I say. If you do not like the rules I set, then by all means leave." She hadn't meant to sound rude, but it had come out that way.

"I thought you did not want me to leave. I think you said I would not make it to the doorway with my injury."

Essie gave him a look that would have spoken volumes to each of her siblings. She was usually the quiet Sinclair, the peacemaker, the even temperament among six fiery ones. Why, then, was she struggling to find that calmness with this man?

"I only want to help you, sir, and to do that you must allow me to know what is best for you." There, that had been spoken in her usual calm, rational manner.

"I shall try, but invalid food has never agreed with me."

Essie did not buy the contrite look on his face, but she remained silent.

"Why has your brother left you alone?"

"He will return in a few hours, and I am not alone. I have three servants, and how do you know my brother has left?"

"Josiah told me. Where is the rest of your family?"

"They are in London, where I shall be in a few weeks."

"You are to go to London?"

He seemed surprised by that.

"I am. Why do you ask? Do you perhaps live there, sir?" She could read nothing in his expression.

"I live nowhere."

His answer was frustratingly evasive. She wanted to know more about this handsome stranger, and yet had no right to push for answers, especially if, as she suspected, he was poor, with no possessions to his name. It would be wrong of her to pursue the matter, especially if it embarrassed him.

"You miss them, your family?"

Essie nodded, her throat suddenly tight as she thought about her siblings. She did miss them. After the disaster of her first season, she had then endured another, but had pined for Oak's Knoll, and her eldest brother had told her that if she wished to go home for a while, he would not stop her. Cam had joined her, in between trips to visit friends.

"Very much."

"Then why live here, and not with them?"

"You ask a lot of questions, sir."

"You interest me."

"There is little to interest anyone, I assure you. And like you, I do not like to discuss my personal life."

"So you do not believe you are beautiful or interesting? I wonder who has made you believe these things that are obviously untrue."

"No one, and this is a silly conversation. Please do not attempt to flatter me with empty words. I assure you I am not easily fooled."

Essie did not want to be of interest to anyone, and most especially not this large, disturbing man. She needed to keep her exposure to him to a minimum from now on. Bertie and Josiah could care for him. She did not want to feel her pulse race anymore, nor the unsettling feelings he produced inside her.

"If there is nothing further you need, I shall leave."

Max made himself move, then hissed in pain... loudly.

"Are you in pain?"

"Some," he said, feeling no guilt for his words. He'd been shot, stabbed, and his body had been beaten badly, so he was used to pain. But what he wasn't used to was the need to have the woman touch him, or the need to have her close. So he would do what he could to achieve that.

She intrigued him. More than that, she made him hungry

for her, and no woman had made him feel that way... ever. He understood lust, and he understood greed, but he doubted Essex Sinclair understood either.

Max knew people, and his experience had taught him that most wanted something when they came in contact with him. Rarely did they want just companionship or friendship. However, he had a feeling Essex Sinclair was different. In fact, he thought that perhaps Essex Sinclair was exactly as she seemed, a beautiful woman with a good heart. Was it true? The thought was disturbing, because Max had not met any such people in his life before.

"Your bandages are not too tight."

He tried not to react as her finger slid under the bindings and touched his skin.

"Your body has suffered a trauma, sir, it will likely be painful for some time. But to ensure a full recovery, you must rest."

Max schooled his features to look solemn. "I shall try to do as you say, Essex."

"Miss Sinclair," she chided him, but it was accompanied by a sweet smile. He felt as if he'd received a treasure.

Christ. What the hell is happening to me. Has she created some potion to enslave me?

"Essex," he said, a bit more sharply than intended. "I will call you that."

Her lips tightened, but she said nothing, and then left the room.

Max had learned early that to survive you had to be the strongest and meanest of those around you. He'd become that and more. He was never weak, and subtleties and gentleness were beyond him.

Swinging his legs over the edge of the bed, he made himself stand. Dizziness had him holding one of the posts.

When his head steadied, he made himself walk slowly around the room. He needed to be ready to leave here, and to do that he had to get his strength back.

"I often marvel at the stupid acts of men. I can now add you to the top of that list, sir."

Essex was standing in the doorway, hands on hips, green eyes fired with anger. Max wanted to go to her, to wrap an arm around her slender waist and kiss that angry snarl off her lips. Instead he made himself walk back to the bed.

"I need to keep my strength up, as I must leave here soon."

"I told you to rest."

"I do not take orders from anyone."

"Then leave my house, for I have no wish for you to stay if you will not accept my word."

She had not yelled, but he heard the anger in each word. She then left him again. Minutes later he heard the front door shut. Easing himself gently back into the bed, Max felt his heart thudding hard in his chest, as if he had been running. He was weak, there was no doubting that, but he was never laid low for long; this would be no different.

Max had not had a woman speak to him as Essex Sinclair just had in many years, and wasn't entirely sure how he felt about it... or her. The smile that shaped his lips told him that perhaps he liked it. Her anger was refreshing. He would need to apologize, of course.

His smile grew.

He must have dozed, because when he woke he heard voices in the room next to the one he lay in.

"I'll not be getting off it, Elder Sinclair. I need to tend my animals."

Curious, Max threw back the covers and was about to get

out of bed when a man entered. He had the look of the other one who had brought him his morning meal, well-built with the same smile.

"Good day to you, sir, my name is Bertie."

Max nodded.

"I would not advise you to leave your bed yet, as Miss Essex was most displeased when she found you walking about earlier."

"I wish to stand." Max didn't take orders.

"You'll not be strong enough to."

Max slid his legs to the floor. As he pushed upright, his head swam again and he grabbed the bedpost.

"Are you wishing to go anywhere particular?"

"What's going on in there?" He nodded to the doorway through which he'd heard the noise.

"Miss Essex is treating a patient."

Hating to admit he was feeling weak, and hating to have another man see him in such a state, he rested a hip on the bed.

"She is the only healer nearby?"

"There is an elderly lady in the next village, but as that's a full day's ride, the locals from Crunston Cliff are happy to have Miss Essex back. Her family have been here for centuries, and one has always been a healer."

"Back?"

The man's face remained pleasant, but his eyes were suddenly guarded. Loyalty in a servant was an excellent thing, even if it stopped Max getting the information he wanted.

"Can I send word to anyone to collect you, sir?"

"No, there is no one." Max continued to endorse the fact he was alone. "Is my horse still here?"

"Yes, we have settled it in the paddock behind the stable.

Now, if you need no further help returning to bed, I shall leave you."

Max waited until the man had left, and then struggled back into bed. He then listened for the next two hours as Essex treated people. He caught snatches of conversation; there was a boil on a knee, a pain in the stomach. A small child had hurt her wrist, and another had an infected cut. The man she treated now was being lectured, and not liking it one bit.

"You'll not be telling me to stop, Miss Sinclair. I have no time to sit about like a lady drinking tea."

"All ladies do not sit about drinking tea, Mr. Clever. Some of us are even intelligent enough to raise families, run households, and work."

Her words were clipped and colder than a winter's day, and had Max smiling. He wished he could see the fire in her green eyes.

"While I would not care if your health affected only you, I do care about your wife and five children. Therefore, I am telling you that if you do not take today to rest, you will have to do so for a great many more if your injury gets infected and your stitches tear. Now, I have no intention of seeing my work ruined, so if your wife cannot talk some sense into you, then I will tell your mother, and she will."

"Oh now, there's no need to do that, surely?"

"There is every need if you do not immediately go home. And I shall be checking."

Max muffled his snort of laughter. *Lord, what a woman.*

"I-I'll be heading home at once then, Miss Sinclair."

"A very sensible move, Mr. Clever."

Her next patient was a woman called Emily Brunt. Her voice was soft, and Essie talked to her gently, so he could not pick up a great deal of the conversation, except that she had lost another child, and that was when the smile fell from his lips. Essie talked to the woman for some time, and then Max heard sniffing, which suggested the woman was weeping. He closed his eyes. Crying women were something he had never been able to tolerate.

CHAPTER 4

"I have food." She came after her patients had gone, with the shaggy dog on her heels, and settled a tray on his lap. Her expression was polite, and held none of the fire he'd seen or heard in her while she was treating her patients. She'd changed her dress, and this one was lavender. No lace or frills, no ribbons or trimming. Just a plain dress that fitted her lovely breasts and fell to the floor. Her hair was in a braid and hung over her shoulder. A piece of wool was tied around the end.

"Do you not have ribbons?"

"Pardon?" She lowered the teapot and looked at him.

"You have wool tied around your braid."

"Ribbons come undone."

"Then you have some?"

She nodded. "Why do you ask?"

"You do not dress extravagantly, and I wondered if you do not have the funds to do so."

She laughed. More a giggle, actually, and it was a lovely sound. Her face softened and her eyes twinkled, and Max felt the urge to sigh. But as he was not one who did so, he gritted his teeth instead. The woman was far too appealing.

"My brother is a baron. And while we once did not have money, I assure you that is no longer the case. I like to live simply when I am here, and there is nothing more to it than that."

Her family were nobility. He searched his memory for a Lord Sinclair, and located one. Why had he not connected them? It was unlike Max to not do so. This woman had robbed his wits.

"I intended no insult," he said in a gruff voice. "You would look beautiful in a sack."

She blushed, the color filling her cheeks. Max grabbed her arm as she turned to leave, and his fingers slid down to circle her slender wrist.

"You are beautiful, Essex."

"H-how does your injury feel this afternoon, sir?"

She still did not believe him, and it frustrated him that she could not see what he could.

"It is better, thank you." Max did not pursue the matter. It wasn't his way to do so. The problem was, he had found himself doing and thinking differently since arriving in this house and meeting this woman. He cared that she did not see her beauty, and that was not like him. Max cared for nothing and no one.

"Excellent." She laid a palm on his forehead. He felt something when she touched him, a tingling through his body, and what followed could only be described as hunger. He had known her for less than a day, and he wanted this woman with a desperation he'd never before experienced.

Why?

He had lain with plenty of women, and most were wealthy and bored. Some of noble birth, others, daughters and wives of rich merchants. All dressed in expensive gowns and smelled of sweet perfumes. Essex Sinclair smelled of her herb garden, and wore frumpy gowns, and her hair in a single braid that hung to her waist. What the hell was her allure?

"And you have no pain?"

"No." He snapped out the word with more force than was required because she unsettled him. The dog growled at his tone, so he glared at it.

"What is that animal's problem?"

"Myrtle is an excellent judge of character. She also does not like raised voices."

"She needs a haircut."

"No, what she needs is a wash after Cam threw a mug of tea over her."

The dog looked from Max to her mistress and back to him again.

"Now, sir, rest is the best—"

"God's blood, call me Max, woman." He reached for her as she turned away. Wrapping his fingers around her waist, he pulled her back. "After what we have shared, I insist upon it."

"Let me go, please."

He didn't; instead he gave her a tug, and tumbled her onto his chest. Before she could say anything, his lips were on hers. One of his hands cupped her head, the other her waist, and the feel of her pressed to his chest made his head swim. He'd wanted this, her lips pressed to his, since this morning when he'd woken with her in his arms.

"Essex," Max sighed into her mouth. He gentled the kiss, coaxed instead of demanded, and soon he felt her response, but it was her tears that stopped him.

"Why are you crying?" He held her shoulders, her face close to his. Tears spilled over her lids and down her cheeks. "Tell me." His words came out raspy as he brushed the tears aside.

"I-I don't want this."

"This, being kisses? This, being held by a man who wants you very much?"

She managed a nod, but her eyes remained on his, almost as if she was begging him to understand what she had not said.

"You are a stranger. I know nothing about you, and yet…."

"You are aware of something between us, as am I," Max finished for her.

"How is that even possible when we have known each other no more than a day?"

Max shook his head, unable to answer. It was a mystery to him also.

"I would never hurt you, Essex."

"Yes, I know."

"You can't know that," Max said, contradicting himself. "And it is wrong of you to trust so easily."

"I have known bad men, and you are nothing like him. I can sense that if nothing else."

Him. Jealousy and rage lanced through him. Someone had held her like this. Kissed her soft, sweet lips. The thought made him furious.

"Who hurt you? Tell me his name."

She braced her hands on his chest and pushed back, and Max reluctantly released her.

"It matters not. What matters is that I will never allow a man to break me as he did."

"Any man who would hurt you is no man at all, Essex," Max said, taking her hand in his. Lifting it to his lips, he kissed the palm. "Tell me his name and I will make him pay."

"He is dead. Now I must go, another patient has arrived."

She was lying; no one had arrived, because Max would have heard them.

"Max." She turned back at the door.

"Yes."

"I understand you have no place to go, and no one to tend you, so please stay here as long as you wish."

The words humbled him. That she would offer her home in such a way when he had just kissed her was foolish and far too trusting. She knew nothing about him, yet he knew so much about this woman already. He should not be surprised that she would open her home to a stranger.

Essex Sinclair was everything he was not. Innocent and caring, and from a noble family. He would be best to leave here now, today, and ride as far away from the beguiling woman as he could.

He heard a snuffle and found the dog beside his bed.

"Your mistress has left, I suggest you follow her."

She jumped on the bed and planted two paws on his chest, then stared at him through strange blue eyes. Max lifted a hand and stroked the long silken fur, then scratched the dog behind the left ear.

"Myrtle is a ridiculous name for a dog."

She whined softly and closed her eyes as he continued to scratch. He'd never had a pet, and saw no need for one.

"And now you can leave," he said when he'd finished. Instead the dog leaned forward and licked his cheek, before going to the end of the bed and turning a few circles before lying down. She then huffed out a breath and closed her eyes.

"As long as you're comfortable," he muttered, moving his feet. "Don't mind me."

He needed to get away from Essex Sinclair and this place. Away from her soft, caring hands and beauty. Being near her had made him weak, and Max would never allow himself to be that again.

CHAPTER 5

Max slept, and when he woke he felt a great deal better. The sky told him it was dusk, and the rumble in his stomach told him it was time to fill it.

Nudging the still slumbering animal off his feet, he received a sleepy-eyed look, then her tail thumped by way of a greeting.

"You are a lazy creature. Surely there are rabbits to hunt?"

Another thump, followed by a yawn that made him smile.

"What am I doing?" he muttered. "I have never smiled as much as I have since arriving in this place." He could not remember a time when he had rested so much, either, even with a bullet hole in his side. He needed to leave here; Oak's Knoll was making him vulnerable.

The sound of raised voices had him swinging his legs out of bed and standing. Myrtle huffed out a breath and joined him. Had the brother returned?

"I'll not have you near her!" The loudest voice was angry. Pulling on the clean shirt Essie had left him, he walked slowly out the door with the dog on his heels. Cursing the pain in his side with every step, he made his way up the hallway.

"You may have others in the village fooled, but I know you Sinclairs are dangerous. I've seen things happen that shouldn't, and unlike others I won't ignore them. You're a witch, and I'm here to tell you to stay away from my wife, or I'll see to it others know what you are!"

Max increased his pace as anger gave him strength and took away the pain. Only one woman, beside the maid, lived in this house. And no one had the right to call that sweet creature a witch.

"Your wife is sick, Mr. Brunt, and unless she is treated, allowed to rest, and left alone by you, she will not heal."

Essie's words were calm, like she was speaking to one of her bloody patients instead of an angry man. Where the hell was the brother? Had he yet to return?

"Back away, Mr. Brunt," Josiah said, sounding nothing like the man who had tended him earlier. There was now a mean edge to his voice that Max liked.

"I'll make you see reason!"

Max reached the doorway, and parted the Hemple brothers by placing a hand on each shoulder. He then stepped between them and around Essie in time to see a burly, angry man coming toward her with a hand raised. He didn't speak, just acted. He plowed his fist into the man's jaw, sending him backward to land on his ass.

"Max!"

Ignoring Essie's shriek and the hands she wrapped around his arm, he walked forward, taking her with him.

"Never speak to her that way again! Never darken this door, never even look at her!" Max roared, reaching down to grab the man. "She tends the sick for no other reason than she is kindhearted. How bloody dare you be anything but nice to her!"

"It's all right, come away now, Max. Your stitches—"

"She's a witch, everyone knows it!"

The man had blood pouring from his nose, but still glared defiantly up at Max.

"She's a bloody angel!"

"My wife can't give me children, and I blame her!" The man pointed at Essie, who was now at his side.

Max dragged the man to his feet by the neck of his shirt and shook him hard.

"You're an idiot if you believe that! Go home and treat your wife better, and do as Miss Sinclair says. Only then may you be blessed with a child."

"I'll not do it!"

"Then rot in hell for all I care," Max snarled. "But if word ever reaches me that you have so much as raised your voice to her again, I'm hunting you down, and there will be nowhere for you to hide."

Before Max could strike him again, the man shook himself free and ran. Myrtle followed, barking loudly.

"Myrtle, come here!" Max roared, following the man to ensure he left the property. He did not want the dog to get a boot to the head.

"Max, stop now. Please."

It was her "please" that stopped him. The word held desperation. Turning, he looked down into Essie's face. Worry had drained it of color, and her eyes were damp with tears she fought to hold back.

"Did he hurt you?" He cupped her cheek, her unshed tears affecting him more than they should. "Tell me!"

"He did not hurt me, I promise."

"Don't cry."

She sniffed loudly. "I'm not going to."

As the anger began to drain from his body, he felt the

pain return. Swift and searing as fiery pokers, it stabbed into his side, taking his breath.

"Christ!"

"Bertie, take his other side." Essex moved to his left and wrapped an arm around his waist.

"You will not be able to hold me if I fall."

"I'm stronger than I look."

"Come now, Max." Bertie took his other side, careful to stay away from his wound.

"I can walk," Max muttered

She said nothing further as they reached his room. She silently helped lay him on the bed, and then checked his wound. He had not pulled the stitches, surprisingly. She left, and returned minutes later with a cup.

"Drink this, it will help with the pain."

"I need nothing."

She lifted the cup to his mouth, and he would end up with it all over him if he didn't open. He knew the determined look she wore.

"Essie, about—"

"Thank you for defending me." She had not met his eyes yet.

"Look at me."

Instead she went to pat her dog, who was once again at the foot of his bed.

"And now I must go, Max."

"Where?" He reached out to grab her, but she had stepped from his reach.

"I shall send Bertie in with your meal."

"Essie!" he called to her as she left the room, but she didn't stop, just kept on walking, leaving him alone again with his thoughts.

. . .

Max slept, as whatever she had given him had insured that. He felt better upon waking, and felt his strength was returning. He would be able to leave here soon. Could ride a horse if necessary, and knew that it was fast becoming imperative that he put some distance between him and Essex.

She was becoming a fixation. Far more alluring than any well-dressed lady of London, she touched him in places he was sure no woman had ever reached before.

She had infiltrated him, broken through his barricades and found the raw places. The places he wanted her to soothe.

Climbing out of bed, he made for the windows. Darkness had long since fallen, but he still felt it, Raven Mountain looming over him like a menacing shadow.

This whole place unsettled him. The mountain, the people. He had the strange feeling he was meant to come here, and could not work out why.

"Max?"

He turned to find Essex in the doorway, holding a candle. She wore a dressing gown and slippers, and had obviously been roused from sleep, as her hair was tousled and her eyes still unfocused. *Sweet*, he thought, achingly sweet. Max felt his body stir in reaction to the picture she presented.

"Are you all right, Essex?" He made himself stay where he was and not go to her, which his body was begging him to do.

"I-I…. Did you call out to me? I thought I heard you."

"No."

"Are you hurting?" Lowering the candle to a chair, she took a step toward him. "I can take a look at your side, and make you something if need be."

His feet moved before he could stop them, and seconds later he was at her side.

"I am in no pain."

"Oh. Well then, I shall return to my bed."

Max cupped her cheek when she made no move to leave.

"You need to go now, sweet Essex. Leave me before I do what my body is yelling at me to do."

She swayed toward him, one of her hands resting on the bare skin of his chest through the open shirt. Her touch made him shudder.

"Wh-what do you want to do?"

"To take you," he whispered. "Lose myself in your body, as I have wanted to since I woke with you in my arms."

She did not pull back, and her eyes were clear now. But Max saw no fear, only a need that matched his own.

"Go back to your room." His words brushed her lips. "Hell, Essex, I'm begging you to go back to your room." The words were wrenched from Max. "I have no willpower around you."

"I don't want to leave. I want you too. Want this need inside me to be extinguished. I've never felt this way before, never experienced such passion for a man."

Christ, he was shaking like some innocent youth about to make love for the first time.

"I-I have no right to ask this of you, Essie, as I have nothing to give you. I can make you no promises beyond tonight."

Her eyes held his, open and honest. She did not look away or behave coy.

"I want this, to lie with you. Beyond that I ask for nothing, either, as I have no wish to marry. What I want is to experience what can be between a man and woman."

"Last chance," he rasped, cupping both her cheeks.

She rose to her toes and kissed him. The touch was fleeting and innocent, and beast that he was, he would take what she offered. Seizing control of the kiss, he teased her lips with gentle caresses that eased the tension from her spine and had her clinging to him in seconds.

"Open for me, Essex."

His tongue slipped inside to caress hers, and Max's head spun. Just kissing her was causing a frenzy inside him.

He undid the tie at her waist and pushed off her dressing gown, then worked the ribbons at the back of her night shift loose. Sliding a hand inside the opening he had created, he caressed her back. Her skin was warm and silken to touch, and he wanted more.

"You inflame me."

He tasted her sigh as his hand swept the swells of her bottom and up the line of her back, stroking each knuckle on her spine with infinite care. Stepping back, he looked at her.

"Take it off for me, Essie."

She didn't hesitate at the husky command; she reached for the hem and dragged it up her body and over her head.

"Sweet Christ, you're exquisite," Max whispered, his gaze devouring what she had uncovered. Candlelight only enhanced her beauty. She was a vision of lush curves and pale satin skin. He pushed a handful of hair over her shoulder, then ran his fingers down her chest to cup the fullness of a breast.

"Look at me, Essie," Max whispered. She lifted her eyes to his. "Tell me you see your beauty as I do."

"Max, it's all right, you have no need to speak that way."

Taking her hand, he led her to the mirror. Placing Essie in front of him, he gathered her hair and draped it over her shoulders, exposing her to their eyes.

"This," he said, caressing the side of her face, "is perfection. I have travelled thousands of miles and not once have I seen the color of your eyes in another, or the sensual curve of your lips."

She watched his hand as it traced her lips.

"I do not like to look at myself like this."

Max held her still as she tried to turn away. "Let me show you what I see, Essie. Please."

"The others in my family…." She turned her face away from the mirror. "They are so much more than I am." She whispered the words, and he knew they caused her pain.

"I don't believe that." He turned her face back to the mirror. "No one could be so much more than you. Your skin is sun-kissed, unlike the other pallid ladies of society. Smooth as silk," he whispered into her ear. "I long to worship every inch."

Max trailed his fingers down her arm and over her stomach, and her eyes followed.

"When I woke with you in my arms my first morning here, I watched you for minutes while you slept. You looked like an angel… my angel. The neck of your chemise had swept low, and I could see this." He stroked her ribs as he moved upward to cup a breast. Max looked at the scar that ran along the length of his hand. It appeared big and brutish against her soft, unblemished skin.

"Feel what you do to me, Essie." Max groaned, placing a hand on her stomach to pull her back against him.

"I-I feel it," she gasped as he pressed his hard arousal into the curve of her buttocks. Max knew that, unlike other innocent woman, Essie had experience of the body. She'd tended many conditions, and knew what people looked like without their clothes. She was not embarrassed or shy.

"You do this to me, Essie."

"Max, I-I— These feelings…."

"I won't let you hide from me, Essie. I will not allow you to hide what you are feeling here in this room from me."

"What of you, are you hiding things from me?"

He held her eyes. He had lied, and he was hiding things

from her, but not this. Not what he felt being here in this room with her.

"What I feel for you here in this room, here at Oak's Knoll, I am not hiding from," Max said, and it was all he could give her for now. He prayed it was enough.

"We barely know each other, and yet I want to be with you," she whispered, placing her hand on top of his where it sat on her hipbone. "I am not afraid of you, or this, Max."

Max kissed the side of her neck, tasting the sweet nectar of this woman. Moving his fingers inward, he parted the soft folds between her thighs.

"Look at my hands on your lovely body, Essex."

"I'm looking." Her head fell back onto his chest.

"Let me love you now."

"Yessss," she hissed as the tip of one finger stroked the hard bud between her thighs, making her shudder.

"Tell me you're beautiful." How could she not see what he did? Were all the men she encountered fools, to not see her beauty?

"Yes, Max, you make me beautiful."

"I can wait no longer, Essie, I need you now."

"Then take me," she urged, turning in his arms to wind her own around his neck. "Kiss me, Max."

CHAPTER 6

Both were breathless in seconds as their kisses grew fiercer. Slowly they moved backward as one, until Essie felt her thighs touch the bed.

"I don't want to hurt you, Max. Your injury... we must go carefully."

"You could never hurt me."

"But—"

He pressed his fingers to her lips. "I want this... I want you, Essie."

"Will you let me take off the shirt then, let me touch you, Max?"

"No... I—"

"I've seen the marks on your back. I hate that you suffered to get them, but they are part of you," she whispered. "Let me touch you."

"I-I want that, but no one has ever touched me there before."

Essie heard the vulnerability in his voice. She would not touch him there tonight if that was his wish. But next time...

if there was to be another. He would trust her enough to allow that intimacy, she vowed.

"Let me help you take off your shirt." Her fingers were unsteady, yet they never faltered as she pulled the hem over his head.

"Last night when I saw you, and took off your clothes, I remember thinking you were the most beautiful man I had ever seen. A warrior," Essie whispered, running a hand down his chest, carefully avoiding the bandage. "I thought you looked like a lion. Fierce and proud. Your eyes glinted gold in the firelight."

"No one has ever called me beautiful." His laugh was unsteady as she reached the opening of his breeches.

"You are beautiful. A beautiful lion," Essie whispered. She kissed his chest, her touch causing him to inhale.

She felt different suddenly, emboldened by the beauty he saw in her. Essie wanted this... wanted more. For the first time in so long, she was certain of something. She wanted this man, and tonight she would take him and have no regrets, just as he would take her.

Reaching for his breeches, she undid the button, and ran her hand over his stomach. It was flat and hard; she found no spare flesh. Her fingers brushed the tip of his erection, and the breath hissed in his throat.

"You know the male body well, Essie, and yet I think this, what we are about to do, is new for you?"

"It is, and yet I would not want to be anywhere else. This, being here with you, Max, it feels right."

She saw a flash of doubt on his face.

"I care nothing for what you have or don't have. Possessions, wealth, and property mean very little to me." Essie touched his cheek, making him look at her. "Forget about what lies outside the door awaiting us."

His hand was in her hair, and with a gentle tug her head

fell back, and he was kissing her once more. Essie lost the ability to think; she could only feel. His hand was on her body, tracing each curve and cupping her breasts. His fingers stroked her nipples and sent ripples of pleasure through her.

She felt his hot breath on her neck, and then lower, until he was licking one of her breasts.

"Oh" was all she could manage as he took one of her nipples into his mouth. His hands continued to touch her, stroke the secret place between her legs, and all Essie could do was hold on as the tension inside her escalated.

"Max!" Her body spiraled tighter as he pushed a finger inside her. It was exquisite, and she shuddered as pleasure swamped her.

"Christ, you are beautiful," he whispered against her lips as he eased her back onto the bed. "And I want you very much, Essex."

"I want you," she whispered. Her hands pushed his breeches down his thighs. Essie was not afraid of the human body; she had seen it in many different forms. Max had a beautiful body, so powerful and strong.

"God!" He threw back his head as she touched the hot flesh of his arousal. She trailed her fingers up and down the skin, and then wrapped a hand about it and stroked him.

"Sweet Christ, that's good." His hands cupped her face and tilted it upward. She saw the savage expression, but felt no fear. Max would not hurt her. His hands circled hers and eased them away from his body.

"Trust me, Essie."

"I-I do."

Starting at her neck, he began to kiss his way down her body, and by the time he reached her stomach, Essie was writhing, her fingers clenching handfuls of the covers. Lifting one of her legs, he kissed the inside of her thigh.

"Max?"

"Just feel, Essie."

She felt his breath there. The hot sweep of his tongue and warmth of his breath, and then she could think no more as sensation after sensation swept through her. The pressure was exquisite, and then he eased a finger inside her once more, and she shattered for a second time.

"You must take me inside you, sweetheart. My injury will not allow me to brace myself on my arms too long." He urged her to her feet, then sat on the side of the bed and pulled her onto his thighs, her legs straddling his. Cupping her face, Max kissed her, and then lay back on the bed.

"Lift up on your knees."

She did as he ordered, and felt him pressing at her entrance. Easing down, Essie felt him slowly enter her, stretching her wider. Silken muscles clenched as he stroked forward. There was discomfort, but also wonder. *So this is what happens.*

"God, you feel good, Essie."

She felt his hands on her waist as he met her maidenhead, then he took control and pushed through, pulling her down onto his chest as she cried out at the pain.

"Sssh, sweetheart, it will ease," he soothed.

The feeling was unusual, and yes there was discomfort, but there was also pleasure that she was now joined to this man. His hands were stroking her back as she listened to the steady thud of his heart beneath her ear.

"Sit up now, Essie."

She did as he asked, and then he was lifting her hips, easing her slowly up his arousal, and then back down. The silken glide of his flesh inside her stirred her body to life once more. Max gritted his jaw as his hips drove up to meet hers as she came down. His hands cupped her breasts, and Essie came down harder and faster, eager to reach that pinnacle she had found before.

Max's hoarse cry met Essie's as she threw back her head; together they flew over the edge.

Breathless, Max wrapped his arms around Essie and held her close to his chest. He felt the brush of her breath on his shoulder as she struggled to steady herself. He wondered what had just happened, how an innocent had made him feel something no other before her had managed. For the first time in his life he'd lost control, felt lust so powerful he had been beyond reason. She had touched his back, touched the welts that had been inflicted on him as a child, and he had not shuddered. What did that mean? How was it possible that this woman had come to mean so much to him in such a short time? The panic began in the pit of his stomach.

"Max?"

"It's all right, Essie," he soothed, easing the grip he had on her hair.

"What's your name, Max?"

"You know my name," he said, trying to get control of himself. She deserved to know more, but he could not tell her... not now, after what they had shared. He had deceived her by withholding information he should have shared. Guilt settled on his shoulders.

"No, your full name."

"Max Hunter." *Another lie.*

"It suits you," Essie said, kissing his chest, which felt way too good and right for Max's peace of mind. They lay there in the dark, he holding her body on top of his, and he thought what a fool he had been to make love with this woman, because he had a terrible feeling that he'd never want to let her go.

"Do you wander the earth a free man, Max? No people or

buildings to tie you in one place? Will you tell me of your life? Some of the personal things."

"No. I do not speak of my life."

She rested her hands one on top of the other and looked down at him. He saw no shyness in her gaze, and no regrets over what they had done. The regret was his alone.

"You are not like other women."

"If you mean why am I not horrified and cringing in maidenly modesty, then yes, I am different. I am a healer. I know the human body, be it man or woman. I was also raised with a family who are not like others. We are for the most open and honest with each other."

He touched a curl, wrapping the silken strands around his fingers.

"Max, I care nothing about your past, or your possessions. I care nothing if you are a wanderer, with no fixed abode. But should you need a place to rest at any time, then I offer you this one."

Christ.

"Essie—"

She placed her hand over his mouth. "Do you believe a girl who wears wool in her hair and grubs about in the earth cares about wealth or prestige? That I care if you have nothing to your name? I care nothing for that, only what I know. You are a good man, Max Hunter."

He closed his eyes rather than see the emotion in hers. She was open and honest, and he... well, he was a lying bastard who would never be good enough for this woman. He needed to tell her the truth. It was the only way.

"Tell me that you now see your beauty, Essex." Those words came out instead of the right ones, and Max knew why. He wanted her soft and pliant in his arms for a while longer. Believing that he was a good man. Another hour, no longer, and then he would send her back to her bed and leave. It was the only way. He would hurt her if he stayed, and he could not do that, not to her, not when he owed her so much.

CHAPTER 7

Essie braced herself to enter Dev's bedroom and see Max. She found a smile as she imagined what she would see: him resting on the pillows, his tawny mane of hair tousled, eyes sleepy. Big body warm beneath the blankets.

What they had shared last night had catapulted her into a world of sensual pleasure that she had never experienced before. Yesterday, Essie knew, had changed her completely. Max had changed her. His touch had ignited her, his kisses had melted her, and she wanted more.

She'd thought Tolly had broken her, left her unable to feel anything for another man. Max had changed that last night. His lovemaking had left her reeling.

"Does that make me a hussy?" Essie giggled. Likely it did, but then she cared nothing for that. She would take what snatched moments she could with Max. And in the time she had with him, she would try and persuade him to stay.

He had challenged Murray Brunt, and then punched him, with a bullet hole in his side, and all because Brunt had said horrid, threatening things to her. Surely that meant he cared for her a little?

She had finally left his side as the gray streaks of dawn filtered through the window. She had kissed his lips softly and left him slumbering peacefully, and vowed she would return to that very place again soon.

Opening the door, she walked inside and found the bed empty. Pressing a hand to her heart as it started thudding hard inside her chest, she looked around the room but saw no sign of him. Running out, and down the hall, she checked every room, arriving in the kitchens last.

"What is amiss, Miss Essex?" Bertie was stirring a pot on the stove.

"Max, he is not in his bed." Panic was filling her because even as she did not want to believe it, she knew he had gone.

"Go to the stables, perhaps he is there seeing his horse, and I shall check upstairs," Bertie said.

She did as he said, and ran all the way, but all she found was Myrtle sitting outside the empty stall that had held Max's horse. She dropped to her knees and hugged the dog, who whined softly.

"H-he's gone, Myrtle, and Lord, it hurts."

She had known him for such a short time, and yet the impact he'd had on her life was immense. Last night he had treated her as if she was the angel he professed her to be, and then after he had taken her innocence he had fled like a thief in the night.

"How could you," she whispered into Myrtle's fur. Did what they had shared mean nothing to him at all—or had he left because in fact it had meant something?

Essie made it back inside; she even appeared composed when she told the Hemple brothers Max had gone.

"I'm going to wash up now, and will be back shortly."

They did not question her, and Myrtle followed as she climbed the stairs. Only when she closed her door did she let the tears flow. Silly, useless tears for a man she knew nothing of except what her heart had told her. He was kind and gentle, and protective. Was she wrong again? Had she misjudged another man?

"No, I won't believe that," Essie whispered. *He cared for me and Myrtle, and I will not believe differently.* He'd told her he had nothing to give her, and she had accepted that. The shock was that he had left before she awoke, but she had to admit he had promised her nothing.

"I wonder if we will ever see him again?" She hugged the dog close.

He was alone by his own admission. Alone, with no possessions or home, and had promised her nothing. She had last night as a wonderful memory, and that would be enough. It was certainly more than she had ever believed she would have.

"Are you in there, Essex?" The words were followed by a heavy fist banging on the wood.

Rolling off the bed, Essie knew if she didn't answer it, Cam would knock it down. Wiping her eyes, she forced a smile onto her face and opened the door.

"Cam, why are you roaring at such an early hour?"

She stepped back and away, so he could not see her, but his hand stopped her. He turned her to face him, then her chin was lifted.

Her brother's eyes roamed her face, taking in the devastation she was sure he saw there.

"Why are you crying?" Cam went still when he was truly worried, and his voice lost all the lightness and humor he was known for.

"I am merely exhausted."

"Tell me the truth." He shook her.

"He... Max has gone."

"And this upsets you enough to have you crying?"

She nodded, then bit her lip as more tears threatened. "H-he is injured, and I fear for him."

The green Sinclair eyes narrowed.

"No, there is more to this sadness than just that. What did that man do to you?"

She forced a laugh from her lips, but it was more a sob.

"How can he possibly have done something to me in two days, and with a bullet hole in his side?"

"That I do not know, but I plan to find out."

"I-I— He can't mean anything to me."

"And yet he does?"

"N-no." Essie refused to weep again. "I will be fine, Cam, it was merely a s-surprise to see him gone this morning. I worry he will open the stiches and get an infection."

"You were always the worst liar in the Sinclair clan." Cam opened his arms, and she walked into them simply because she wanted to be held by someone who loved her.

"I'm all right, truly, Cam. Unstable, and not s-sound of mind, but all right." Essie tried to make light of the situation. "Tiredness is making me weepy."

"Of course you are, but you're all those things and my sister, and if someone has hurt you, I will have to hurt him."

"I am not hurting, it was a shock." Essie tried again to convince her brother.

"Well considering what Bertie told me about Brunt, I can understand you have had a trying time of things.

"He is a nasty, mean man."

"He is at that, and I believe I now owe this Max a debt of gratitude for flattening him with a good punch."

She nodded into his shirt. "I fear you will not see him again to thank him."

"You don't know where he has gone then?"

She shook her head.

"Come, let us go out to your garden. You're always calmer there."

Essie let Cam lead her outside, and felt the sun on her head as he walked to her gardens. Reaching the bench seat she and Eden had built, he lowered her onto it.

"Cry your tears, Essie, and then we shall talk, you and I."

"I don't like crying, it makes my head hurt," she said, leaning into his arm. "And really I have no reason to do s-so. I am not the weeping Sinclair, as you very well know, I am the calm Sinclair."

"Who wrote that rule?"

"It is the way of things, Cam. I settle arguments and soothe ails."

"I had no idea you were so boring. Remind me again why I am here with you?"

"You know what I'm saying."

"No, I really don't."

She looked at him, and saw the look on his face was genuine.

"I-I'm not like you, Dev, and Eden."

He studied her, running his eyes over her hair and face. "You certainly look like us."

"I just don't have your..." Essie struggled to find the right words. "Charisma."

"I wouldn't be too upset about that, as not many people do," Cam bragged.

Essie snuffled into his shirt.

"Are you wiping your nose on my clothing?" Cam always knew how to make her smile even when she had no reason to.

"I arrived downstairs this morning to find the Hemple brothers wringing their hands and murmuring about this sainted Max, he who felled Brunt with one blow. It's enough to put a man off his food… were he any man but I, that is."

Essie sighed. "I am all right, Cam. It was just a shock to find him gone."

"I know you, and this is more than shock."

"I don't want to feel things anymore." Essie struggled to put her thoughts into words.

"A trifle hard when you live in a family of emotive people, love."

"That is not my meaning. I meant I never want to feel anything for a man again. I decided this after Tolly broke my heart."

"You were born to love, Essie, it's in your nature."

"I don't want that. Don't want the pain and heartache that goes with it. I have seen our siblings struggle with emotion, and while Dev and Eden are now happy, they suffered to get there."

Cam sighed. "It is part of the process, Essie. You cannot simply wake up one morning, meet your mate and live happily ever after. Not if it is true love, anyway. Some of those marriages in London make me shudder, all about connections and family ties. Cold and unemotional unions are not for a Sinclair."

She looked up at him, but his eyes were on Myrtle, who had followed them outside and was foraging about in her gardens.

"Do you want that, Cam?"

He was quiet for a while as they listened to the sounds around them. Essie could hear the waves crashing against the rocks some distance away, and the gulls screaming, the rustle of leaves in the trees. The smell of her herbs wafted around them. All were as familiar to her as breathing.

"I'm not sure I have it in me to love like that, Essie. I'm not sure I want to ever feel that way about a woman either." He looked down at her.

"You know that when you sigh like that, you of all my

sisters, it breaks my heart," Cam said in a soft voice. "When that bastard Tolly hurt you, I wanted to raise him from the dead for the pain he inflicted on you."

"I know, just as I know you and Dev would do what needed to be done to protect me."

"How has this man who left in the middle of the night hurt you in such a short time? Can you tell me that?"

"He did not hurt me," Essie denied.

Cam snorted. "I know you well enough to see the hurt, sister."

"Brunt hurt me with his words, and I hurt for Beth, and yes, perhaps I did feel a little something for Max, but he was nothing but a gentleman to me."

"Then why are you hurting? It makes no sense."

"Because he made me feel something. An awareness that I had hoped to never feel again," Essie said. *And when he made love to me, I was sure he touched my soul.*

"I understand what you mean. Women have come and gone in my life who have made me aware of them. A touch or look shared. It's disconcerting," Cam said.

"Is there a particular woman in your life now who makes you feel like that?"

He shook his head. "Oh no, no, no, we are not discussing me, sister, but you."

Essie sighed again. "Every man who has come into my life, I compare to you and Dev. Every one usually fails, but yesterday I realized that Max is like you both. He is a protector, for all he appears the opposite. He was kind to Myrtle, and she in turn loved him, and h-he punched Murray Brunt when he dared to call me a witch."

"Now that I wish I had seen," Cam said.

"Brunt called me a witch, Cam."

Her brother got to his feet and stalked away from her. She watched as he plucked several heads off flowers and shredded them. Myrtle came to his side and pressed herself against his leg. Cam being Cam, he bent to pat her head. Even in anger, her brothers would never turn from those that loved them.

How had she known in such a short space of time that Max was the same?

"And you say you felt something for this Max?" Cam stalked back to stand before her.

"I-I— Yes," she said honestly. "But more an attraction, I think you could say," Essie lied. It would do no good to let Cam believe any different. "And as I know you have felt the same many times, I'm sure you understand."

"Of course, I feel attractions to women all the time, but they do not upset me as much as you are upset."

"I told you why I feel upset, Cam. Beth and then her husband, and then finding Max gone. I have had very little sleep also." No good would come of him becoming aware of just how much she and Max had shared. "Truly, Cam. I was just being pathetic this morning because I was weary."

"No." He shook his head. "You are one of the strongest women I know. Never be ashamed of your emotions, or sharing them with me, no matter how uncomfortable they make me feel."

She found another laugh.

"It will pass, Cam. As you have said, I knew him two days; a person cannot form an attachment in such a short amount of time. We will go to London and I shall forget all about him and the Brunts."

"You give so much of yourself to others, Essie. Everything you do, you do with your heart on your sleeve, and we love you because of that. If some man can't see what you are, then he is not worth your heartache, sister. Although this seems an odd conversation to be having, considering the circumstances."

She regained her feet and took the hand he held out to her.

"Why can't I find someone like you or Dev, or even James?"

"Well of course there is only one of me," Cam said, smiling as she scoffed. "Dev and James are far too uptight for you, love. Not to mention they are family. I worry about you, Essie. You are vulnerable around men."

"One man does not make me vulnerable. Yes, I was a fool with Tolly, but then he was the first man I had cared for. Perhaps in light of that I was blinded to his true self."

"Two men now."

"No. I did not love Max. How could I after two days? So you see, there is no need to worry for me." Did all her family feel like this about her? "I am no fool, Cam."

"Fool, no. Innocent, and generous of spirit, yes. If I may suggest, when you find your heart weakening again, as surely it will, you come to me and I shall check the man over thoroughly. If he passes, you may proceed."

"Idiot."

"And now we must prepare ourselves to once again walk in society. You must throw off those hideous dresses and actually tie your hair with a ribbon, or have your maid style it with flowers."

Essie looked into her brother's eyes. "Thank you for caring, Cam."

"Always," he said, placing a kiss on her forehead.

And this, Essie thought, *should be enough*. It had to be, as once again she had made a fool of herself over a man. She vowed to never do so again.

CHAPTER 8

"You received a letter from Dev today, Cam? What did it say? And furthermore, why did you not tell me?"

He and Essie were taking their evening meal. The night was warm, so they forwent a fire, but sipped from mugs of tea.

"I was giving you time to compose yourself."

She waved a hand about. "I am now composed, so tell me what Dev said."

"Women are such fickle creatures. One minute you are heartbroken, and then next it is forgotten."

"I was not heartbroken, and after a good sleep I am once again hearty." She did not tell him that thoughts of Max had plagued her all day. "Now, tell me what our brother said."

"That our presence is required in London."

Tea sloshed over the brim of her mug as she quickly sat upright. "But we are returning soon anyway. What has happened to want us earlier?"

"Nothing bad, I assure you." He waved her back into her seat. "It is merely that you are to be an aunt, and James and

Dev want you to come to London to watch over their wives until they are ready to leave and travel to their estates."

"I'm to be an aunt!" Essie leapt to her feet. "Both are expecting?"

Cam nodded, his smile telling her he was pleased with her reaction. "And let me tell you that I am not entirely sure I wish to spend the next six months in the company of either man. They are already protective, they will now be insufferable." He looked disgusted. "It is decidedly off-putting to see such powerful men brought to their knees."

Essie found a laugh. "I'm telling them you said that."

His smile fell away, and the look that followed was suddenly serious, not something she usually saw on this brother.

"That is the first genuine smile I have had out of you today, sister, and it pleases me to see it."

"Oh, there is much to plan now before we leave! Excuse me, brother, I have lists to write."

"Again it is just you and I, Myrtle. But then, you always were my one true love."

Essie was smiling as she left the room.

Essie drew her eyes from the passing scenery to look at her brother, who was lounging on the opposite seat. No easy feat when you were over six foot, but he always managed it. They had finally reached London, after many last-minute preparations.

"Mrs. Toots has assured me she will watch over my patients until I return, and Mrs. Beadle, Josiah, and Bertie know enough to help should they be needed," Essie said as the carriages entered the outskirts of London. "My fear is—"

"Enough, sister!"

Essie's eyes widened at Cam's harsh words.

"God's blood, Ess. I have watched you rush hither and yon doing what you feel must be done. I now know more than enough about every ailment of the residents of Crunston Cliff, and believe I could have done without picturing old Mrs. Lemon's festering sores. Please, I beg of you, allow me some peace, so I may arrive in London in a pleasant humor."

Essie poked out her tongue.

"I know you worry, and that is entirely natural, but Crunston Cliff survived without you when last you came to London, and it will survive now. Should there be an emergency then they will ride to the next village and get help there. Now have mercy on me, and shut your mouth."

Essex huffed out a breath, then gave her brother a rueful smile.

"Thank you."

"For what?"

"Being my brother. Loving me, when I know sometimes I do not make that easy."

His smile was gentle, and she wished others saw what she and the rest of their family did, the man with a big, generous heart.

"Compared to the rest of our family, my sweet, loving you was never difficult."

She gulped down the tears.

"If you cry I may revise that opinion."

She saw the changes in him that she had not taken the time to notice earlier due to her preoccupation with her patients. Cam had put on weight, but it suited him. His hair was still overlong and stood off his head in a tousled mass. He wore clothes effortlessly, like their elder brother, and Essie was relieved to see he did not have silly high collars and overly bright waistcoats. He was a handsome man, and she knew that he would be a wonderful husband one day.

"I love you," she said softly.

"Love you right back."

She took the hand he held out to her and squeezed it.

"Look at that silly animal."

Myrtle was seated beside Essie, her head out the window, tongue hanging from the side of her mouth.

"The children will be pleased to see her."

"Undoubtedly."

Her eldest brother lived on the same street as their aunt and uncle, and James and Eden. People thought it odd that they were living that way, but it suited them. The youngest Sinclair siblings could flit between houses whenever they wanted to see a particular family member.

"You know that Dev and Lilly buying that huge house at the end of the street has made us even more peculiar in the eyes of society," Cam said.

Essie shrugged. "We have always been different, Cam, and I don't remember you caring what people thought of us before."

He waved a hand about. "I don't care, and I'm so highly regarded I could walk about wearing pink satin with feathers in my hair, and I would still be universally loved. I was merely alerting you to the facts."

"You are not universally loved. Pitied, more likely."

"Harsh, sister, but I understand that your hurtful words spring from the well of jealousy inside you."

She was still laughing as the carriage drew to a halt, as she was sure was his plan. Cam did not like to see his family hurting in any way.

"Before we get out, Cam. I must ask you to promise not to mention this business with Max, as there is really nothing to it."

"Of course, if that is your wish. After all, you know how much I love keeping secrets from Eden and Dev."

"Idiot."

"I'm sure my back has a permanent crick in it from several days of travel." Cam arched as he stepped down.

"Essie, Cam, Myrtle!"

Looking up the large brick-fronted house, Essie saw the faces of her twin sisters. Aged ten, Somerset and Dorset were frantically waving down at them.

"Pull your heads back inside, you hoydens!" Cam scolded them. "You'll bloody well fall and land on me if you lean out any further."

They giggled and retreated.

"I see they are still shy and retiring," Essie said, slipping an arm through Cam's. She took Myrtle's lead in the other.

"I don't know how we shall present them in society when the time comes. Timid little dormice that they are," he drawled.

Dev and Lilly's house had needed a great deal of work to bring it up to scratch after they'd purchased it. Months later, it was now as they wanted it to be, an extension of the love they shared. The warmth of the house wrapped around them as Cam lead her upstairs, their feet sinking into patterned carpets. Walls were in peach and gold, and paintings of landscapes hung in shadowed alcoves.

"It's so lovely, don't you think, Cam?"

"It is, and suits the mighty Lord Sinclair."

"He and Lilly are so happy now. It is so wonderful after the lives they both lived."

"Aye, I cannot disagree with that, sister."

"Essie!"

She caught her youngest brother, Warwickshire, when he ran at her. Bending, she hugged him close. He had grown, she realized with a pang of regret that she had not been here to witness it. Next came the twins, and they hugged her together, like they did everything

Arms around them, she followed Warwick into the room where the rest of her siblings waited. Myrtle was adding to the mayhem by barking and turning circles.

"Essie." Devonshire Sinclair was the eldest of their clan, and had carried the weight of responsibility for them for many years after the death of their parents. Tall and broad shouldered, he had the Sinclair dark hair and stunning green eyes, and to Essie he was one of the most handsome men in England—alongside Cam. She pushed aside Max as he slipped into her head. He would never be anything to her now. In fact, she doubted she would ever see him again.

"Dev." She leaned into him as his arms closed around her.

"What has happened?" He held her shoulders and looked deep into her eyes, as only an elder sibling who had known you since birth could do.

"Nothing, I am merely tired from traveling."

The hand that cupped her cheek was warm and made her eyes close.

"No, there is more to this than fatigue, but I will not pursue the matter now. There will be time later."

"There is nothing more. Now, let me tell you how lovely your house looks, and that I am so happy for you and Lilly, Dev. When is the baby due?"

He didn't speak immediately, just lowered his head and kissed her forehead.

"I'm so pleased you are here."

"As am I," she managed to get out around the lump in her throat. "And I am sure I shall say this more than once. Please do not worry. Lilly is strong, and everything will be all right."

Dev exhaled loudly. He was one of the strongest men she knew, until it came to his wife or family. Then he was irrational and fiercely protective.

"Will you tell her that she must rest and not overdo things, Essie?"

"Do not listen to him, Essie. I told him not to make you come to London, but of course my words were ignored."

Lilliana Sinclair was a beauty. She had thick blonde hair, eyes the color of lavender, and she and Dev were the perfect match in every way. After turbulent beginnings, they had forged a bond that Essie knew would never break.

"Hello, Lilly, and please do not give it another thought, as I was coming to London anyway."

The smile, if possible, made her more beautiful.

"You are glowing," Essie said, tamping down the bite of jealousy. She would never carry a child, but she had no right to be bitter when those she loved did. "And I am very excited about one day soon meeting my niece or nephew."

Nephew, Essie thought. Lilly carried a boy, but she kept that to herself.

"I am healthy as an ox, but still your brother worries."

"That is what I am supposed to do, my love." Dev slipped an arm around his wife's waist and kissed the top of her head. "It is my job through the confinement, I believe."

The love they shared was so strong, she felt it settle over the room.

"Excuse me while I see to refreshments." As Lilly excused herself, Dev pulled Essie to his side.

"She seems in excellent health from what I could sense, Dev."

"Does she?" The relief in his voice was clear for everyone to hear.

"I never thought you one for vapors, Dev. Are we to carry smelling salts for you too?" Cam drawled.

"I am not having vapors, brother, it is concern for my wife. One day you will know the difference."

"Not for many years, is my fondest wish." Cam's eyes brushed over Essie. "This love business is far too painful for me. I will remain a self-centered, perfectly eligible, and may I add, highly sought bachelor for many years to come, thank you."

"I can see the baby's color." Dev said the words quietly, so only Essie and Cam heard. Their younger siblings were playing cards at the table, loudly, like they did everything else.

"You can see the color already?" Cam whistled.

"It is my match," Dev said, and Essie heard the wonder in his voice.

The Sinclairs were not like other people; they had heightened senses. Supposedly this anomaly came about centuries ago, and while Essie liked some aspects of her gift, she loathed being different from other people, and having to hide that fact.

Dev's gift was sight. He could see things from great distance, and also at night. He also saw people in colors when he changed to his other sight. Eden had the gift of hearing, which was why she wore earplugs, as she could hear someone whisper from some distance away. Cam's was smell, and Essie's, taste. Each had other variations on that sense that had evolved over the years. Essie would sometimes taste fear or danger seconds before it happened. If she touched an expectant woman, she could tell they were carrying a babe and the sex of that child. The only sense they did not have was touch, but Lilly had that, and they knew this was why she was now wed to Dev.

"What am I to have, Ess?"

Essie smiled up at Dev. "That is for me to know only, brother."

He laughed, a deep rumble of joy. "Very well."

"She will bloody well tell me what I'm having!" Shortly after those words reached them, in through the door came the Duchess of Raven, formerly known as Eden Sinclair. Dark haired like all of them, Eden was the only sibling to have gray eyes. At her side walked her husband, the Duke of Raven. With Dev's build, he had dark hair and brown eyes, and had once been a serious, conflicted man with little reason to smile. Eden had changed that.

"Eden!" Essie hurried to hug her sister. She felt the babe, and acknowledged her niece silently. "You too are glowing. Cannot one of you carry a greenish tinge and look off-color, like so many women in the early months of their pregnancies."

"She has a greenish tinge in the morning for an hour, if that helps," James said, kissing Essie's cheek.

"Oh it does, immensely."

Eden made a pffting sound, and took Essie by the shoulders as Dev had done. She inspected her thoroughly.

"What has happened?"

"Nothing has happened." Essie smiled. "I am just weary from traveling."

She watched her sister's eyes lift over her head, and knew Eden shared a brief look with Dev and Cam.

"Lilly is approaching, and tea will arrive shortly," Eden said, still studying her.

"Excellent, I'm famished." Cam stepped to Essie's side and accepted a hug from Eden.

"When are you not famished?"

"When I sleep."

Essie left her siblings talking, and went to see Warwick, Somer and Dorrie, who were reacquainting themselves with Myrtle, who in turn was loving the attention. She did not like lying to her siblings, but in this she would stand firm. No one need know she had once again made a fool of herself over a man, and that this one she had only known for two days.

CHAPTER 9

*E*ssie had been in London two weeks before she decided to venture out alone. She had hoped the memory of Max and what they had shared would have eased by now, especially since she had left Oak's Knoll, but it had not. In fact, she worried for him constantly. He had no money or home, and was staying she knew not where, and surely that would not help him heal. Was he even now lying somewhere, mad with fever?

She worried about infection, she worried that he had no one to love, and she hated that she worried. He was nothing to her. He had not even told her he was leaving for pity's sake. That alone should be enough to force the man from her head. He had wanted nothing more to do with her.

She had spent the days since arriving in London with her family, reading and playing with her younger siblings, and venturing to the park that lay a five-minute walk from Dev and Lilly's house to run Myrtle, or for a picnic. She had visited with her aunt and uncle and generally caught up on family news. For now, she had managed to avoid the questions about what had upset her, and for once Cam had held his counsel. She had no doubt he had done so under duress, as Eden and Dev would have questioned him relentlessly.

"I wish to replenish my medical supplies, Dev. May I use the carriage, please?"

"London is not a place for a young lady to travel about alone, Essie."

They were seated at the breakfast table, Lilly, she, and Dev, and their three younger siblings.

"How fortuitous that I am not a young lady then, Devon."

She watched his jaw clench briefly, while beside him Lilly gave her a wink, then continued to eat her eggs.

"You are my younger sister, and as such my responsibility."

Dev had always taken his responsibilities as head of the family seriously.

"And yet I live in Oak's Knoll without you. How on earth did I survive without my big brother watching over me?"

"You had Cam with you, two Hemples, and a maid," he snapped.

Dev sat across from her, close enough to Lilly so he could touch her if he wanted. The three younger Sinclairs were engaged in consuming their food and insulting each other. Something of a Sinclair sibling tradition.

"Raise your head, Warwick, I have no wish to listen to you slurp your food directly from the plate."

"Why must I, Dev, when there is no one to see?"

Warwick needed a haircut, Essie thought as his fringe fell over his eyes. Peas in a pod. The three little Sinclairs would grow up to look just like the older ones.

"We are here, and as we are the people who love you, I should think we are more important than anyone."

"How do you do that?"

"Do what?" Dev questioned his little brother.

"Be telling one of us off, but notice when another is doing something you do not like?"

Lilly snuffled, and received a sharp look from her husband.

"Plenty of practice is how. Now lift your head."

"Cam has arrived and is hungry," Warwick said, hoping to distract his brother. "He said to tell someone to replenish the food."

"It wouldn't matter how much food there was, he'd still need more," Somer said.

"Uncle says he has hollow legs," Dorrie added.

"Highly likely, girls, so I suggest you eat up before he arrives."

"Yes, Dev," they said in unison.

"If only every member of this family was as accommodating as you two," he said, smiling at them.

"Universal adoration is not good for anyone, but most especially not you."

"Hear, hear." Lilly lifted her teacup to Essie.

"You are not leaving this house without one of us," Dev continued with the dogged determination to remain on task that had always infuriated his siblings. He had a fiendishly good memory also, and never forgot a conversation. "The places you will go are not safe, therefore I will not allow it."

"Dev," Essie sighed. "I will have my maid and your carriage. Surely they will suffice?"

"God's blood, my hunger is savage this morning." Cam wandered in, yawning loudly after those ominous words. His lodgings were next door to their aunt and uncle, in a house gifted to him. He looked like an eligible young gentleman should, and Essie was sure if any unwed young ladies were present they would sigh at the sight he presented.

"Good morning, heathens," he said, picking up the twins and kissing them loudly, which made them giggle. He ruffled

Warwick's hair. "Which Roman emperor was defeated at the Battle of Chrysopolis?" he threw at them as he made his way to the loaded sideboard.

Essie looked at Dorrie, Somer, and Warwick. Her siblings, like the elder Sinclairs, were sharp-witted and could hold a great deal of useless information in their heads. Challenging them was something she, Eden, Cam, and Dev did often, as boredom led to trouble. She knew this, as the elder Sinclairs had been no different.

"I know!" Lilly said.

"Licinius I, who reigned from 308 to 324," Dorrie said quickly, before Lilly could beat her.

"He was executed by Constantine I," Warwick added, with his mouth full of food.

"Do you know that you three are more intelligent than any number of the adults I know?"

Somer and Dorrie smiled at Lilly's compliment. Warrick continued to eat.

"Tell your sister she is not leaving this house without a companion, namely you."

Cam's eyes switched from Dev to Essie as he settled into a seat with a loaded plate.

"I'm sure there is an inch of room there." Essie pointed to Cam's plate. "Surely you could have crammed something else on it?"

Cam frowned. "Perhaps you are right. I shall be sure not to make the same mistake when I replenish my plate."

"Don't try and change the subject, Essex."

"I gather you are the sister concerned, as the other one is married to an overprotective duke, and these two would never leave the house without company?" Cam indicated the twins.

"Dev is being overprotective yet again. I will take my maid, and I merely wish to visit apothecaries. I need supplies that I cannot source in Crunston Cliff. I have no wish to have one of you accompanying me and constantly moaning about the time I am taking. Therefore, at age twenty-seven, I feel more than capable of going out alone. After all, just last week I treated Mr. Bundle's boil, and it was situated—"

"Essex!" Dev thundered. "You will keep the rest of those words inside your head, if you please. We are eating."

Essie popped her last piece of toast in her mouth and chewed slowly.

"Therefore, I feel more than capable of entering a few establishments. Plus, and I repeat for possibly the fourth or fifth time—"

"At least ten, surely?"

Essie smiled at her sister-in-law before continuing. "I will have your driver, Bids, watching over me, and we all know how studious he is in that duty."

Dev looked at her, those amazing green eyes of his seeing everything. She knew he had switched his vision and was seeing if her color was healthy. He did that often with his siblings. Strong color meant a healthy person, pale meant something was not as it should be.

"At least your color is good now. When first you rejoined us, it was weaker. Of course, as yet I have not been given the reason why." He glared at Cam, who ignored him and continued to shovel in food.

"Dev." She reached across the table for his hand and squeezed it. She felt the usual jolt she always did when she connected with one of her siblings. "I need you to let me go now. I am old enough to live alone at Oak's Knoll, and more than capable of a trip to some stores. Please," she added.

"It's only because I love you."

"And because I have terrible taste in men." Essie tried to lighten the mood, but saw Cam scowl. He had kept his word and said nothing about Max, and for that she was grateful, because really, what was there to say? "So I will go, and then I will return," she added quickly.

"Very well." Dev sighed as Lilly leaned into him. "But two hours, and no more. If you are longer, I will come looking with Eden. Now please excuse me for a few moments, there is a matter I must attend to."

That threat had been used often on the Sinclair siblings, as Eden could hear a great distance. She was hell to play hide-and-seek with.

She watched him leave the room as he did everything... with purpose.

"He worries about you two, you know," Lilly said.

"I can understand worrying about her, because I do that." Cam nodded to where Essie sat. "But why me?"

"He needs to worry about someone other than me, so as you two are not settled into happy unions, I'm afraid it will stay that way until you are."

Cam snorted. "He's worse than a father."

"Why do you worry about me?" Essie questioned her brother. "There is no need, surely?"

He raised a brow, and his silence told her he was alluding to the business with Max.

"I am fine, for pity's sake. I am rarely without a family member watching over me, and while this may surprise you, I am actually quite intelligent. Some days I even put on matching shoes."

"Do you really?" Cam drawled. "That is exceedingly clever of you, and I must say this look is a better one than your attire at Oak's Knoll. Why, you almost look pretty."

Lilly laughed as Cam continued to needle Essie.

"Essie is one of the most beautiful ladies in all of London." Warwick lifted his head to utter these words, before lowering it to his plate once again.

"Thank you, darling, that is quite the loveliest thing anyone has ever said to me."

"What are you after, you little toad?" Cam lunged across the table at his little brother and tickled him under the arms until the boy was squirming.

"Tonight we go to Aunt and Uncle's ball," Dev said, reentering the room. "So have mercy and return in time to have a rest, so she will not yell at you if you yawn."

"Of course, although I do not need my beauty sleep like some," Essie said.

"I hope you are not referring to me?" Cam said, grabbing Dorrie and hauling her into his lap, making the girl shriek. "As we all know I am beautiful no matter the situation."

"Christ," Dev muttered. "I'm sure her screams could burst an eardrum."

"How exciting, a ball," Essie lied, getting to her feet. She loathed society functions, but this one she knew she must attend.

"Your enthusiasm is overflowing, sister."

"It's all right for you, Aunt will not be thrusting any available man with good teeth into your path, as it is quite acceptable for you to still be unwed. Whereas I am practically on the shelf, but unlike other women, happy to be there."

"Aunt means well, Essie," Dev said. "And you are too pretty to be on the shelf."

"Besides, that rules out Tickersly," Cam said. "His teeth are missing in the front."

"And Culliver, his are crooked," Dev added.

"Yes, thank you, there is no need to outline all the undesirable men. Your sister is no fool," Lilly interrupted.

"Well, actually—"

Essie glared Cam silent.

"I will have Grace get your dress ready, Essie," Lilly said before the conversation could continue. "And we, your family, will be there to ensure you dance with no one unsuitable."

"Thank you, my most favorite of sisters-in-law." She kissed Lilly's cheek, then her siblings'. "I love you too," she whispered to Dev, and then left the room.

"She's your only sister-in-law!" he roared as she walked down the hall.

Family, she thought. You had no time to be maudlin surrounded by so many of them.

She went to her room, got her bonnet and gloves and slipped on a spencer, then made her way downstairs. It was there she found Eden. Humming softly to herself, she was rearranging the flowers that had just been arranged by one of Dev's staff.

"Hello, sister," Eden said without looking up. Of course she had heard Essie approach.

"Hello, sister."

Giving the flowers a last tweak, she turned to face Essie as she walked down the stairs. Eden, as always, looked beautiful in a long coat in pale peppermint. She wore a cream dress beneath, the skirts exposed through the opening below her waist. Her bonnet matched the coat and she looked as she always did, exotic, intriguing, and beautiful. Eden was all those things and more. Outspoken and vivacious, she was the Sinclair men fawned over and liked to look at. Pregnancy had merely enhanced the allure that had brought the Duke of Raven to his knees.

"Why are you rearranging flowers in Dev and Lilly's entranceway?"

"I'm waiting for you."

Sighing was really the only thing she could do. So she did, loudly.

"Dev sent word, didn't he? What did he do, stand outside on the road and roar your name?"

Eden slipped her gloves back on.

"Don't be silly, he would never make such a spectacle of himself. He went into the gardens behind the house and roared."

Eden snorted.

"It was no hardship, and as I was lolling about in the breakfast room annoying James while he attempted to read his morning paper, it was a welcome distraction."

"Where are Emily and Samantha?" James had two half sisters that had come into his life late.

"Taking lessons. Emily asked if she could join in, as she wanted to continue her learning, and James thought it a wonderful idea."

"It is," Essie agreed.

"I missed you, Ess, and therefore we shall spend a lovely day shopping for your supplies, as long as there is a cup of tea and delicious treat at the end of it."

"You wish to spend the day shopping for herbs and other medical supplies?"

"Lovely," Eden said, with absolutely no enthusiasm.

"Come along then, and don't say I didn't warn you."

"Eden, how lovely to see you. This is a surprise!"

Essie looked up at her eldest brother, who was leaning over the railing looking down at them. The satisfied look on his face had Essie itching to stomp up the stairs and give him a piece of her mind.

"You could at least try and sound convincing," she said.

"I have no idea what you mean."

"You are happy for Eden to accompany me, but not a maid?"

"Eden has excellent hearing," he replied.

The sisters snorted, and then Essie lifted her nose in the air and led Eden outside. Her brother's laughter followed her.

They climbed into the carriage and were soon rolling through London to their first destination. As Eden was with her, she had left Grace behind.

Midmorning had the London streets busy enough that the trip to the first store was a slow one.

"So I have waited for you to tell me, but it seems I must ask."

"About what?" Essie looked at her sister.

"Whatever you left behind in Oak's Knoll."

"I left nothing behind, I was merely tired."

She was subjected to the Sinclair look from the only gray eyes in the family.

"Beth Brunt came and saw me the day before we left." Essie decided on a half-truth. She was not lying if she omitted all details about Max, surely?

Eden's eyes softened. She, Essie, and Beth had played together as young girls. Those days had seen Beth happy and healthy; she was no longer either of those things.

"She has miscarried many times, and is thin and weak, and that brute of a husband of hers will give her no peace!" Essie felt the anger again.

"Oh no, Essie. That is so horrible."

"Murray Brunt came to Oak's Knoll that night to tell me to stay away from her. He called me a witch."

"Dear Lord, did he threaten you?"

"He tried, but I had Bertie and Josiah with me, and a patient was also there, so Brunt was all bluster." See, not a lie; she had told the entire truth without bringing Max's name into it.

"What patient?"

Damn.

"A man, you don't know him. He and the brothers got rid of Brunt. Plus Myrtle, who chased after him growling savagely."

"What was this man's name?"

"I told you, it was Murray Brunt."

The thing about a Sinclair was that they were relentless in their pursuit of answers until they were satisfied, and could rarely be deviated from their course. Essie did not like to lie to her siblings, for no other reason than they always knew when she was. She would do so otherwise in a heartbeat, if the lie was only a small, insignificant one.

"As you very well know, I did not mean that fool. I want to know the patient's name."

"I don't like to talk about my patients, you know that."

Eden leaned forward and gave Essie the full force of her glare.

"You are evading answering me, and I want to know why?"

Essie looked out the window as she felt the carriage slow.

"Wonderful, we are here!"

Opening the door, she clambered out with more haste than elegance. Eden followed, looking as if she were royalty.

CHAPTER 10

"We must walk up the lane, Eden, as it is too narrow for the carriage."

"I have not finished with this conversation, Essie."

"I have."

"I will find someone to watch the horses and accompany you, your Grace, Miss Sinclair."

"No need, Bids. We are quite capable of walking the short distance to that shop you see there." Waving a hand down the lane, Essie did not make eye contact with Dev's driver. The man was a terrible worrier.

"But—"

"Honestly, Bids, there is no need for all this fretting."

"You never know who's lurking about, your Grace."

"We will scream should some miscreant approach. Will that ease your fears?"

"Very well, your Grace."

Essie could see he wasn't convinced, but she and Eden struck out anyway.

"His poor wife is expecting their first child any day now, and can you imagine what he is putting her through, Essie?"

"Oh dear, yes I can." Essie knew Bids would be smothering his wife with concern. "I shall have a chat with him, and try to reassure him."

The air was not as clean as in Crunston Cliff; in fact it was filled with the scents of chimney smoke, cooking, and many others, all mingling to create an odd yet strangely invigorating aroma.

She climbed the two rickety steps that lead to Mr. Riley's Apothecary Shop, then opened the door and entered.

"Good morning to you, Miss Sinclair."

"Good morning, Mr. Riley. This is my sister, the Duchess of Raven."

"Your Grace, it is an honor." The man bowed deeply.

"If you will fill this order for me, I shall see what else you have that may interest me." Essie handed him her list.

"I shall see to it at once."

This shop was one of only a few that Essie believed held truly excellent supplies. She could find most things here, and what wasn't readily available, Mr. Riley would source for her. She had stumbled across it on her first visit to London, and had returned often since.

Essie inspected instruments in cabinets and selected two carboys. The clear glass vessels would be excellent for use at Oak's Knoll. She moved to a shelf lined with books, and saw one that caught her attention.

"I shall take this copy of *The English Physician* also, please Mr. Riley. I have long sought a copy."

"Oh indeed, its lists of plants and herbs, preparations and usage, are unsurpassed." The man took it down from the shelf and added it to her rapidly growing pile of goods.

"I would also recommend to you a building on Nettle Lane, Miss Sinclair. Recently opened, it has a large quantity of herbs and other medical supplies, plus several books that may interest you. You will get burdock and anemone juice there, as I am out of those at this time."

Essie took the card Mr. Riley held out to her.

"Huntington's Supplies." She read the black lettering. "Have you been there, Mr. Riley?"

The man rocked back on his heels as he nodded. Not overly tall, he barely reached her chin.

"Oh indeed, and I purchase a great deal from there, I assure you, Miss Sinclair. The owner is a wealthy merchant, and he has many business interests in the United Kingdom, from what I gather. There are three warehouses filled with many different things, but the one of interest to you is the first you will come to."

"Well, thank you, and I shall return to your wonderful store before I leave again."

"And I shall have your purchases sent directly to Lord Sinclair's address."

"Essie, come and look at this."

She moved to where her sister was looking down into a glass-topped cabinet.

"Performance enhancer," Eden whispered. "For men who... well, you know."

"Eden!" Essie glanced over her shoulder, but Mr. Riley had his back turned to them. "Come away at once."

"James certainly has no need of that." Eden giggled as they left the shop.

"I cannot believe you are discussing that"—Essie waved her hand about—"in public!"

"It is hardly public with only one man in the shop, and he was not listening. Besides, we have discussed such matters before."

"You're carrying my niece or nephew. What will it make of your scandalous behavior?"

"I'm sure it cannot hear me, or for that matter understand what I say."

"I wonder if it will have your hearing." Essie took her sister's arm as they started walking back down the lane. She missed this when she was parted from her family, the familiarity born from years and years of living with her siblings. "How are Emily and Samantha?"

"Samantha is wonderful, full of life, mischievous as ever, and Emily is still shy and quiet. But sometimes, Essie, when only Samantha is with her, she changes. It's as if she comes to life. I hear them laughing and doing silly things when she thinks no one is listening, which I assure you James and I often are. He is very gentle with her, but there is still a barrier there that he cannot breach."

"Time and patience will get him there, I am sure. Her life was a very difficult one, from the little I have learned."

"Does it still hurt to think about Tolly, Essie?"

Tolly had been Emily's brother, and it had been he Essie had believed she loved.

Gently prodding around in her heart, she thought perhaps it didn't hurt anymore. She thought about Max then, and hoped he was healing well, and not alone. This had worried her more than anything when he'd told her. Everyone should have someone to turn to, surely?

"No, it hurts no longer."

Eden squeezed her arm. When she reached the carriage, Bids looked relieved. Honestly, he was worse than Dev.

"We wish to go to this address now, if you please, Bids," Essie said, handing him the card she'd received from Mr. Riley.

"Oh but—"

"At once, Bids, and you'll stop your bellyaching," Eden said, motioning Essie into the carriage. "Honestly, we are grown women, and it is daylight!"

Essie looked at the buildings as they passed. Some narrow, others tall or small. People bustled about, some earning their keep, others strolling at a slower pace with little but a day of leisure before them. The carriage rolled on slowly while she sat beside her sister in companionable silence.

She'd thought about her reaction to Max often. It had been instant and unsettling, almost uncomfortable, like wearing a shirt covered in hair. His touch had made her shiver; just a brush of his fingers and she had ached for more. How had she reacted so to a stranger she knew nothing about?

Was she starved for affection?

Thinking of it now, she felt incredibly foolish about her reactions, especially when she'd found him gone. Essie was the clearheaded Sinclair. She was the reliable one. She didn't fall about the place in vapors, or lust after men. That just wasn't her way.

Perhaps she had still been vulnerable? What had happened with Tolly must have left her exposed, and she had been there with only Cam, so her thoughts had not been occupied with her family, but only her own. Yes, that was the reason, surely. It wasn't just Max, it could have been any man and she would have reacted in the manner she had. Hardly flattering, and it had cost her her innocence, and yet she would never regret that. The night they'd shared was a warm memory and would stay that way for as long as she lived.

"What are you thinking of to make you frown so?"

"Do you consider me weak and vulnerable, Eden?" Essie answered her sister's question with one of her own.

"No! Good Lord, where did that come from?" Eden looked genuinely horrified. "You are strong and resilient, and twice the person I could ever be."

Essie wished she'd kept her thoughts to herself. "Now you're just being silly."

"I'm not being silly. You are a wonderful, strong woman, and I often envy you."

Essie flicked her fingers, dismissing her sister's words. "Even my sense is a silly one. Who needs accentuated taste buds?"

"I'm not sure where you are going with this, Essie, but I have never thought of you or your sense as silly."

Neither was she, so she plowed on. Now she'd started, she could not back out, and perhaps it was time to say how she felt. She'd touched on the subject with Cam, and he too had been vehement in denying what she had always believed about herself.

"I have always felt inferior to you, Dev, and Cam. Not as vibrant. As if I am constantly in the shadows."

Eden was struck speechless. Her mouth fell open as she grappled with what Essie had said.

"You'll trap something in there if you do not close it," Essie muttered when Eden remained silent.

"I cannot believe you feel this way, Essie. Cannot believe you do not see yourself as we do. Strong and silent, yes, but intelligent, and resourceful. You are the important piece in the Sinclair family. You're our strength. Only you could do what you do, tend the masses."

"Hardly masses, Eden. You're exaggerating again, and please forget I said anything. I'm not sure why I did."

"You would not have said those words if they hadn't been bothering you for some time."

"It matters not. It was silly to bring it up."

"It matters to you, my dear, infuriating sister. You need to understand that without you, Essie, we, the family, are not whole."

Essie swallowed several times. "I— That was a lovely thing to say, Eden."

"And the truth!" her sister snapped crossly. "Honestly, you are a goose sometimes, Essie. How could you even think that way, when every day we show you what you mean to us. There is not an hour goes by where someone is not asking you something."

She thought about that and realized that in fact it was the truth.

"When you and Cam left for Oak's Knoll, Dev came to visit me with Lilly later that day. He was morose, and I felt the same. We both felt as if someone had lopped off a limb."

"Charming," Essie said, but inside she was warm.

"How long have you felt that way?"

Forever.

"Not long."

Eden leaned forward and studied Essie, her lovely eyes serious. "You're lying to me, but I shall leave that for now, and instead say that the thought of going through this," she pointed to her stomach, "without you is quite frankly terrifying."

"I will be here for both you and Lilly, Eden."

"Because you are you, I know that. So let us have no more of this other rubbish, if you please. Quite simply, you are our linchpin, Essex Sinclair."

Essie nodded, feeling ridiculously happy. She wondered why she had never spoken the words before.

They traveled the rest of the way in silence, both women deep in thought. When they stopped, Essie climbed down and went to stand below Bids. The man had a strained look on his face as he scanned the area around them. Essie suspected he was looking for undesirable people who at any minute would appear and attack her and Eden.

"Bids, I understand your wife is with child. Please allow me to congratulate you both."

He dropped his eyes to her, and the color leeched from his face.

"Yes, w-we are... I mean, Mrs. Bids is expecting a child soon, Miss Sinclair."

"I need you to listen to what I am saying now, Bids. Listen very carefully. Can you do that for me?" He nodded, eyes wary. "Woman deliver happy, healthy babies daily here in London. Wife and child all do well, with no mishaps."

"I understand that, Miss Sinclair, but—"

Essie raised a hand. "I know you have heard stories, we all have, about things going wrong. But I want you to also know that I will stay in London until your child is seen safely into this world, Bids. I am available to you at any time of the day or night, and more than capable of helping your wife should she need it. I have delivered too many healthy babies to count."

The man's mouth opened and closed several times as he fought for the right words.

"I-I can never thank you enough, Miss Sinclair, for that offer. It's true I'm right worried, but knowing you are near will relieve my mind."

"Excellent. Now you must listen to my next piece of advice very carefully, do you understand, Bids?"

"Yes, Miss Sinclair."

"You must not upset your wife by continually worrying her about her condition or what she is doing. She will know her limitations, and does not need them pointed out to her. Let her stay healthy and relaxed whenever possible. If you have any concerns regarding her condition, come to me instead."

He nodded eagerly. "Oh indeed, I will. Perhaps you would

have a tonic I can give my Ellie, as she's been awful tired of late."

Essie smiled. "Indeed I do. I will prepare it as soon as I return to the house." She saw the tight look on his face ease as Bids smiled down at her.

"'Tis very kind of you, Miss Sinclair."

"And you think you are weak," Eden scoffed, linking her arm through Essie's. "Well done, sister, I do believe you have just done Bids' wife a great service."

"Let us hope so."

Three large brick buildings stood before them. A path had been laid to the doors, and the place looked neat and tidy, with no piles of rubbish. The windows were clean, none broken, and it boded well for what lay inside. She felt her anticipation gather as she and Eden headed for the front door of the first building, where Mr. Riley had told her to go. Knocking, they stood back to wait.

"Good morning." A young boy appeared. His clothes were tidy, cap on straight. His fingers were clasped around a cane.

"Good morning. I recently visited Mr. Riley's Apothecary Shop, and he directed me here, as I am in need of purchasing some medical items."

The young boy smiled, and it was as he turned his head that Essie realized he was blind.

"Good morning to you. Please come inside, and I shall call someone to look after your needs."

Essie felt a surge of excitement as she entered the large warehouse and smelled the scents emanating from inside. Dried herbs hung from racks, and tables were laid out with a myriad of things that made her eyes widen. She found jars, bottles, and bandages. Further down the table she saw more books.

"I hear your surprise," the boy said.

"Yes indeed, there are a great many things on display."

The boy smiled again. "Yes, Mr. Huntington thought that people would like to have all their needs catered for under a single roof.

"In the next warehouse we have household supplies, and next to that fabrics, trims, and everything required for garment making."

"Really? How wonderful! It is incredibly forward-thinking of whoever is behind this endeavor."

"Mr. Huntington is a forward-thinking man, madam, and something of a visionary in many things. His work in steam power is unsurpassed."

"Really? My brothers and husband would be intrigued to hear that," Eden said.

"Please excuse me while I get someone to look after you."

"Can you not do that?" Essie asked the boy.

"Of course. However, some people would rather have someone with the use of their eyes helping them."

"Not us." Essie looked at her sister.

"No indeed, young man. We are fully aware of just how strong the senses are when one is removed."

Eden's words surprised him, and Essie guessed he had come up against a great deal of prejudice in his life.

"In that case, then let me lead you to the first grouping of products. My name is Silver."

"What a lovely name," Essie said, following him. Soon she was lost in the wonder of what was on display before her, and all other thoughts were pushed to one side. This was all she needed in her life. Her vocation would keep her focused and busy.

CHAPTER 11

"The only lease I could procure for the season is for that house, Max. Lord Alverson has been forced to leave town due to ill health, supposedly, and yet I have it on good authority he's leasing his house at an exorbitant price as his finances are dwindling fast."

"And it is on a street where many wealthy nobles live? You know how I feel about that, Edward."

"And yet it is the only one available on short notice."

Max looked across his desk to where his steward and friend stood. A head shorter than he, and thin, having not yet developed into the man he would one day be, at twenty Edward believed he often knew better than Max. Max had made his steward aware on many occasions that was not the case.

"And you say the repairs to my town house will take many weeks?"

"The fire destroyed a great deal before it was put out, Max. You could always remain at the hotel?"

"I have no wish to remain at the hotel. There is very little privacy, and the staff need to be resettled."

"Then shall I say yes to leasing it? After all, it has never bothered you before to upset nobility. If any of the boys visit, I'm sure they will be on their best behavior."

"No, it has not, and they are better behaved than most of those nobs and their chinless progeny, anyway."

"Well then, it is settled. I will organize the move for as soon as possible," Edward said. "Now, about the mill you have just purchased. Are you sure about the acquisition, and conversion from water to steam, as it will take all your time—"

"Edward," Max said in a voice that made his steward's eyes widen. "If I wish to buy all the ice in the United Kingdom and leave it out in the midday sun, then that is my choice to do so. Your job is to say, yes Max. I like the mill, and while it is run-down in its present state, with changes it will produce great yields. Therefore, I believe the matter is now closed."

Edward gave him a small smile. "You hired me to advise you, so I will continue to do that, Max."

"I hired you because you can calculate figures quicker than me, and like me you are not bound anywhere. Plus, there is the matter that no one else will have you, so I feel duty bound to keep you employed."

"You are lucky to have me," the younger man scoffed.

Edward and Max had known each other for many years, but he did not speak of his past, and as Max did not like to either, they made excellent friends.

"Upstart."

"I live to please, and on that matter, there is a wonderful room facing the gardens in Lord Alverson's for those rare nights I am forced to work into the early morning hours and have no energy to drive home."

"As long as mine is better, you can have it," Max said.

Edward bowed deep, which he knew annoyed Max, and let himself out of the office.

Max sat back in his chair and looked around him. Once, this small room would have seemed like a palace to him. Now, he kept offices all over the United Kingdom in various properties and businesses he owned. Some big, others smaller, all fitted with what he needed. Today had found him here, as he had wanted to see how the three warehouses he had set up were running. Plus check on the staff who ran them for him.

"Mr. Huntington, if I may have a word?"

"Of course, Mrs. Floyd." Max waved the woman inside. She looked after the warehouses and oversaw the staff, most of whom were young boys he'd rescued from ships.

"Peter is not well, Mr. Huntington, but putting a brave face on."

"His breathing again?"

The woman nodded.

"I'll come and see him, and we'll get the doctor to look him over."

She was a solid woman, as round as she was wide, and one with a great deal of sense.

"Any doctor is going to tell you he's got a weakness, and try and take more of his blood, but that doesn't help him breathe easier, and only makes him weaker."

"Then we will keep searching until we get him help."

She nodded, face solemn. It took a great deal to make Mrs. Floyd smile.

"I'll go and see to the ladies now then, and leave the matter in your hands."

"Ladies?" Max felt a shiver pass along his spine, and could find no reason for it.

"They just arrived, and Silver is showing them around the

warehouses, as they were happy for him to do so. But I want to be there should they ask any questions he can't answer."

"Very well." Max nodded.

He wasn't sure what had him on his feet. Intuition, longing, or just a need to stretch his legs. But seconds later he followed Mrs. Floyd out the door, and walked to where he could look down into the warehouse.

He had been restless since leaving Oak's Knoll in the early hours of that morning. Restless and aching. His clothes felt uncomfortable and his skin the wrong fit. It was her fault, of course. Essex Sinclair. Just thinking about her heated his blood. He'd known the woman for two days. How was it possible he could think of nothing but her?

Did she think of him? Had she been upset and angry when she found him gone? She had every right to be so. After all, he'd taken her innocence and fled, after convincing himself his actions had been for the best. Strangely, with time and distance that thought had not comforted him.

The night they had made love had recreated itself inside his head so many times now that he loathed going to sleep in case she visited him again. The colors of her hair and eyes, the taste of her lips and skin. Her smile, and the sounds she had made as he'd run his mouth over her body.

He'd left, vowing never to think of her again, and thought of nothing else.

Guilt sat heavily on his shoulders for what he had done, and yet had he not left then, Max feared he would never have found the strength to do so, and that would not do.

"I rely on no one."

His eyes ran over the shelves and rows of plants, then down the tables laden with supplies.

"Essie." The name left his lips as he saw the back of a woman's head.

How he knew it was her, he knew not. Only that for the

first time since he had left her his heart felt light, and the ache inside him began to ease.

His feet didn't seem able to move, so he stood and watched her as she walked down the rows. Bending occasionally, she'd sniff something, or brush her bare fingers over an item. He remembered how they had felt on his skin.

"Turn around," he whispered, and was rewarded seconds later. Although he could not see her face clearly, the impact made his hands clench. His need for this woman had not eased by even an inch. He had dreamed of her, lusted after her, and longed for her every day since leaving her at Oak's Knoll.

"Damn you, why?" he whispered. "What is about you that has caught and held me?"

Max usually bedded a woman and then never thought of them again, but not this one.

He'd known she was coming to London, but had doubted their paths would cross; it seemed he was wrong. Was she here to replenish her supplies? Or was one of her beloved family sick or injured? Was that why she was now walking about in his warehouse, just feet from where he stood?

"And yet you can never have her," he whispered.

She wore a deep, rich burgundy bonnet and spencer, the latter covering her lovely breasts. Breasts he had laved in kisses, and pressed to his chest. Her dress was cream with burgundy stripes. Max knew fabrics, and this, he could tell, was good quality. Gone was the woman who often had her hair falling all over the place or bound by wool, and wore worn dresses. Essex Sinclair was now an elegantly dressed young lady of London society. Her gloves were off, he guessed so she could feel and smell. Looking down the row, he found another woman. Would it be the sister, or sister-in-law, or another?

He didn't hesitate; in seconds he was taking the stairs

down. She would be shocked to see him, and yes, likely angry, but he cared little for that; he wanted to see her. The sense of anticipation thrumming through him should have been enough to keep Max where he was. No good could come from this, but still his feet carried him toward her. Approaching quietly from behind, he stopped a foot from her.

"Hello, Essex."

She had a handful of dried sage in one hand, and he heard the crackle as she crushed it, sending a waft of scent into the air. Her shoulders rose and then fell before she opened her hand and dropped the herb. Turning, she looked at him.

"Max... Mr. Hunter?" He saw the flare of joy as her eyes ran over his face, and then it was gone, replaced by confusion. "Why are you here?"

"You look beautiful," he said, not wanting to give her an answer. He'd let her deliberately believe he had nothing to his name. No money or house, when the truth was very different.

"I-I— Thank you." Her eyes ran over his clothes, taking in the cut of his jacket and shine of his boots. He saw the moment she came to the right answer.

"Y-you're Mr. Huntington?"

"Essie, I never told you about my life because—"

"Mr. Huntington, this is Miss Sinclair and the Duchess of Raven."

Silver interrupted him as he made his way to where Max and Essie stood. At his side was Eden, Essie's sister.

"Your Grace." Max bowed low, and when he rose he saw the hurt and anger on Essie's face.

"You are Mr. Huntington?"

"I am." Max watched her expression as she slowly came to the realization of just who and what he was.

"Is this your warehouse, sir?"

"Essie—"

"Please answer the question."

"It is."

"Y-you played me for a fool." The whispered words made him wince.

"I never denied or confirmed your words, Essex. You came to the conclusion I was penniless on your own."

"You told me you had no one and nowhere to go. You told me your name was Mr. Hunter. That is a lie!"

Max winced. Yes, he had said those words.

"If you will just give me some time to explain, I—"

"I have had more than enough of men making a fool out of me to stand here and listen to more lies." She was furious now the shock had worn off.

"Essie, what is going on here?"

This was the sister she believed outshone her in every way. Yes, she was pretty, but her beauty could not compare with Essie's.

"What is going on is that we are leaving, Eden. Come along," Essie said.

As Max was standing in her way, she could do nothing but glare at him.

"Please move."

"Let me talk, I deserve that much." He touched her simply because he could not do otherwise. The shock traveled up his arm as their skin connected, and then she was stepping back and away from him.

"There is nothing to discuss, Mr. Huntington. Good day."

So cold and polite; all the fire had gone from her. The lovely healer was treating him to the disdain that he deserved. *You took her innocence and left. How is she meant to behave?*

Before Max could stop her, she'd turned and was dragging her sister by the hand down the row of trestle tables. They then came back up the next.

Frustrated, and yes, aroused from just seeing her, inhaling her scent, Max spoke. "I never believed you a coward," he said as she drew level.

"I call it self-preservation, sir." She looked at him briefly; her eyes were no longer expressionless, they were now charged with the heat of anger. "You see, I tend to trust on short acquaintance, and the results are never in my favor."

"Essie, I just want to talk." She seemed almost unreachable, miles apart from the woman he had met at Oak's Knoll, the gentle, kindhearted healer. In fact, she looked just like him on any given day. Everything shut away, no weakness showing.

"There is nothing we need say to each other, Mr. Huntington, and please call me Miss Sinclair."

Max was used to getting what he wanted. He rarely, if ever, failed, but looking at that elevated chin, he thought that perhaps he was going to have work a great deal harder with Miss Essex Sinclair. It surprised him that he wanted to do just that, especially as any path that led to her would surely spell trouble for him.

"I will leave if you wish to purchase your supplies, Miss Sinclair."

"No, thank you."

"Stubborn to the point of stupidity," he snapped, his own temper tweaking. "I had thought you more intelligent than that." Max resorted to needling her to get a response. He knew he had no right to feel the bite of anger and frustration, and yet he did. "A healer does whatever they must for their patients, I believe you once said to me."

She looked at him briefly; he saw the flare of emotion, and then she had closed herself away once again.

"A healer must also do what it takes to keep themselves safe, sir."

"I am no threat to you!"

"As you will never be again, Mr. Huntington."

With those words she continued on down the row and out the door, leaving Max alone, as he'd always been, only this time it was not by choice.

CHAPTER 12

"To hell with that!" Max roared, stalking after her. He reached her carriage as she did.

His hand stopped the door from opening.

"I need your help."

"I do not want to help you ever again, Mr. Huntington. So please step away from the carriage."

"I have a boy in there," he pointed to the warehouse next to the one she had just left. "He is sick, and unless I can get him help, he will likely die."

The duchess was looking from Max to Essie, eyes wide as she tried to understand what was taking place.

"Call a doctor."

"Essie!" Her sister looked horrified.

"I am not asking you to speak to me. I merely want you to look at Peter. He struggles to breathe, and today he is worse. I want to help him, as I'm sure do you, but unlike you I do not know how." Max knew her soft heart would never allow her to walk away.

"How do I know it is not another lie on your part?"

"I would never lie about something as important as this, as you very well know."

She faced him. "I know nothing about you, and do not care to."

"Then care for the boy and leave." Max knew he'd won when her shoulders slumped.

"Very well, take me to him, but I have nothing with me to tend him."

"As you see, I do," Max said, which made the sister's lips twitch, but not Essie's.

"Do you wish to stay here, Eden?"

"Not on your life," the duchess said, taking her sister's arm. "Lead on, Mr. Huntington."

No one spoke as he led the way into the second building. Peter, he knew, would be seated down the end, sorting supplies. He could do little else, as his strength let him down, and while Max continually told him he need not work when he was feeling unwell, the boy insisted upon it.

Max was proud of what he'd achieved, and usually happy to walk through his warehouses, but not today. Today he wanted to turn and look at Essie, soak in her beauty and see her smile at him again. Something that was not looking likely in the near future.

He located Peter, and the boy struggled to his feet as they approached. The wheeze in his breath made Max feel helpless.

"Don't rise, boy." Max laid a hand on one bony shoulder and settled him gently back in the seat. Small and thin, Peter had pain etched in every line of his face. He was twelve years old, and his eyes were those of a much older person.

"You t-told me I cannot sit in the presence of ladies, Max." His speech was labored, his breathing choppy.

"I know, but as one of them is here to look at your chest,

you'll just have to sit when she tells you to, so you may as well stay there," Max reasoned with him.

"One of them's looking at my chest?" The boy looked worried. He'd suffered far too much pain in his life already for one so young. "But that doctor you took me to last week said he couldn't help, and that was after he'd taken more blood."

"I know, Peter, but I think Miss Sinclair may be able to."

"Hello." Max stepped aside as Essie moved closer. "Will you let me help you, Peter? I know quite a bit about tending people, and I promise you there will be no more bloodletting."

The smile she gave the boy made the muscles in Max's stomach tighten.

The boy nodded, still looking wary.

"Does it hurt to inhale, Peter?"

The boy nodded. "It's hard to breathe sometimes."

Max watched as she dropped to her knees beside him. She tore off her gloves and threw them to the floor beside her, uncaring where they landed or in what.

"I'm going to lift up your shirt now, dear, and look at your ribs."

Peter's body was painfully thin, and Max cursed again the man who had mistreated him. He watched the skin suck in between his ribs with each breath he struggled to draw.

"Is your breathing worse when it's cold, Peter?"

He nodded.

"And when you are sick, or have the sniffles?"

He nodded.

"Is it always clear fluid that comes from your nose?"

The boy nodded again, although color had ridden high in his cheeks. Max could hear the rasp of his breathing as he tried to draw air into his lungs.

"Blanket, please," Essie said, lifting her eyes to look at

Max, cool and impersonal. "And a length of soft material that he can wear around his neck. It needs to be long enough to wrap around twice."

"I'll get it, Mr. Huntington."

"Thank you, Mrs. Floyd," Max said to the woman.

"Now, Peter, I want you to get on your knees and lean on the chair. Can you do that for me?"

The boy looked to Max, who in turn nodded. So he struggled to rise, with Essie's help, then got to his knees. She positioned his arms as she wanted them.

"You see, the problem is, Peter, that when you tense your body and hunch your shoulders, you are closing your chest, and then it is harder to breathe. In this position, you have opened the airways."

Max saw instantly that Essie was right, and wondered again how she could not believe she was special, not believe she was an angel.

"Now this is the tricky part, Peter, but between us we will get through it. I am going to rest my hand on your stomach, and I want you to breathe deeply and push it out. Because what is happening is that you are only taking small, shallow breaths, when in fact you need to be taking big deep ones, right through your body."

"How do you know my sister, Mr. Huntington?"

Max looked at the duchess, who had moved to his side. She had gray eyes, unlike her sister, and they were narrowed and focused on him.

"Pardon?" Max kept his expression carefully blank.

"My sister knows you, Mr. Huntington, and I want to know from where," she whispered. "Her reaction to you was instant, and her behavior tells me she is not happy with you. Tell me why?"

"I'm sure if your sister wishes you to know the details she will tell you, your Grace."

"She's terribly closemouthed," the duchess said, surprising him. "And getting information out of her that she is unwilling to share usually takes a great deal of skill and bribery."

That surprised a snort out of him, which he was immediately ashamed of.

"Forgive my rudeness, your Grace."

"Mr. Huntington, I have three brothers and three sisters. None of them, I assure you, would give a thought to snorting in my presence, therefore there is nothing to forgive... unless of course you have upset my sister in any way I find unforgivable. Then, I assure you, snorting will be the least of your worries."

Max shot the duchess a look to see if he'd heard her right. She was smiling, but not with her eyes.

"For pity's sake, Mr. Huntington, smile, and don't show my sister we are conversing in any but a polite manner."

"Most would be surprised were I to smile," he muttered, doing as she asked.

"Now, tell me how you know my sister."

"Can we perhaps leave it that we do know each other, but it is up to her to tell you how?" There was no use in denying it, as Essie had shown her hand when first they met.

The duchess did not look happy with Max's answer.

"I'm with child, Mr. Huntington. Surely you can see how easily I am upset. My nerves, you know...."

Max couldn't help it; he snorted again.

"Now, your Grace, that may work on your husband, however it will not work on me. But please, allow me to offer my congratulations for the happy event... whenever it may be."

Her mouth pursed, and there was definitely a sparkle in her eyes, which she tried to blink away.

"How frustrating." She sighed. "You're not related to my husband, are you, as he is not easily manipulated either."

"I don't think there is a duke in my lineage, no."

Her eyes studied him for long drawn-out seconds, and Max resisted the urge to shuffle his feet at the intensity of her gaze.

"Very well, I shall have to resort to bribery to get the information I want."

"It's probably your best bet," Max added.

"Peter is not pleased to have someone else examine him, but my sister has a way about her that soothes people. He is already telling her what she wants to know."

Max couldn't hear a thing from where they stood, as Essie had her head lowered and Peter was whispering, but he knew how gentle Essie was when she was caring for someone.

"I have excellent hearing, Mr. Huntington."

"So do I, normally."

She smiled, and he saw Essie in the look.

"Clear the table, please, and lay the blanket on it."

Essie didn't look at the man behind her, she focused all her attention on the sweet little boy who was struggling to breathe. Max, she would think about later, when she was alone in her room.

"Does your breathing feel easier now, Peter?"

He nodded, and she could hear it was, although it was still loud and raspy.

"Now, I am going to lift you onto the table, Peter. I assure you what we are about to do is no less taxing than what you have done, so there is no need to worry."

"I will lift him."

"Your injury?" Essie said as Max moved closer.

"Is healed."

Max lifted the boy gently into his arms, and held his free hand out to her. Not taking it would be churlish, which was exactly how she was feeling. Rising unaccompanied, she directed Max to put Peter down.

"Your breathing is better, Peter," Max said.

She watched as he rested a hand on the boy's forehead, looking down at him. The boy looked at Max with hero worship, and Essie wondered about their relationship. In fact, she wondered about all the boys she had seen in here.

Not that I care. Scoundrel. How dared he mislead her as to his situation! The man likely had more money than her family.

Picking up her gloves, she tucked them together into a ball, and opened her reticule and put them inside. She then lowered it to the boy's stomach.

"I am going to show you an exercise, Peter, and I wish you to do it as often as you can. At least at night before you close your eyes, and in the morning when you open them."

The boy nodded.

"I want you to breathe deeply, and in doing so lift my reticule into the air, and then lower it."

The first breath was too shallow.

"Push your stomach out with the inhale, Peter, and in when you exhale."

By the fourth he was doing it.

"Well, that is impressive." Eden clapped her hands as she moved to Peter's side. "You have picked that up a great deal faster than my sibling, Dorrie. She took at least a week."

"There, you see, Peter, you have impressed a duchess," Essie said, moving closer to Max.

"May I have a private word with you, Mr. Huntington?"

"Of course." He took her arm and led her to a room that

was used to store supplies. It had a door, and a window on the outer wall.

"I shall return shortly, Eden. I need to speak with Mr. Huntington."

"Go." Her sister waved her away.

Max ushered her into the room; once they were inside, he closed the door behind them.

"Please open the door. I merely wish Peter not to hear us converse."

"Your hands are shaking, Essex. You have no need to be nervous around me."

She pushed them behind her back when he reached for them. She never wanted this man's touch again.

"Miss Sinclair, and I am not nervous around you, my worry for the boy made them shake." Essie cursed herself for a fool for saying the words. No one knew how scared she sometimes became treating patients.

"Why?"

"Be quiet and listen, please. I wish to discuss the boy."

"But I wish to discuss why your hands are shaking. Does this happen often? Or is it when you treat very sick people?"

No one knew how she sometimes reacted after dealing with a very ill person, and she did not want this man to be the only one.

"If you will not tell me that, then let me say I did not deliberately mislead you, Essex."

"Miss Sinclair, and that has no bearing on the boy."

He moved closer to where she stood, and she took a backward step.

"I left Oak's Knoll—"

"What are Peter's living conditions?" she interrupted him, her eyes on his left shoulder. "It is imperative that he not live in a damp, moldy room."

"As of two weeks ago, warm and dry."

"Good, and is there plenty of nourishing food? Fruits and vegetables?"

"There is."

Essie nodded, hating that she was so aware of him, this man she knew nothing about—actually, that wasn't true, she now knew he was a wealthy merchant. Her brothers or uncle could likely fill in the rest of the gaps, were she to ask them, as they knew a great many people just like him.

"Essie, I left because—"

"I don't want you to speak about that. I want to hear no more lies, plus my sister has excellent hearing, so please lower your voice."

"She can surely not hear from where she is standing?"

Yes, she can, but Essie did not say the words out loud.

"My sister-in-law runs a house for children who live on the streets. If at any time Peter is not able to have those things I spoke of, please let me know, and I will send him there."

"I will look after his welfare."

"He is far too thin, and I fear the smog and damp will harm him. It is vital he is kept warm and dry."

He wrapped his hands around her shoulders.

"I don't feel things for people. I have found it is better that way."

"I don't want to hear any more of your lies. Release me at once!"

"No."

She tried to shrug free, but his fingers remained on her arms.

"H-he needs a drink of cloves and honey. The cl-cloves must be boiled and the honey added. It will help him."

"Look at me."

She shook her head.

"You made me feel things, and I have found it better not to, so I left Oak's Knoll."

She looked up at him then, and fought against the invading weakness being near him caused inside her once again. "I don't even know what that means. How can you just decide not to feel things?"

His eyes held hers, the tawny depths mesmerizing.

"It has always worked for me."

Which told her that he had never been loved, or had a close relationship with anyone. In that, he had not lied. The lion was alone in this world.

"Release me, please."

His hands moved, rubbing circles on her shoulders, and damn her to hell, she could feel her body softening and her defenses lowering.

"I'm sorry I left you after what we shared, Essie. I had no right to do so, but—"

"It matters not." Essie cut him off. "You are nothing to me, as I am nothing to you. Now, please tell me why these boys are here?"

"You should be nothing to me," he said, and she saw the confusion inside him.

"The boys...."

"Do you believe I am mistreating them, Essie? Do you think me capable of such deeds?"

"I know nothing of you, how am I to know what you would do?"

"What does your instinct tell you about me?"

"I-I don't believe in instinct, I believe in fact. You, Mr. Huntington, lied to me, so I will never trust you again. However, for some reason I do believe you are not hurting those boys. Am I right?"

"They are cabin boys... or were," he said softly. "They have each been mistreated."

"So you rescued them?"

"Yes."

"You are right to be wary of me, but know that I would never hurt someone with a soul as beautiful as yours."

"Stop it," Essie hissed. "Stop talking like I mattered to you, as I know I did not. What is important now is Peter, and ensuring he recovers."

His grip on her tightened, and then he was pulling her forward until her breasts touched the hard planes of his chest.

"Let me go now. My sister is...." The words fell from Essie's lips as he lowered his head.

The kiss was everything she remembered and more. The feel of his lips on hers, the scent of his large body. She felt it again, the wonderful ache inside her that only this man had ever made her feel.

He lifted his lips and she saw the passion in his eyes.

"When I saw you in my warehouse, all I could think was that I wanted you in my arms again." His breath brushed her lips. "And yet I know I have no right to touch you this way."

She fought for sanity, fought against the drugging need to close the gap between their mouths once more.

"Let me go," Essie whispered.

His eyes ran over her face, and whatever he saw had him releasing her.

"This cannot happen between us again. Will not," Essie said, then turned away and walked from the room.

Eden threw her a glance as she returned, but she did not answer the questions in her sister's eyes. Of course, there was every likelihood she had heard the conversation that took place in the storeroom, anyway.

"Now you may sit up, Peter, and I want you to listen to me carefully, as I have some things I need you to do."

Max arrived in time to help the boy rise. Essie kept her eyes from him.

"I need you to stay warm at all times. Wear scarves, and if possible woolen jumpers. If you go out in the cold weather, or the air is very cold, then I want you to breathe through your scarf, Peter. Can you do that for me?"

"I-I can try."

"I have a chest rub, and a tonic I want you to take. Plus, I have told Mr. Huntington that boiling cloves and adding honey will help ease your breathing. I will come back and see you soon, Peter, but if at any time your condition worsens, then someone will come for me."

"I will do so."

She did not look at Max, but nodded to say she had heard.

"Clean air is the best thing for you also, Peter. If the smoke is thick, then breathe through your scarf again. If you are sick, then take extra care to dress warm, and do not exert yourself. If you are struggling to breathe, then do not exert yourself."

"He will not be allowed to do so," Max said.

Essie patted the boy's thin shoulder.

"Thank you, I am feeling better, Miss Sinclair."

He looked it, Essie thought, but was still a long way from healthy.

"I have the material you wanted." Mrs. Floyd arrived.

Essie took it, and wrapped it twice around Peter's neck, and then tucked it down his shirtfront.

"Use this until I send you some woolen scarves, Peter. Remember to breathe into it if the weather gets cold."

Essie then brushed a hand over his head, and turned to collect Eden, who had wandered off to look around the warehouse.

Max walked at Essie's side as she made her way to Eden.

"Thank you for caring for Peter."

"I will prepare some things for him today and send them over, then I would like to see him again. I will go to his lodgings."

"Because you have no wish to see me again?"

Essie was the nonconfrontational Sinclair. She hated conflict, but she made herself stop walking and face him.

"That is for the best, as nothing good can come from us meeting again. Good day to you, Mr. Huntington."

She made her way to Eden. Collecting her sister, she headed for the door, and knew Max shadowed her.

His hand reached the door of the carriage first, and opened it.

"Good day, your Grace."

"Mr. Huntington," Eden said, taking his hand. Essie was next, and she realized her gloves still sat in her reticule, so she would be forced to touch him again.

"Miss Sinclair."

Essie looked down at the large hand, palm facing upward, awaiting hers.

"Mr. Huntington." She rested hers on it, and the thrill that accompanied that contact simply made her angry, so she gave him a brisk nod and stepped forward. His fingers closed around hers and tightened briefly. He then helped her into the carriage.

Only when the carriage was moving did she exhale. Looking at her sister, she said, "Not one word."

"I hope you are joking, because after what I just witnessed, I want a comprehensive explanation."

"Well, you are not bloody getting one! I treated him at Oak's Knoll, end of story."

"No, it is not the end of the story. I have never seen you

react that way with a man before. Not even Tolly, who you supposedly loved!"

Essie looked at her sister, and for the first time in forever, wished her somewhere else.

"There is nothing further to discuss. I believed him a different person than he actually is. Believed him penniless, and he did not correct that belief. He spent two days at Oak's Knoll, and what you saw today was my anger at being deceived."

"But why are you so angry he deceived you, if you care nothing for him?"

"Enough, Eden. I wish to speak about him no more." Essie did not yell, but she felt like it.

"All right, we will drop it for now, but I liked him. Are you sure he deliberately deceived you?"

"What does it matter if he did or didn't?"

"He'd make you a fine husband."

Essie stared at her sister in stunned silence.

"Wealthy, handsome, and he is obviously, despite his penchant for fabrication, a good man. He wouldn't be rescuing those ship boys if he did not. Mrs. Floyd told me about them."

"Well, at least you did not listen to the conversation I had with Mr. Huntington."

"I could not get the woman to stop talking loudly so I could do so. It was most vexing."

Thank you, Mrs. Floyd, Essie thought.

"This subject is no longer up for discussion, Eden. That also means you will not speak to Dev or Cam on the matter."

Her sister didn't look happy, but nodded. Essie didn't like her chances that she would keep silent for long, however.

CHAPTER 13

Max watched the carriage take Essie away from him until it had left his sight. It was as if her palm had been an ember, and the contact would remain burned into his skin.

"What is this folly?" Max muttered, returning to his warehouse. "I don't feel emotion, nor do I enjoy the contact of another."

But Essex Sinclair was an angel... angry angel, he added, sighing. He'd never reacted to a woman as he did to her. The yearning to be near her was unsettling. He'd kissed her because he'd had to. Touched her, or gone mad.

"Perhaps I have an illness that is addling my brain," Max muttered. What other reason could account for this irrational behavior?

Edward met him as he entered the warehouse. His limp seemed more pronounced today, which suggested he'd been walking about too much.

"The investigator, Mr. Spriggot, has arrived, along with the Bow Street Runner, Mr. Brown, Max. They are in your office."

"I have heard good reports on both, and thought to have them investigate who wants me dead, Edward. Come and see what you think of them."

"Very well. How do you know Miss Sinclair, Max?"

Max walked a few paces, his eyes going left and right to make sure everything was as it should be in the warehouse.

"How do you know that I know her?"

"She was angry with you. I watched from upstairs, and you were…."

"I was what?"

"Very happy to see her," Edward said softly. "In fact, your reaction to her was something I have never seen before."

"I am often happy to see people," Max protested. But he knew what Edward meant. It was different with Essex Sinclair, and that was not a comforting thought. He'd always believed himself immune to the emotions other men experienced with women.

"Not this happy. Not smiling, and leaning toward a person happy."

Max shot his friend a frustrated look. "Have you been reading nonsense again?"

"Max."

Silver came toward him, using his cane to lead the way. The boy could make his way anywhere in London, and often said he had no need of eyes.

"What is it, Silver?"

"Miss Sinclair helped Peter."

"She did."

"Is she coming back?"

The boy looked straight ahead, but his head was tilted slightly. Like the other boys Max had working for him, Silver had been mistreated as a cabin boy, and Max and Edward had rescued him.

"She said she wanted to see Peter again, so it is likely she will. Why do you ask?"

"I wondered if she may have something for my headaches."

Max rested a hand on the boy's shoulder. "You said they were better."

The smile was small, but held little humor. "I lied."

"Why would you do that?"

"Because you worry, and there was nothing that could be done. But now, maybe there is."

These boys had been mistreated, beaten and worse, and they never complained or asked for anything from him unless their need was great. Silver's headaches must be bad indeed for him to broach the subject.

"I shall speak with her on your behalf, and ensure she comes back. Now, I want you to go up to the room where you take your meals, and rest there."

"I don't need to rest," the boy scoffed.

Max watched him walk away, stick tapping.

"Braver than men twice his age," Edward muttered.

Max didn't speak, because anger tightened his throat, as it always did when he thought how his boys had suffered.

They took the stairs and were soon in his office, where he found Mr. Spriggot, a small, thin man, who to Max's mind was easily forgettable, except for his alert eyes. Beside him sat Mr. Brown, the runner. Blunt-featured and bald, he was larger, but no prettier to look at. Appearances, however, Max had long ago learned, meant very little.

After greetings were exchanged, Mr. Spriggot spoke.

"Please tell us what has occurred, for you to believe your life is in danger, Mr. Huntington."

Max did, relating everything he remembered.

"And you saw nothing or passed no other rider or carriage immediately before you were shot?"

"No. I was riding to inspect a property I'm thinking of purchasing, and the bullet knocked me sideways. I managed to stay on the horse, but as it bolted from fright, I could do nothing but hold on."

"Hurts like the devil to have a bullet hole in you," Mr. Brown said, and this told Max he had experienced the pain firsthand. Because it did hurt like the devil.

"I then managed to control it, and took cover in some trees. There I waited until I believed the way was clear. However, my thoughts were no longer in order, as I was losing blood fast, so I took the wrong road, and ended up in Crunston Cliff. I received help there."

Mr. Spriggot smiled. It was merely forming his lips into a line, but Mr. Brown's was wider.

"Been there myself, to the Duke of Raven's castle. Lovely place, and nice people in Crunston Cliff. Oak's Knoll is where we have clients, Mr. Spriggot. The Sinclairs live there."

"You know the Sinclair family?" Max said calmly, very aware that Edward's eyes were on him.

"I do. Wonderful people. That Miss Sinclair healed my gout."

Essie again, Max thought. She was popping up in his life with more frequency than was entirely comfortable.

"Do you have reason to believe someone would like you dead, Mr. Huntington? An enemy, perhaps?" Mr. Spriggot regained control of the conversation.

Max snorted. "I have certainly annoyed a great many people, and yes, I have enemies, but to find one who would shoot me in such a cowardly manner is another matter."

"If you could make a list of those you believe are your enemies, then I would appreciate it, Mr. Huntington."

"Captain Rutley."

Max tried not to tense as Edward spoke.

"He is dead."

"You have no proof of that, Max."

Captain Rutley had been a cruel, evil man who Max and Edward had been cabin boys for. Max had sought revenge the only way he knew how, by killing him. At least, that was what he'd always believed.

"Captain Rutley?" Mr. Spriggot's expression was calm as he scratched the name on his paper.

"I shot him, and he fell into the sea." Max kept his words cold and emotionless. Inside, however, he was a seething, shaking mass, as he always was when the man's name was mentioned. Not many could reduce him to the boy he had once been, but the mention of that man could.

"I shall still add him to the list of people I need to check, if that is all right with you, Mr. Huntington?"

Max nodded, and then swallowed to ease the tension in his throat.

"This matter is to be kept secret. I want no one aware of what you are doing, only that the culprit is unearthed. Employ as many people as you need to get me a result. Money is of no concern, Mr. Spriggot."

Both men nodded, and then Edward escorted them from the building, leaving Max feeling raw after his encounter with Essie and speaking about the man who had nearly destroyed him.

Rubbing a hand down his side, he emptied his thoughts of Rutley. The man was dead; he'd seen to it personally. Max would not allow him to inflict any more pain on him, even if it was in his thoughts.

Rubbing his side, he eased the ache from the bullet that could have taken his life. Death had never worried Max overly much. If it came before his hair turned gray, again it would not concern him. He had worked hard in his life to rise to the power and wealth he now had, but he had formed few connections along the way that would weep or mourn his loss.

"I don't even know what that means? How can you just decide not to feel things?" He remembered Essie's words.

Easily, Max thought. Feeling things had only ever caused him pain.

"Work," he muttered. Work would ease his thoughts and calm him, as it always did.

Max worked steadily through the day, only stopping when Edward appeared in his doorway.

"You have the ball this evening, so it is time you left, as it will soon be too dark to ride home."

"I can ride in the dark."

"Not when someone wants you dead."

Max sighed. They had gone over this many times.

"I am not changing my life because of one stray bullet, Edward."

"That could have killed you."

"I don't want to go to the ball." He decided on a change of subject, as they had not agreed the previous five times they had discussed this matter. Max doubted that had changed.

"I understand that, Max, but it is good for you to do so. Lord Wynburg has given you a great honor by inviting you, as you very well know. It would be rude not to attend, and also bad for business."

"Then you go," Max said, getting to his feet. "You'll be better at it than I. You enjoy all that foolish social chatter and false smiling."

"Charming."

"You know what I mean." Max shrugged into his coat. "People like you."

Edward was now leaning on the door, resting his hip, which told Max again that he had been overdoing things.

"They'd like you if you let them."

Max snorted.

"Perhaps your Miss Sinclair will be there."

The thought was far more appealing than it should be.

"She is not my anything."

"Well, I did some investigating on Lord Wynburg as you asked, and his nephew is Lord Sinclair. He also has two other nephews and four nieces, one of whom is married to a duke. No doubt the same duchess who was in this very warehouse today."

Christ.

"So it is likely that she will be at her uncle's ball."

"I still have no wish to attend," Max lied. He grabbed his hat and slapped it on his head. "Now, good evening, Edward. Please leave directly, as I can see your leg is causing you discomfort and I have no wish for you to take yet another day off tomorrow."

"I've never taken a bloody day off!"

Max smiled as he made his way down the stairs. Annoying Edward always made him feel better.

Would Essie be there? Her uncle was the rare breed of nobleman who embraced change and those that came with it. He accepted merchants *and* nobility into his house, as was evidenced by Max's invitation to his ball.

Would she be there?

The journey to the hotel was not a great one, and after stabling his mount he walked to the building and climbed the impressive steps to where awaited an equally impressive entranceway.

"Good evening, Mr. Huntington."

"Good evening." Max passed the reception and made for the stairs. Reaching his rooms, he found his valet had laid out his evening clothes.

"Good evening, Max, you are late."

"Good evening, Phillip, and I had work to do."

"Your carriage will be arriving in twenty minutes."

"I do not need a great deal of time to ready myself, as you very well know."

Phillip, like Edward, had been with Max for many years. He had collected him, also like Edward, on his travels, and he had stayed with Max since. Valet was his official position, but he was so much more. Unlike Max, he'd been raised in an affluent household, and when he reached the age of ten his life had changed for the worse.

"Your day was fruitful?" Max asked his friend when he was soaking, however briefly, in his tub.

"Sylvie told me she thought you were the most handsome of the guests staying here at the moment."

"Sylvie being?"

"One of the maids. Apparently, they run a poll on the matter weekly."

"What's the prize?"

"As to that I'm unsure, but I did offer myself, and she said she would give it some consideration."

Phillip was short and round, with straight gray hair. His smile could make a woman sigh from a hundred feet, and he could talk his way out of any situation and under any woman's skirts.

"Your generosity knows no bounds, Phillip."

His valet smiled, then handed Max a drying cloth as he stepped from the tub.

"Sylvie also said that you should be married. A man like you should never be alone."

Max thought about Essie. She would not be a comfortable wife; not that he ever planned to marry, or that she would have him if he did. She was a nobleman's daughter, and deserved to marry a man of her standing. The thought of her with another man made him want to strike at something, but as he had no claim to her, her marrying another was inevitable, even if she believed otherwise.

You will marry, Essex Sinclair; no man could resist you.

"You marry first, and test the waters, and I shall see how it works, and follow," Max drawled, making his friend snort.

He dressed, and Phillip fussed until he was happy with how Max looked.

"Sylvie will swoon if she sees you."

"Something to aspire to, I am sure."

Max shrugged into his overcoat, nodded to his valet, and then left the hotel. He missed his own house. There, he could hide away in his study and read; here he did not have that luxury.

When the carriage stopped, he stepped down and told his driver to come back in a few hours. He would not be staying late. Max never really felt comfortable around noblemen, as he was sure they did not around him.

The house was as it should be for the man who lived within it. Elegant, large, and grand, and he wondered if she was inside already. He walked through the open door and was greeted by the butler, and he felt his tension rise. She was here, he could feel it. Which should be enough to have Max turn and leave.

"My name is Mr. Huntington," he said instead.

"Please come this way, Mr. Huntington."

He removed his hat and followed the butler up a grand staircase. Max rarely wore gloves; just another thing to set him apart from noblemen. He found them restrictive and often too small for his large hands. Tonight was no different, which would surely turn up the noses of the nobility present.

He let his eyes wander as he followed the butler. The paintings and trappings of years of wealth and title were everywhere. He thought it must be nice to have such an illustrious line of ancestors at your back, who had handed you your power and wealth. Unlike Max, who had worked his fingers to the bone to receive his.

He heard the hum of voices as he approached a door.

"Mr. Huntington," the butler called, and he entered the room filled with guests. There were hundreds of them, all talking and laughing. Primped and pampered, the woman draped in jewels and fine dresses, the men in evening clothes. The people closest turned to look at him, and then a man disengaged himself to walk forward. Max let his eyes circle the group Lord Wynburg had left, and found her.

CHAPTER 14

Essie stood with her family as the other guests arrived at their aunt and uncle's ball.

"You know, of course, that aunt has great hopes for both you and me this season. She told me we were going to be a sensation, and I... well, I already create a stir wherever I go, but she believes my freedom is coming to an end, and some woman will drop me to my knees."

"That sounds painful," Essie said.

"And I have no wish to hurt her, but you know my feelings on the matter, sister."

Like Dev and James, Cam looked his usual immaculate, handsome self. Tall men, they carried clothes well and had an assurance about them that made women look.

"I told her that I have no wish to wed for at least five years, possibly more."

"And I never wish to wed," Essie said.

"Never is a long time," Eden said. Dressed in ivory silk, she looked stunning. Her hair was pinned into a mass of curls and decorated with diamonds.

"As this conversation has absolutely nothing to do with you, you can stay out of it."

Eden merely smiled at Cam's words, and moved closer to Essie.

"I think you have just not met the right man... or maybe you have," Eden whispered in Essie's ear.

"What are you two whispering about?"

"You look wonderful, Lilly," Essie said, hoping to deter her sister-in-law. "Like Eden, you are positively glowing."

Lilly was beautiful in emerald velvet with a matching band in her hair. She had changed a great deal since marrying Dev. Both of them had, actually, Essie thought, looking at her eldest brother, who was staring at his wife with that special look couples in love often shared. Or at least the three couples she knew did. Her aunt and uncle, and the marriages of her siblings.

"Dear Lord, what is that odor?" Cam looked round him, sniffing loudly. "Christ, it's that bloody Kippley again. He's bathed in a bottle of scent."

"You should see the color of Lady Griffin's dress," Dev drawled, joining the conversation. "It is something my wife would once have been very proud to own."

They all laughed, as Lilly had once worn hideous clothes to deter suitors. Of course that had not worked for Dev, as he had seen through them eventually.

"I overheard the Earl of Stathern telling his son to behave, before entering the ballroom. It seems, he overindulged at the Griffin musicale, and was not found until the following morning—under a table and covered in the previous night's overindulgence."

Having heightened senses meant her siblings saw, heard, and smelled a great deal, and they only shared those things with each other. Never did they let anyone else hear their conversations—except James, who was the only one among them who did not have heightened senses.

"Well now, this is interesting." Eden's words made Essie follow her sister's gaze. Dear God, suddenly she couldn't breathe. Max was here, and he looked ridiculously handsome in his evening clothes. So much larger than those around him, he should look out of place; instead he appeared at ease in the ballroom crowded with people.

"What is interesting?" Cam demanded.

"That Mr. Huntington is here."

There were rare times in Essie's life when she wished to be an only child. For instance, when there was only one portion of apple-and-plum pudding left, and she was not quick enough to secure a second helping... and now.

Max was here, and today he'd kissed her again.

"Is he? Where? Uncle has told me about him. Apparently he has a remarkable head for making money, and is involved in many innovative enterprises," Cam added.

"Who is innovative?" Devon said.

"Mr. Huntington." Eden smiled at Essie. "He is here."

"I'd like to meet him." James joined the conversation. "Supposedly he has several steam-powered mills up and running now. Your uncle said he's a great man to invest with."

Max was talking with her aunt and uncle, a polite smile on his face as he listened. He wore a black jacket and white evening trousers. His waistcoat was black with ruby stripes, and like today, the clothes suited his tall, muscular body. His hair was still a little too long, and slightly untamed. Not that she cared. *He could wear a flour sack and it would not matter*, she reminded herself. *Look away, for pity's sake!*

"Essie knows Mr. Huntington."

Glaring at Eden, Essie prepared for the questions that would follow.

"How do you know him?" Dev was first.

Essie had thought about how to answer this after seeing Max today, and dealing with the possibility of maybe doing so again in the future when she was with her family. She decided on honesty... for the most part.

"Cam has met him also," she said.

Cam dragged his eyes from the nearest pretty woman. "No, I haven't."

"He was shot, and you helped me carry him in to Oak's Knoll," Essie said, proud of how calm she sounded.

"What! I don't remember you telling me about anyone being shot at Oak's Knoll!" Dev thundered. Eyebrows now lowered, as he glared at his siblings.

"That was Mr. Huntington?" Cam looked around him once more, and Essie knew he was searching for Max. "Good Lord." His eyes then came back to Essie, and she knew that he also realized that Mr. Huntington was the Max who had made her cry. She gave him a look that she hoped he interpreted to mean, "say nothing more or I shall make you pay for it later."

"He was not shot at Oak's Knoll, Dev, but found his way there, and I tended him."

"There is more to this than simply a chance meeting and you tending him, Essex, and I want the entire story... now."

"I have nothing further to add. Only that he was wounded, and then he left. End of story."

"There by the door," Cam said. "I'd recognize that big brute anywhere. He's as heavy to carry as he looks. What I didn't realize was that we knew his last name," he added, shooting Essie a look that suggested he wanted to know why she had left that out.

The eyes of her family members then turned as one toward the door, where her aunt and uncle were still conversing with Max.

"We encountered him today, in one of his warehouses." Eden entered the conversation once more, looking extremely happy that she knew something her brothers did not. "Essie was not aware he would be there, and he of course was surprised and pleased to see the woman who saved his life."

As Essie had told her sister very little about how she knew Max, Eden was having a wonderful time ad-libbing, and there was nothing she could do to stop her, as the truth would never be aired.

"Indeed, he was quite effusive in his praise for our sister — Ouch!"

"Oh sorry, dear, did I stand on your foot?" Essie's smile was more a snarl. Eden just looked smug.

"You went to a warehouse?" Dev and James said in unison.

"It was a clean warehouse, and we were in no danger, my love." Eden patted her husband's arm. "It had supplies that Essie needed, and as it turned out, it was owned by Mr. Huntington. Essie then looked after one of the children working there. She was wonderful."

"Yes, thank you, Eden," Essie said, with a calm she was far from feeling.

"She saved this young boy's life, and Mr. Huntington was eternally grateful."

"It matters not if it was clean," James said. "What matters is that you went there with only Essie. Furthermore, I know nothing of this Huntington."

"And Bids."

"Pardon?" James snapped.

"Bids drove us." Eden smiled at her husband.

"And my driver makes three," Dev muttered. "Well, as you are both standing here, obviously nothing heinous befell you."

"I will have more to say about this later," James whispered to his wife, loud enough for everyone to hear.

"You have no idea how good it was to hand her over to you. I now only have three sisters to worry over," Dev added.

"And your brothers are of course paragons," Essie said, smiling sweetly through her teeth.

"We need to thank Huntington, actually," Cam said to Dev, but Essie heard and tensed, as she knew what was coming.

"Why?"

"Brunt called, and yelled at Essie after she tended his wife. The Hemples told me he raised a hand to strike her for interfering, and Huntington intervened. Brunt also called her a witch."

"He did what!" Dev thundered. Eden winced and stuck her fingers in her ears, forcing her earplugs deeper. Several of the nearby guests turned to see who had made the noise.

"I am unhurt, and thank you, Cam. I thought we were not discussing that incident."

Cam shrugged, then leaned to whisper in her ear. "Don't think I don't remember how upset you were when Huntington left either, sister. We shall discuss this later."

"I was upset about Brunt!"

"No, you were not, so don't try and fudge me."

"You knew about this business with Brunt and didn't tell me!" Dev glared at his brother.

"I knew too."

Essie wondered if anyone would notice her hands slipping up around her sister's neck and squeezing.

Dev spun to impale her with his fierce green gaze. Had she not been the recipient hundreds of times before, Essie would admit it was intimidating.

"You told them and not me."

"Cam was there when it happened, and I told Eden today after meeting Mr. Huntington again, Dev. Don't make a fuss."

"Sssh, all of you, Aunt and Uncle are approaching with Mr. Huntington," Eden said, her eyes snapping with excitement, and suddenly Essie wished she were anywhere else but standing here, about to see Max again.

"Allow me to introduce you to my family, Mr. Huntington."

Max couldn't draw his eyes from Essie. Beautiful seemed too simple a word for how she looked. Her dress was pale apricot satin with a soft floating overskirt in a matching color. A twist of braided satin ran down the center and banded cap sleeves. Her hair was swept high and styled in a mass of curls, and as she turned to look at her brother, he saw a stem of flowers in gold and emerald set in the back. Around her neck sat a thin gold chain that held a heart-shaped locket.

Digging his toes into his shoes, Max resisted the urge to lean forward and inhale her scent. He wanted to place his lips in that spot at the base of her neck.

Stop it, Max!

This had to stop. He could not have this woman in his life even if he wanted her. Her family would never allow that, and if they knew what had already happened between them, he would likely end up hanging from a noose. *Or beaten and thrown in the Thames*, he thought, looking at her two large brothers. The eldest looked not exactly inhospitable, but it was a near thing.

"My niece and her husband, the Duke and Duchess of Raven," Lord Wynburg said, and pride rang loud and clear in his voice.

"Your Grace, your Grace," Max said hoping he was addressing them correctly. His tutor had spent many months teaching him how to behave when he was around nobility, and he remembered most of it... he hoped.

The duke was a big man, almost Max's size, and the way he lowered his head was regal enough for the title he carried.

"How wonderful to see you again, Mr. Huntington, and so soon."

Essie's sister, however, may look regal, but by the wicked sparkle in her eyes, he thought that perhaps she was anything but, and had cost her brother many sleepless nights. The duchess was enjoying this encounter between him and Essie. Max wondered what, if anything, Essex had said to her sister about their acquaintance.

"And you, your Grace."

"My nephews, Lord Sinclair and Mr. Cambridge Sinclair, and niece Miss Sinclair," Lord Wynburg continued.

"My lord, Mr. Sinclair, and Miss Sinclair." He looked briefly at Essie, but she did not meet his eyes.

"Mr. Huntington, I hope your wound is healed."

"Yes, thank you, Mr. Sinclair, and thank you for coming to my aid." This man had carried his unconscious, bleeding body into Oak's Knoll. The thought that he may have seen his back was an unsettling one. The green eyes gave nothing away, however.

"And by no means the last of our family members, but the last one here this evening, is Lady Sinclair, my nephew's wife," Lord Wynburg finished.

She was the only fair-haired one among them, and her smile the most welcoming.

"My lady." Max bowed again.

"I hear my sisters visited you today, Mr. Huntington?"

"Indeed they did, Lord Sinclair."

"I also understand that my siblings tended you after you arrived at Oak's Knoll with a bullet in you?"

"Right again, my lord. It's my hope the sheets to your bed

are changed before you sleep in them again." Max wasn't entirely sure why he said the words, but they came out just the same.

"I beg your pardon?" Lord Sinclair's eyes were the most startling green he had ever seen, piercing in their intensity.

"Well, I was hardly carrying him up the stairs to mine," Cambridge Sinclair drawled. "Good Lord, look at the size of him. My back would have ached for a month."

Lady Sinclair muffled her giggle behind a glove. Her husband shot her a dark look.

"Your bed was the only one he could fit in, Dev."

Essie said the words, and Max knew that she was the peacemaker in this family. The soft, calming influence. Strangely, she did not have that effect on Max. He felt anything but calm when she was near.

"May I ask who shot you, Mr. Huntington?"

Max swung his eyes to the duke. He spoke in the smooth, cultured tone of a man who had been raised with the assurance his every need would be met... and met well.

"I don't know who shot me, your Grace. It happened as I was riding to view a property I was interested in purchasing. My horse bolted, and I was unaware of much after that, only that I had the good fortune to end up at Oak's Knoll."

"If I may have this dance, Miss Sinclair?"

A man in naval uniform had joined the group, and it was he who asked Essie to dance. Max watched her brothers look the man over, the eldest staring intently at him. Cambridge raised his nose and sniffed the air, looking like an animal catching a scent.

"Of course, Captain Hilliard, I would love to dance."

Max looked away as Essie placed her hand on the man's arm, and called himself every kind of fool for feeling a bolt of jealousy travel through him.

"I have heard of your houses, Mr. Huntington."

Lady Sinclair had moved to his side, and Max dragged his eyes from the sight of Essie being escorted onto the dance floor by Captain Hilliard.

"You are doing wonderful work with those boys."

She had a lovely smile, and eyes the color of the heather that he had seen growing wild on the hills and valleys of Scotland.

"I'm not sure how you came to hear about my houses, Lady Sinclair."

Her smile only increased her beauty, but it had no effect on Max, unlike Essie's smiles. Those made his toes curl inside his boots.

"I look after children who live on the streets, Mr. Huntington. It has been a passion of mine for many years."

"Yes, Miss Sinclair told me about your house today."

"When she and my wife visited your warehouse?" The duke joined the conversation.

"They were in no danger, your Grace. I would not have let harm befall them."

The air expelled loudly from the duke's lips, in a very unnoble way. "I do not blame you, Mr. Huntington. The women in this family are a force of nature. I have learned that you can't barricade them in, you need to simply keep a close eye on them."

"Well done, darling, you are learning," his duchess called from several feet away, and Max wasn't entirely sure how she heard her husband's words so clearly.

Lady Sinclair laughed. "I am impressed by your capacity to understand the female mind, cousin. Perhaps you could speak to my husband now, so he can learn also."

"After years of keeping my sisters safe, I am not about to change now, my love," Lord Sinclair said, holding out his hand to his wife. "Now come and dance with me."

"Seeing as you asked so nicely."

Max shook his head. He had never encountered nobility quite like this group. They weren't rigidly polite to each other like many he knew. In fact, they seemed comfortable in speaking exactly as they wished, even with Max in hearing distance.

"I'm not entirely sure why my sister was upset when you suddenly disappeared from Oak's Knoll, Huntington, but she assures me it is her business and not mine."

Max found Cambridge Sinclair at his side. The man wore a pleasant expression, but his green eyes were deadly serious.

"But as I wish to know about this steam-powered mill," he said conversationally, "I will not pursue the matter at this time. However, if I find you have hurt her, then I will come calling."

"I don't like threats, Mr. Sinclair." *Even if they are warranted,* Max added silently.

"Excellent." The man slapped him on the back. "We understand each other, then. Now tell me more, Huntington."

He was serious, Max realized. Shaking his head, he dismissed his first thought, which was to leave, as the lure to talk about one of the few things in his life he was passionate about overrode all else. He was soon lost in the world he loved. Technology, and what it offered those bold enough to embrace it.

"Advancements in tools and machinery are improving steam power rapidly, Mr. Sinclair."

The duke and Lord Sinclair soon joined their conversation, and Max answered the questions they fired at him. These noblemen were surprisingly intelligent and had a vast knowledge of the industry. He wasn't sure how long he stood there, but when the Duchess of Raven coughed loudly, the men turned to find her frowning at her husband's back.

"Forty minutes is quite long enough for this conversation,

don't you think, gentlemen? While this has been extremely entertaining for you men, I assure you Lilly and I are near bored to tears."

"Excuse us, Mr. Huntington," the duke said. "We have neglected our wives for too long."

"And there are several women in dire need of my attention also," Cambridge Sinclair said, walking away.

Max found himself alone. He should leave; there was nothing else for him here. He had made an appearance and now it was acceptable for him to go. His gaze found Essie a few feet away. She was standing with her aunt, chatting. *One dance*, he told himself. Just one.

"May I have this dance, Miss Sinclair?"

No!

"I... ah, well, as to that—"

"She would love to, Mr. Huntington."

Essie couldn't glare at her aunt, as she had no idea why she had no wish to dance with Max.

"Miss Sinclair?"

He held out his arm, and Essie placed her fingers on it. Of course it would be a waltz; why had she believed otherwise. Bracing herself, she let him turn her into his arms.

I did not just shiver, it's merely cold in here.

"You have an interesting family, Essex."

"Miss Sinclair," she said. "And yes, they are very important to me."

"You are lucky to have them in your life, then."

She wanted to ask him about his life, but no good could come of her engaging him in conversation. She would get through the dance and then leave his side.

"Peter is doing a great deal better. Thank you for your care of him today."

"I am glad."

"Silver asked me to talk with you about his headaches."

She looked up and found him smiling down at her.

"I knew it would take speaking about the boys to have you look up at me."

"Don't toy with me, Mr. Huntington. What happened between us should not have, but as it did, we must now move on and I wish to never think of it again."

"Is that possible?" He spoke softly.

"Yes, very much so."

"Then you have more control than I."

Essie looked away from him, to watch the other couples dance by. Dev and Lilly moved to her side, and she saw her brother's questioning look. She smiled in reply, which seemed to appease him.

"Your family are very protective of you."

"It is our way."

"It must be both stifling and comforting."

It was, but she would not have it any other way.

"I love my family, Mr. Huntington."

"I did not say otherwise."

They danced in silence, and Essie focused on his necktie. She was no simpering, silly maiden to swoon over a man. Control, she realized. Control was what she needed, and for most of her life she had managed to achieve just that, so surely she could do so now around this one man.

"How are you different, Essie?"

She had told him the first night they met, that the Sinclair's were different.

"I'm a healer, Mr. Huntington, my family are not. That is how I am different."

His look told her he was not convinced. "And how is your family different?"

"Even on such short acquaintance, I'm sure you have seen that we are not a regular family," Essie said calmly.

"Yes, they are certainly different, but I had a feeling there was more to it than that, when I heard you speak on the matter."

"You were delirious with fever, Mr. Huntington. I'm not sure you could remember what I said that night."

"I remember."

And Essie had a feeling he really did, and the thought was not a pleasant one. Her family had secrets, and she had no wish for this man be aware of them.

"Are we to forget all that lay between us also, Essie?"

"It was you who walked away, Mr. Huntington, not I. And that, I now believe, was for the best. I would ask that you respect my wishes and speak of this matter no more."

"I wish I could. But as yet, I have been unable to put you out of my head." His words were deep and steady.

She looked at him then, and saw the flare of passion. He felt this dangerous need they had for each other, too. So she would have to keep herself safe by avoiding him. It was the only way.

"You lied to me and walked away. I want nothing further to do with you." She made herself look at him. "Thank you for the dance, Mr. Huntington." Essie dropped into a curtsy as the music finished, and fled.

Essie knew her aunt and uncle's house well, as she had lived there when she first came to London. Leaving the ballroom without her siblings being aware, she made her way to the stairs, and climbed.

Her body had betrayed her in Max's arms. He had awakened something inside her that night in Oak's Knoll, and now when he was near she responded to him. Surely if she just kept her distance, all would be well. She wanted no man to have control over her ever again. *Distance*, Essie thought. She must keep her distance from him. And if she was forced into his company, then she would ensure she always had someone with her.

She had watched him talking with her brothers and James, confident and comfortable in whatever discussion was taking place. He had also been comfortable with those boys at his warehouse today, leaving her in no doubt he was helping, rather than harming them. Again, she wondered at his story. How had he ended up living the life he now did? He had suffered, his back told her that, but risen above that suffering to be a powerful, wealthy man.

She found the small terrace off the end of the hall, opened the doors, and walked out. The cool air was a relief after the ballroom, with its scents and body odors.

"I must stay away from him," Essie whispered, gripping the railing. He made her weak, he made her feel, and she could not allow that. Could not allow him to lie and manipulate her again. "Put him from your thoughts," she whispered.

"Essie."

She spun to find Max walking through the doors behind her.

"Why are you here?"

"I followed you."

Essie couldn't read his expression as he drew closer.

"Why?"

"Ask me instead to recite a few Latin proverbs. I assure you that would be easier."

He walked closer, and she was pressed to the stone balustrade, with no escape.

"You look like an angel tonight."

"No." Essie shook her head. Holding a hand out before her, she kept him at bay. "Go away, Max. I told you I wanted nothing to do with you."

"Why can't you accept a compliment?"

"Why can't you leave me alone?"

He trailed a finger down one cheek, and Essie could do nothing to stop the betraying shiver of awareness.

"You should not be here," Essie whispered. "What happened between us is over... done with. This, what was, can no longer be, which I know is what you wanted when you left Oak's Knoll in the middle of the night."

"That's not why I left."

"It matters not. You lied to me, and I will not forgive you."

"As you shouldn't, because I am a man who does not deserve to touch one such as you." He cupped her cheek and leaned closer. "But you tempt me to do what I shouldn't."

"I don't want to tempt you."

Essie felt her body lean toward him, telling him her words were a lie. *Lean into that wonderful strength.* She'd never before felt this frenzied need to be close to a man.

He kissed her again, deep and long, and she lost the ability to do anything but feel. He held her pressed close to his body, and she wanted to open his jacket and slide her hands inside.

"I've watched you dance tonight, and battled the need to plant my fist in the face of each of your partners."

His hands moved to the front of her body, and up. She gasped as he cupped her breasts.

"I am no good for you, Essex Sinclair. I'm savage, and have a darkness in me that would destroy you." His words were deep and dredged from deep inside him. "You are right to keep your distance, but God help me, I cannot stay away from you."

"What darkness?" Essie wrapped her arms around his neck and fisted her fingers in his hair. Tugging his head down, she kissed him.

His hand touched the skin above her bodice, brushing softly from side to side, until her body was a furnace of need.

He then tugged the material down and took her breast into his hands, and Essie moaned.

"God, I'm a fool!" He stepped away from her. "I have to leave here now."

"Then go, and d-do not toy with me again!" Essie cried, sounding like the heroine in a dreadful novel. "I am a nobleman's daughter, damn you! I-I will not be treated this way!"

And as quickly as he'd arrived, Max left her. Head reeling, body aching, Essie tried to grapple with what had just happened.

She remembered his words then. *"I'm savage, and have a darkness in me that would destroy you."*

"Dear Lord, what am I to do?"

Entering the ballroom when she was back in control, she found her family.

"Hello, where have you been?"

"Chatting," Essie said to Cam.

"I know that it was Huntington who upset you, Essie, but what I don't know is why? I spoke to him at length earlier. The man is intelligent, articulate, and I did not gage him to have a mean spirit. So why were you so upset when he left Oak's Knoll?"

"I have no idea now." She dismissed her brother's words with an idle flick of her wrist.

"Yes, you do, and if I had to hazard a guess, I would say that both you and Huntington are very aware of each other, and I'm not entirely sure how I feel about that fact."

"Cam!" She looked around them to see if her siblings had heard. Eden was smiling, which said she had, but then that was nothing new.

"He's a smoky character, and harbors secrets, I've no doubt, but I can't help liking the fellow."

"Who?" Dev appeared at her side.

"Huntington. I can't help liking him."

"And Essie should care about this, why?"

"Because she and he have been trying the entire evening to not look at each other, and failing miserably," Eden said.

"Good Lord, is there any possibility that a conversation can be held in this family without each and every one of you involving yourselves?" Essie said, instead of denying what Eden had said. She couldn't, because for her part, her sister's words had the accuracy of an arrow.

"Are you interested in Huntington, Essex?"

"No!" Essie managed to sound outraged enough to deny her brother's claim.

"It was a simple question," Dev said calmly. "There is no need to deny it so vehemently."

"Why are you yelling, Essie?" James said.

Eden patted his cheek. "You really must try to keep up, darling."

Essie was thankfully asked to dance, so she had to endure no more questions. She wished she could shut off her thoughts as easily.

CHAPTER 15

*D*ev and Cam let Essie accompany them to the docks to see Dev's new ship, but only because she had told them she wished to visit the markets. If they did not go with her, then she would go alone, so they relented.

"It's a beauty, brother. You must be proud."

The three siblings were standing on the deck of *The Lilliana*.

"I am, Cam. When I think how far we have all come, it is hard to believe."

Essie listened to her siblings while she looked around her. The air carried the noise and bustle of what was taking place around them. Vendors, hawkers, and sailors, the sounds were a cacophony of pitches—which was why Eden never came here.

It had been five days since her aunt and uncle's ball, and thankfully she had not run into Max again. Nor did she ever plan to. She had spent that time with some of Lilly's children, healing sniffles and coughs and cuts and bruises. She had treated a few of the staff in her family's houses. And that, she realized, was what she loved; she needed nothing else in her life.

She heard a shout to her right, and found four men on the deck of a ship. The one with his back to her could only be one man. Max. She knew no one else that big, and if his size had not alerted her, then the tingle of awareness she felt would have.

"Did you say something, Essie?"

She shook her head as her brothers came to her side, but she kept her eyes on the ship. Something wasn't right. Acid had filled her mouth, and she found it hard to swallow.

"Dev, is that Mr. Huntington having an argument with those men?"

Her brother focused, and she knew even from this distance he could make out every man's expression.

"Yes. He is not yelling, but the other man is. Mr. Huntington is alone, but the other man has three men at his back," Dev added, watching intently.

"Oh dear, the man just pushed him, didn't he, Dev?"

"Do we like this man Huntington, Cam?"

Cam, who was also watching the scene, nodded. "I believe we do, Dev. Not entirely sure I know why I like him, but strangely I do. Although considering what he has on his back, perhaps it's respect for his survival."

Essie remembered the feel of those scars lacing Max's back, each welt deep and formed many years ago. They had been inflicted in rage, she had no doubt.

"What does he have on his back?"

"Welts," Cam hissed. "Hundreds of them, and Essie believes he received them as a child."

The men were moving in on Max, Essie could feel her fear escalate. "I taste danger."

"I can smell it in the air," Cam said softly.

"Damn," Dev whispered. "You," he pointed at Essie, "don't move!"

She watched as Dev and Cam ran down the gangway and along the dock. Lifting her skirts, Essie pulled out her pistol and followed.

"Where is he, Hoyt? I know he's here, because I had word last night. I also know you beat him almost senseless when he was too ill to work."

"I own the boy, Huntington, so get off my ship!"

Big, with a bloated belly, Captain Hoyt was a man who wielded authority with a fist. Word had come from another cabin boy that a lad named Tiny was on board and in a bad way. Max had come to collect him as soon as he could.

"I'll pay you for him."

Greed was a currency men like Hoyt understood.

"Take your do-gooding ass off my ship, Huntington, I have no need of your interference. The boys understand the order of things on board, and Tiny is no different."

Max looked to the sailors at Captain Hoyt's back. They would do as their master directed because they wanted to keep their positions. But he was sure a few of them had received the same treatment as Tiny at some stage.

"I'm not leaving without him."

Max braced his legs and tensed, readying himself for what was to come. His pistol was tucked in his boot, and if he'd been thinking clearly, he'd have it in his hand by now. But bending to get it would signal his intent. They would likely beat him senseless, as he was outnumbered, but he'd inflict a few bruises himself first. He'd been foolish to come without his men. The problem was, he'd slept badly, thinking about Essie, dreaming of her lying beside him, on top of him, and every other scenario that had him hard, and as a consequence, he hadn't been thinking clearly. Something else he rarely did. That woman was messing with the order of things. Max didn't get distracted; his life was on a set course, and he wanted no deviation.

"Then we'll be throwing your body off when we're done with it."

Captain Hoyt bared his teeth. Max wasn't worried; he'd taken beatings before. What concerned him most was that below the decks was a boy who lay suffering somewhere, and no one but he cared if Tiny lived or died.

"I'll be leaving with the boy, Hoyt." Max deliberately left out the word captain to infuriate the man.

"Captain Hoyt!"

Max braced himself as the burly seamen began to advance.

"Need a hand, Huntington?"

He turned, and saw the Sinclair brothers had arrived on deck.

"This is no place for the likes of soft noblemen," Max said as he once again looked at the sailors. He did not want Essie's brothers injured because of him. She had enough to hate him for already, without adding to the tally.

"I'm not entirely sure I like what you are inferring, Huntington."

Max didn't turn at Lord Sinclair's words. The fight was about to begin, and he was more than ready.

"No indeed. Nothing soft about either of us, brother."

Max only had time to grunt at Cambridge Sinclair's words, as the first sailor was swinging a fist at him.

The fight was dirty, and he could spare no time to look at the brothers, but when he did catch a glimpse from the corner of his eyes, they were acquitting themselves well, using their feet and fists. They fought dirty like him, much to his surprise.

"You'll all stop now!"

Max ducked a fist, then turned to see Essie standing on a crate.

"Get off this boat, woman!"

Ignoring him, she aimed the pistol in her hand at the captain, who had not entered the fray, but stood to one side watching.

"Stop them now or I shoot, and I assure you I am accurate."

"Stop!"

Max hauled in a breath as the man he was fighting backed away. He then stalked to where Essie stood.

"What the bloody hell did you think you were doing, boarding his ship! Anything could have happened to you, Essex. These men do not have the same code of honor your precious, soft-bellied nobles do!"

He reached up and grabbed her around the waist, then lowered her to the ground. Taking the pistol from her hands, he shoved it into his pocket.

"Give that back," she demanded.

"I had no idea you were still carrying that about." Lord Sinclair moved to Max's side to scowl down at his sister.

"Of course I carry it. When I visit sick people in less desirable areas, I take it with me."

Max pulled out his pistol, happy that her brother was taking Essie to task for her reckless behavior.

"What undesirable areas are you frequenting alone?"

Max heard Essie curse, and thought any of these sailors would be happy with that word in their vocabulary. Shaking his head, he moved to where Captain Hoyt still stood and pointed the gun at his head.

"You and your men stand over there." He pointed to the bow.

"Mr. Sinclair, do you have a gun?"

"I do, and must object to being called soft-bellied, Huntington, when we just saved you from a severe beating."

Max looked at the man's torn shirt and jacket. He bore several marks from the mill they had just participated in. His smile suggested he had enjoyed it.

"Apologies, I stand corrected, and will add that not all noblemen are soft-bellied as I had once believed. Forgive me also for speaking to your sister thus."

"Think nothing of it." The eldest Sinclair joined his brother. "She deserved it, but the problem is, Huntington, I've delivered her such lectures multiple times with very little success, so you really were just wasting your breath."

Max didn't have time to discuss the matter further, nor the cavalier way Essie's brothers were dismissing her behavior. He had a boy to rescue.

"I would be grateful if you would hold off the men while I retrieve someone, then we shall leave."

"Of course." Lord Sinclair pulled a pistol from his waistband.

"Do all Sinclairs wear arms?" Max had to ask.

"I had not realized my sister felt a need to until today." Lord Sinclair threw a scowl over his shoulder. "But I will address that matter at a more convenient time."

Max heard Essie mumble something that sounded like, "Oh no, you will not."

"Tell me where the boy is, Hoyt." Max moved to stand before the captain, and pressed his pistol into his soft belly. "Now," he said softly.

"He is below," Devonshire Sinclair said.

Looking into Lord Sinclair's eyes, Max saw his pupils had dilated.

"How do you know that?"

"Go now, the boy is in a bad way," Sinclair urged Max.

"His injuries were self-inflicted," Captain Hoyt said.

"I doubt that." Max punched him in the stomach. "That one is for Tiny." He started for the door that would take him below.

"I'll come."

"No." Max did not look at Essie.

"If the boy is hurt, then he may need tending before you bring him up."

"You are not coming, and there will be nothing further said on the matter," Max growled with more force than he should to a lady, even if she had shown no fear and pointed a pistol at a group of sailors. Max refused to be proud of her behavior.

He knew ships, as he'd grown up on them, knew the layout, as he'd walked every inch of several, and then his own. The memories washed through him as he opened the door and started to descend the narrow steps. Some good, others bad, and some too dark to allow himself to remember.

"It is so narrow."

Closing his eyes briefly, Max braced a hand on the wall as he reached the bottom. He turned to see Essie behind him.

"I told you to stay on the deck."

"Yes." She nodded. "I've never been very good at following orders."

He wanted to snarl and look mean, just to show her how angry he was, but instead he found himself smiling. He moved to the last step as she reached a few above. Her bonnet was lavender velvet, as was her spencer today, and she looked so bloody sweet he couldn't stop himself leaning in and inhaling her scent.

"You need to go back up those stairs, Essex."

"I am not here for you, but that boy." She glared down at him.

"Don't be foolish. This is no place for you. Now leave at once." Max ran his eyes over her delicate features, the line of her nose, and soft upper lip.

"We are wasting time."

"So be it, don't say I didn't warn you."

"I think we've established I am no lady, Mr. Huntington."

He had turned away, but her words had him swinging back again. "You think what happened between us makes you less of a lady?"

She dropped her eyes. "It matters not. Please lead the way."

There were so many words he should have said right then. Like, *I am in the wrong and a coward*, and *God you're beautiful*, and *I want to lay you down and lose myself in your lush body*, but all he managed was. "You will always be a lady, Essex Sinclair."

Max then took her hand in his, because he needed to keep her tethered to his side in case she did another foolish thing, but really it was to feel her small fingers in his larger ones.

"This won't be pleasant."

"I know, but then I've seen a great deal of unpleasant in my life."

"What have you seen?"

She waved his words away in favor of her own.

"Were you a cabin boy, Mr. Huntington?"

"Yes." The word was pulled from him. The memories, however, he blocked.

"Are the memories painful?"

They were descending again, Max in front, in case she fell. Thankfully she could not see his face.

"No."

Her hand rested on his shoulder, and in that simple

gesture he found solace, if only briefly, from the darkness inside him.

"Brace yourself," Max said as he opened a door.

Hammocks hung everywhere, and the scent of sweat and other body odors was strong as he entered with Essie behind him. He felt her pressing close to his back, but she said nothing. Here were more memories, of nights spent praying that daylight would not bring another thrashing.

Max found Tiny huddled in his hammock, curled in on himself, no doubt to try and fight the agony he was suffering. His breathing was ragged.

"Tiny." Max leaned over him. "You're safe now, boy."

Essie moved to the other side to look at him.

"I'm taking you away from here."

The boy lifted his head, and pain was etched in his face as he tried to focus through bruised and swollen eyelids.

"Tiny, my name is Essie. Will you let me look at you, dear?"

Her voice softened, as it always did when she treated children. Max called it her soothing voice. She'd used it on him that night her lovely body had warmed him.

"You've had a horrid time of things, Tiny, but that is about to change." She continued talking as her hands travelled over the boy's broken and beaten body. "This man is going to give you a bright new future, Tiny. So you have nothing to fear now."

If he hadn't decided to do so already, if he hadn't bought several houses to save these boys, he would do so for her. Such was the power, he was beginning to realize, she had over him.

"Can you find something to splint his leg?"

Max did as she asked, and returned with two pieces of wood. She untied her bonnet and held it out to him.

"Tear off the ribbons, please."

He did as she asked again.

She tied the wood on either side of Tiny's leg and bound it with the ribbons.

"It will have to do for now. Pick him up gently, Max."

The boy was insensible with pain and fever. Max was sure he had no idea what was happening, as he slid his hands under the painfully thin body.

"Lead the way, Essie."

She did, and he carried Tiny, who winced with every jolt. They arrived up on deck to find the Sinclair brothers standing where they'd left them, and the crew and captain looking enraged.

"Take the bag of coins from my pocket, Miss Sinclair."

She hurried to do as Max asked of her.

"Throw them at Captain Hoyt's boots." She did, and the weight of coins made a loud clinking sound as the bag collided with the wooden deck.

"That is payment for the boy. From this day forth, he is under my protection. And if I hear you have mistreated any more cabin boys, I will return, Hoyt, and this time I will pull the trigger."

He nodded to the brothers.

"You first, Huntington. Essie, you follow."

He did as Lord Sinclair asked, and soon they were off the ship and standing on the dock.

"Where is your carriage?" Devonshire Sinclair said.

"Not far. Please allow me to thank you for your intervention. I should have taken men with me. Also for your help, Miss Sinclair, however misguided."

"I will come with you in the carriage. The boy needs tending."

"Cam, go with them, and I shall follow," the eldest Sinclair directed with the ease of someone who was used to having his orders obeyed.

"There is no need—"

"Lead on, Huntington," Cambridge Sinclair said. "The boy needs my sister's attentions."

He was used to taking the lead in all things, not following the orders of others, but these Sinclairs had a way of wresting the reins from his grasp.

CHAPTER 16

Essie felt every bump as the little boy moaned in pain. She sat with his head on her lap, and Max and Cam sat opposite.

"We should have just shot that bastard!" Cam snarled.

"Even noblemen cannot simply shoot people, Mr. Sinclair."

Max's words were calm in the face of Cam's fury, but she knew better. She saw the fist clenched on his lap, and the banked rage in his tawny eyes.

"You don't have a very flattering opinion of noblemen, do you, Huntington?"

"No."

Just the one word. Her brother snorted.

"I acknowledge that you and your brother may be different, however."

"How kind of you."

Essie did not want to feel anything for Max Huntington but anger at his treatment of her. But in just a few days she had seen so many differing things in connection with the man. The warehouse filled with boys like Silver and Peter, the man dressed elegantly and conversing with a duke at her aunt and uncle's ball, and now this, the avenging Mr. Huntington who was on that boat to save Tiny.

"Not long now, Tiny, and I shall have you feeling better, I promise."

The boy sighed and turned his head into her skirts.

"You smell good."

"It's a special blend I have made," Essie said. "I'm glad you like it."

"I wish more women took your advice in the matter," Cam said.

Essie brushed Tiny's matted hair and stroked a cheek, and the boy shuddered. Her heart ached for his pain. She could not bear to see her little brother and sisters with so much as a sore throat, and here lay this stoic boy who had suffered through so much alone.

"We are here."

Max took the boy from her and stepped from the carriage. Cam and Essie followed. They were outside a large red-brick building. On the left and right were businesses, one belching smoke, the other steam. Max did not stop, he simply walked up to the front door and opened it.

"How the hell does anyone sleep with all that noise going on?" Cam said, placing a hand at her spine.

"Where are we?" Essie asked her brother.

"Somewhere in the East End, I believe."

They followed Max's tall form. The building looked like a shop front, with mullioned windows on both sides of the steps up to the entrance. The inside did not dispel that notion. A large counter ran the length of the room. Max had lifted one end, walked through, and opened a door when they arrived.

"The children would love this place," Cam muttered,

urging her to follow. "They'd play at being shopkeepers all day."

The next room was a large storage room. Here they found supplies stacked neatly on shelves. At the rear of the room was a set of narrow stairs.

"Come," Max said, beginning to climb.

"Not a man to use two words when one will do, then," Cam said.

"Unlike every member of our family," Essie added, following Max. The sound of children's voices grew as they reached the next floor. Walking down a long hallway, they passed a room filled with boys seated around a long table.

"Do those boys all live here?"

Max nodded as he turned into another room. This one held beds lining both sides. He moved to the one nearest the door and pulled back the bedcovers, then gently lowered Tiny onto it.

"Do you have a nightshirt that we can put him in?" Essie said. "I need warm water, soap, and something to wash him with also. What medical supplies do you have here?"

"I shall speak with Mrs. Wand and find out."

Max left, and Essie removed Tiny's shoes and shirt. The boy had his eyes closed now; the trip had obviously taken the last of his strength.

"Oh dearie me!"

A short, thin woman came bustling in with a basket over her arm. Behind her came a short, and if possible, thinner man, carrying a pail of steaming water. Dev was last through the door.

"I'm Mrs. Wand, and this is Mr. Wand."

"Hello, I'm Miss Sinclair, and this is my brother Mr. Sinclair."

Cam came to stand at the foot of the bed.

"Good day, Mr. Wand, Mrs. Wand."

"If you will help, sir, I'm sure the boy will be happier if you clean him." Essie smiled to Mr. Wand.

Between them they washed the boy gently, and she applied some of Mrs. Wand's salve to his bruises, which Essie asked the recipe for.

"I would ask you to rip a rag into strips and find me several sticks, long enough to splint Tiny's broken fingers and leg, please."

Mr. and Mrs. Wand bustled away.

"Dev?"

"Here, love." He moved to her side, his hand at her back.

"How is his color?"

"Weak."

"I need you to check the boy now. Is anything happening inside him that I cannot see?"

Max came back into the room as Dev was bent to inspect the boy's chest.

"What is he doing?"

"Ah...." Essie could find no words.

"He is very good at seeing where bruising forms," Cam said calmly. "Often before it even comes out. He is checking the boy's neck to ensure his airways have not been crushed."

Essie held her breath as Max looked from Cam to Dev. She saw the doubt, but he said nothing as the Wands returned.

Exhaling, she hoped Cam's words had appeased him.

"He is sleeping, but this will cause him pain, so please hold him." The boy had already suffered so much, and now she was to inflict more hurt, but it was necessary if he was to use his hands properly and walk again.

Max stood across from her, his hand resting on Tiny's shoulder. Cam settled his on the ankles, and Dev simply stood silently in support at her side. Essie picked up his abused hand, took the first finger, and straightened it, hoping she had bones aligned. She did so with the next one. Tiny woke crying when she reached the third.

"It's all right now." Max bent over the boy. "Tiny, Miss Sinclair is fixing your hand now, so you may have use of it in the future."

"Yes, nose picking is not a skill anyone should learn to do with their feet," Cam said.

Blurry with pain, the boy looked to the end of the bed and found a small smile.

"You'll not mind him, Tiny. The man's an idiot, but I hear most families have one," Dev added.

Essie tamped down the distress over causing the boy pain, and splinted his fingers and leg. When she was done, she looked at her eldest brother, who shook his head to indicate the boy had no internal injuries.

"Well now, I believe I have finished torturing you, Tiny. I will leave instructions with the very capable Mrs. Wand for your care, and perhaps if you will allow it, I shall come back and check on you soon?"

The boy nodded, but no words came from his lips. Exhausted and in pain, his eyes fluttered closed once more.

"A very small amount of laudanum if you have it, Mrs. Wand. A little broth if he wakes, and if possible keep him drinking boiled water. I shall send over something for his pain and healing as soon as I return home."

"I will see it done, Miss Sinclair, and I thank you for caring for him. Often I have to do so myself, as doctors won't come here."

Essie shot Max a look. His face was shuttered.

"If you have need of me while I am in London, then please send word. My brother will give you his card, Mrs. Wand."

Dev did as she asked.

"Well! I've never had a lord in here before!" Mrs. Wand blushed.

"I assure you we are no different from the next man, and put our trousers on one leg at a time," Dev said, bowing. His words caused the woman to giggle.

They left Tiny in her care and retraced their footsteps through the house silently. Max, Essie noted, followed.

"Is that a printing press?" Dev said as they reached the storeroom on the lower level. He and Cam moved to inspect a piece of machinery in the corner. Essie kept walking through the door and into the shop, sure Max had followed her brothers. She needed a moment alone. Making her way to the window, she looked over the street.

Seeing what had been done to that sweet little boy had upset her, but he had needed her help. Hurting him had not been easy either, as it never was when she must harm someone to heal them.

"Essex, are you all right?"

She didn't turn to face Max as he spoke.

"Thank you, yes, and my name is Miss S-Sinclair."

"Your hands are clenched."

She did not release them, as she knew they still shook.

"If it upsets you to tend them, then why do you do it?" He moved to stand at her side, and Essie felt his eyes on her.

"Because boys like Tiny need to know that there is good as well as evil in this world."

"Yes, they do."

"How c-could that man cause that s-sweet boy so much pain?"

"Breathe in, Essie. That's right, now exhale."

She did as he said, listening to his deep voice. His fingers brushed the back of her fist, and she unfurled it and began to feel calmer.

"I would wish you to never again experience what you did today. However, I doubt you will listen to my words."

"That is not my way."

"And yet I wish it were, as tending those who are very ill hurts you."

How was it he knew this about her when no one else did? Essie watched Bids through the window as he stroked the muzzle of one of her brother's horses. Why did she feel calmer standing here beside the man who created so many conflicting emotions inside her?

"Thank you, Mr. Huntington."

"For what?"

The sound of glass shattering was followed by Max throwing her to the floor. His big body smothered her seconds later.

"Don't move!"

She was saved from answering by her brothers, who hurried into the room.

"Get off my sister!"

She tried to push Max aside, but he would not move.

"Someone shot at me, get down!"

Her brothers dropped to the floor and crawled to where she lay.

"Are you sure, Huntington?"

Essie exhaled as Max braced himself above her. His eyes held hers briefly before going to the wood behind the counter. Rage filled the tawny depths.

"If I'm not mistaken, that is a bullet."

Dev followed Max's gaze, then nodded. "It is."

The shop door burst open suddenly, and in ran Bids.

"My lord!"

"Here, Bids, we are all well," Dev said to his driver.

"A man rode up, fired at the window, and then fled. I could do nothing to stop him."

Max got to his feet and then lifted Essie to hers. Her brothers followed.

"Did you see his face, Bids?"

"It was covered," the driver said, shaking his head.

"All right. Prepare the horses now, Bids. We shall join you shortly."

"Very well, my lord."

She felt the tension radiating off the three men who surrounded her

"Is this the second attempt on your life, Huntington?" Cam asked the question.

"It is." His eyes moved from Cam to Essie. "Are you well, Miss Sinclair? Did I hurt you?"

"No, I am quite well, thank you."

"And who do you believe is trying to dispatch you, Huntington?" Dev asked. He moved to Essie's side and rested a hand on her shoulder. The gesture was to assure himself and her that she was all right.

"If I knew that, my lord, I would have dealt with the matter. However, I have men looking into it."

"Thank you for protecting my sister, Huntington." Cam stepped forward and held out his hand. Max shook it.

"Considering your sister saved my life, and you and your brother came to my aid today, no thanks are necessary."

"Let us leave now, as my sister has had enough shocks for one day."

"I'm all right, Dev."

"I'm not," he muttered.

Max walked them outside, his eyes, like her brothers', looking around them. Essie was hustled into the carriage.

"I suggest you expedite the matter of finding who is trying to kill you, Huntington, before they succeed." Essie shivered at Dev's words. The thought of Max dead made her light-headed.

"Trouble follows that man," Dev muttered, once the carriage had started moving.

"It is hardly his fault someone wants him dead," Cam said.

His eyes were on Essie. "Are you all right? My heart nearly stopped when we found Huntington on top of you. It is not a moment I wish to recreate ever again."

"The bullet was not aimed at me, Cam."

"Accuracy is never to be relied upon in any weapon, sister. That bullet could easily have lodged itself in you."

"God, that thought makes me feel sick," Dev growled.

What made her feel sick was that someone wanted Max dead, and if they kept trying, one day they may succeed.

CHAPTER 17

Max kicked a pebble along the path before him. Yawning, he hoped tonight yielded more sleep than the last one. He was tired for no other reason than every time he closed his eyes he dreamt about Essex Sinclair. He'd not seen her for three weeks, which, considering he now lived on the same street as the Sinclair family, was quite something.

She had personally brought over tonics and ointments for Peter to his warehouse, along with woolen things for him to wrap around his neck or place on his chest. She had also helped Silver with his headaches. Tiny was improving from her care, too. He knew this because Edward told him that according to Mrs. Wand, Miss Sinclair was an angel, which of course Max already knew.

That she had come to visit his properties the days he was elsewhere had made him wonder how she'd known he would be absent. He'd tried to tell himself it was better this way, because she was safe if Max was not there. Safe from a stray bullet. The thought of what could have happened to her that day gave him chills. No, it was better he kept his distance from Essex Sinclair. She was trouble for him, as he was for her. She made him wish for what he could not have. It didn't help that he ached for her, either.

"What fates had aligned to place me minutes from the woman I cannot not stop thinking about," Max muttered in disgust. "I have kept my distance, so why does the burn inside me not ease?"

Max looked to the right as he heard a dog barking, and to his delight saw Myrtle. She was coming his way fast. He climbed over the fence that would put him inside the park, and dropped to his haunches.

"Hello, girl." She put her paws on his shoulders, and he scratched behind her ears. Max was ridiculously pleased to see her. He was sure her blue eyes were smiling up at him.

"Hello."

Looking behind the dog, he found the owner of that voice approaching.

"Good day, madam." Max raised his hat as she giggled. He smiled, because who wouldn't when presented with such a delight? The little girl had black ringlets, sparkling green eyes, and... *hell, another one*.

"My name is Somerset Sinclair, and I saw you walking into a house on our street."

Of course she was a Sinclair; he recognized those green eyes.

"I did not realize the entire street was owned by a single young lady."

She snuffled this time.

"My uncle, brother, and sister have houses there, so it is almost ours, don't you think?"

"I would certainly think you have a stronger claim than any of the other residents, Miss Somerset."

"What is your name, sir?"

"Mr. Huntington, but you can call me Max."

"I like Max, it's a nice name."

"I've always been pleased with it."

"My dog is called Myrtle and she doesn't usually like strangers, but she likes you."

"I've been to Oak's Knoll. Your sister treated an ailment of mine there, and I met Myrtle then. She fell instantly in love with me."

She seemed to consider him for a moment. "I've heard your name mentioned in my brother's house before."

"I hope what was said flattered me," Max teased.

"My brother said you have a smart mind."

"Which brother?"

"Cambridge."

"That was nice of him, don't you think?"

She smiled, showing a row of little white teeth.

"Cam is not always nice, in fact he can be quite wicked. However, he lets Dorrie, Warwick, and me do whatever we like to him. Yesterday, we dressed him in one of Essie's scarves and a bonnet."

Max laughed at the vision. "An ideal elder brother, then."

"Somer!"

The shriek came from behind the little girl. Myrtle left Max and bounded to greet the newcomer.

It seemed his return home was to be delayed. He wondered why he was to be constantly reminded of Essex Sinclair. Was it any wonder he could not remove her from his mind?

He watched another little girl running toward them. Legs churning, arms pumping, she reached them in no time.

"Dorrie, this is Max. Mr. Huntington, Max, this is my twin sister, Dorset."

"Pleasure." Max was now on his knees, as Myrtle had returned and wanted her belly rubbed. He was enjoying the interlude in what had been a taxing day. Just thinking about *her* made his body tense. The woman would not be dislodged from his head, no matter how hard he tried. Of course, he could try harder by moving away from her and having nothing to do with her family, the voice inside his head reasoned.

"You can call him Max, because he likes it, Dorrie."

The twin was cut from the exact same cloth, except her face was thinner.

"Hello, Max."

"Miss Dorset."

"We are to eat our picnic now, Somer, and Ellie is attempting to stop Warwick from starting before you arrive. Emily and Samantha are trying to stop him also, but the task is not an easy one."

Both girls' faces were serious, and Max found them both utterly charming.

"How wonderful, a picnic with your friends on such a lovely day," Max said.

"Emily and Samantha are the duke's sisters, and he is married to our sister," Dorrie said, in that way children had of explaining things. They were very thorough, and if you interrupted they just went back and started again.

Max had not known the Duke of Raven had sisters, but then why would he? He had conversed with the man only briefly, and not on a personal level.

"He should be the size of Mrs. Tiffen by now with the amount of food he eats. It is quite disgusting, Max."

"Mrs. Tiffen being?" Max questioned, as he tried to hold back the laughter.

"She is a friend of our aunt's, and when she comes to tea, we have to get to the cake first or she will eat it all," Dorrie said.

"Yes, and she pinches our cheeks." Somer sighed. "But as she is too large to move from her chair once seated, we have worked out that if we stay several feet away, she cannot reach us."

"Warwick is the same. Dev, our brother, says he has hollow limbs where he stores all the food." Dorrie picked up the conversational reins.

"He is a growing lad." Max felt duty bound to defended his fellow man... or boy, in this case.

"Our aunt says that. But we are growing too," Dorrie said. "Just not at the same rate. Warwick has large feet."

"Does he? Well then, he will likely be a large man."

"My brothers are big, but do you know what, Max?"

"What, Somer?"

"They are soft inside, my aunt says. Because they spoil us terribly."

Max felt an uncomfortable tug of longing to have just once experienced this feeling of family. Looking into the earnest green eyes of these little girls, he wondered what it would be like to have a child of his own. Someone who relied on him for their support and survival.

Dear Christ, what am I thinking?

"We're very intelligent," Somer said, looking at Max. Her eyes weren't sly, she was just stating what she believed to be a fact. "Ask us a question, and we'll answer it."

"Surely you don't know everything?"

"Most things," Dorrie answered.

Two little faces looked up at him expectantly.

"Plus we speak several languages, but if you do not, that's all right," Somerset said, and Max wasn't entirely sure, but felt he'd just been classified as a simpleton.

"Somer, Dorrie!"

Another small girl was now hurtling toward them. This one had hair the color of wheat, and as she drew near he saw twinkling blue eyes.

"This is Samantha, Max. She is the duke's sister."

"Lady Samantha." Max rose and bowed.

"Oh, she's just Samantha, and this is Max."

The blue eyes looked up at him, assessing, enquiring as the twins had been.

"Hello. You have the same hair and eyes as a lion."

"Do I?"

The girls conferred silently, and then nodded.

"You're also very large."

"Well, I promise I neither growl nor bite. Especially not pretty little girls, and especially not on such a lovely day."

"We're very bright," Samantha said.

"I just told him that," Dorrie added.

"Well then." Somer looked at Max expectantly, which he guessed was his cue.

"Spell able," he said in French, sure they would not know the language and were just boasting about speaking several. To his surprise they all made pffft noises, and in unison spelled the word with ease in French.

He went for quartet next, in Italian, because he was absolutely sure that these sweet-faced little girls could not know the language. Again they recited it letter perfect.

"You are not really trying, Max," Somer said. She was now sitting on the grass, small legs out in front of her, while her sister was at her back, braiding her curls. Samantha was plucking grass and building a pile in her skirts. A charming mix of youth and age, the girls were comfortable with him, much to his surprise. But then children, he'd realized early in his life, were not jaded by experience if they had people watching over them to ensure no darkness touched them.

He wasn't entirely sure how long he stood there leaning on that fence quizzing them, but he had to extend himself, and was thankful for the tutors he had employed when he realized that to go forward in the world, he needed knowledge.

He laughed when they were funny and crowed to him about their prowess, and did the same when he won. He watched a woman appear behind the girls. She hesitated, and then started toward them with a young boy at her side. She was slender with fair hair, and the eyes looked familiar. This was the duke's other sister.

"Emily, this is Max, Mr. Huntington!" Somer shrieked, leaping to her feet for no other reason that Max could see, than she could.

"Good day." Max bowed.

"Good day." She gave him a gentle smile. "Now we must return, as Warwick is getting hungry awaiting you."

"Forgive me, I did not mean to occupy them, but we have been quizzing each other."

Emily smiled again. "They have quite a ferocious intellect, Mr. Huntington."

"That they do, but I think I managed to acquit myself adequately."

"We cannot eat until you come back, so hurry!" The youngest male Sinclair was glaring at the three young girls. He had knobbly knees, and his black hair was flopping over his eyes, but Max saw his siblings in him. One day he would be the size of his brothers.

"Don't be rude, Warwickshire. We are speaking with Max," Somer scolded.

"Good day to you." Max nodded to the boy.

The boy moved closer and looked at him. "You've just moved into our street. I heard you talking the other night."

"Yes, I have." Max wondered where the boy had been to hear him talking. "And now I must bid you all goodbye, as I have an appointment."

"Goodbye, Max!" the little girls cried. Warwick grunted something, took his sisters' arms, and dragged them back to the maid.

"Good day, Mr. Huntington."

"Good day, Lady Emily." He vaulted back over the fence.

The smile fell from her lips. "I am not Lady Emily. My name is Miss Tolly."

"Forgive me," Max said, but she had already turned and walked away, leaving him feeling like he'd hurt her in some way. It was not a comfortable feeling, which was odd, considering he did not even know the woman, and if she was the duke's sister why was she Miss Tolly?

Max shook his head, pushing the incident aside. He had enjoyed the brief interlude with the children, but now he had work to do. Looking up the road, he saw his house, and then his eyes went to the duke's, and further down the street to where Essie was staying. He was a fool for doing this, moving in here where he could see her.

He'd almost reached the end of the park when he heard the piercing shriek. It had not been one of pleasure or excitement, but fear. He didn't hesitate, but leaped back over the fence and ran into the park as fast as his legs would carry him.

CHAPTER 18

*E*ssie lifted her face to the sun, enjoying the warmth on her cheeks. Her aunt was not here to scold her, just Grace.

"You will get freckles if you keep that up."

"It feels lovely, Grace."

"I'm sure it does. However, it is not good for your complexion, Miss Sinclair."

Sighing, Essie lowered her face and continued walking. She had just passed Eden and James's house, and was going to the park to see the children. She knew Max now lived on this street, as he had told Cam he was moving there. But as yet she had not seen him, nor did she plan to. She had been sending one of her brother's footmen to check if Max was in his warehouse or the boys' home before she paid calls. Thus far she had avoided him, and hoped to continue to do so.

Every day she prayed that whoever wanted him dead failed. Hoped that they had been caught. Thus far he was safe. She knew, because Tiny had told her he visited every day to check on his recovery.

"Something is wrong," Essie said suddenly as an acid taste filled her mouth.

"Essie!"

Up ahead she saw Warwick running toward her. His little face was anxious and pale.

"What is wrong, Warwick?" She gathered him close as he threw himself at her. "Tell me."

"It's Samantha, sh-she fell in the w-water, you must come quick."

Essie didn't hesitate. Picking up her skirts, she clasped her little brother's hand and ran. She had managed only a few feet when she saw Max approaching with Samantha in his arms. Dorrie and Somer were crying, and Emily looked scared.

"Essie, help her!" Max's words were desperate as she approached.

"Is she conscious?" Essie touched the little girl's cold cheek.

Max shook his head. He had no jacket or hat, and his clothes were wet.

"I heard a cry and ran into the park, and found her in the water. Miss Tolly was about to throw herself in when I arrived."

"I-I can't swim, but I would have tried for Samantha."

"It's all right now," Essie said to Emily. "We will have her well in no time." She prayed she was right. "Run ahead now, Emily, and inform James and Eden of what has happened. Once inside the house, open the door to the closest room that has a table, we will be on your heels."

As Emily ran back to the house, Essie urged Max on. "We must get her to the house at once, Max."

"She's not breathing, Essie," Max said, softly so as not to frighten the children.

They ran, with him clutching a limp Samantha to his

chest. James was running out the door with Eden on his heels as they arrived seconds later.

"There is no time to waste!" Essie cried as they reached her.

She heard the thunder of feet and knew it would be her brothers and Lilly. They would have sensed something was not right. Max ran through the doorway and into the room Emily indicated, with everyone on his heels.

"Lower her to the table, and then step back, please." Essie moved to the little girl and touched her neck. There was no pulse.

"Everyone in a circle around the table, hold hands," Essie said. "No, Lilly, you cannot heal carrying a baby." She urged her sister-in-law back as she stepped closer. "Form part of the circle. Children in too, we need your strength." No one made a sound, just did as she said.

Essie moved over the still little girl, and placed her hands on Samantha's chest. She felt Lilly's hand on her neck, and knew behind her the others would be taking hands and forming a circle around the child. When Dev wrapped his fingers around her wrist, completing the circle, the surge of strength and power came.

"Come on, sweetheart." Essie lifted Samantha's chin, opened her mouth, then inhaled and exhaled into the girl's mouth. The child's chest rose and fell. She did it again, and then pressed down gently on Samantha's heart and felt the surge of power come from her family, through her and into the child. No one spoke, but she could feel the tension as she repeated the process. After the second time, Samantha started to cough.

"Samantha, I need you to open your eyes for me now. It's Essie, sweetheart, open your eyes, come on." The eyelids flickered.

"Samantha, come on, love, please." James's words were thick with emotion.

Her lashes fluttered upward, and she tried to focus on Essie.

"Hello, darling." Essie turned Samantha onto her side, where she proceeded to be violently ill over the carpet. Essie felt Dev's hand briefly in her hair, and then the connection was broken.

"Christ!" James expelled a loud breath.

"I feel sick, Essie."

"I know, love," she soothed the child.

"James." Samantha's voice was weak.

Essie moved aside so James could get closer. He lifted the child into his arms and held her close. Essie saw the relief as he closed his eyes briefly and lowered his face to his sister's damp hair.

"Emily?"

"I am here, Samantha."

"Eden?"

"Here also, sweetheart."

Raised without love or support, when she was scared or ill, Samantha needed all those she loved dearest close.

"Everyone is here, Samantha," James said, holding her close. "Your family are all close."

"We need to warm her up now, James," Essie said. She could not allow herself to feel the fear yet; she had to hold on to it and remain strong until she was alone. Clenching her hands briefly, she fought the shivers that wanted to consume her. "A-a bath, and then some broth, b-but nothing too heavy, as her stomach will be sore. I will make a tonic for her."

"Essie." Cam stepped to her side and pulled her into his arms. "It's all right now, love."

Closing her eyes, she absorbed his strength, and then eased out of his arms, feeling calmer.

"W-we must get Samantha to her room."

They all trooped down the hall and up two sets of stairs, and soon Samantha was settled in her own bed.

"Check her colors, Dev."

"She's a bit weak, but they are strengthening."

"Her lungs are clear," Eden said next, after listening to Samantha's chest.

The little girl sat solemn-faced in her big bed, nodding as James started his lecture.

"I have told you many times about getting too near the water, Samantha."

"I know, James, but there was just the right stick floating by."

"God's blood." James huffed as he slumped to the bed beside his sister. "You scared us, sweetheart." He wrapped his arms around her.

"Our new friend saved you, Samantha." Somer said the words softly as she climbed on the bed with Dorrie.

"New friend?" Cam asked.

Essie looked around her, only now realizing that Max was not with them. When had he left? More importantly what had he seen?

"Max stood with us for a long while," Dorrie said. "Quizzing us with tricky questions, and then he left and we went to have our picnic, but we stopped by the water for Samantha to get the stick."

"Did he now," Eden said, throwing Essie a look. "Mr. Huntington is a man of many talents, it seems."

"He speaks several languages, but he asked us questions about steam engines, which Samantha pointed out was unfair. But he said that he was not allowing us to beat him, so he had to pose a few questions that we didn't know."

"But we are going to learn about steam engines now," Somer said. "Uncle will be able to help us."

"Come and see Samantha, Warwick." Eden urged all the children onto the bed, which left the adults alone to talk.

"I can never thank you enough, Essie." James hugged her hard. "You saved my sister's life."

"Actually, we all did that. Without their strength, I'm not sure I would have succeeded."

"What was that thing you did with your mouth?" Cam asked.

"I read something about it two months ago, and I remember thinking at the time that it made perfect sense, putting your air into a body that is not breathing."

"You've never tried it before?" James said, running a hand through his hair.

"No."

"Well, my dear sister-in-law, can I say how pleased I am for your thirst for knowledge."

"He saw us," Essie whispered suddenly. "Saw what I did... what we did."

"Who?" Lilly looked around.

"Mr. Huntington. He saw what I did, what you all did."

"I'm not sure that he did, he may have left by then," Dev said, coming to Essie's side. "And what did he see but family supporting each other?"

"I said I needed your strength," Essie whispered. "And told Lilly she could not heal, as she was carrying the baby." Ice sluiced through her veins.

"It will be all right, love." Dev settled a large hand on her shoulder.

"He cannot begin to understand you Sinclairs. Christ, I still can't work it out, and I'm married to one," James added. "One thing I do know, however, is that I owe him a debt of gratitude for getting Samantha out of the water."

"He has left the house," Eden said. "Jenny, one of the maids, is telling the housekeeper about him. Apparently Mr. Huntington is fiercely handsome, almost as handsome as her master and those Sinclairs."

"Oh come now," Cam scoffed. "There is no way that man is more handsome than us."

"Vanity is a sin," Emily snapped.

"This is not your fault, Em," James said to his sister.

"I should have stopped her, James, but she is quick, and fell before I could do so."

Essie could see Emily blamed herself for what had happened. Another who had been raised in an unhappy and unhealthy situation, she still bore the scars.

"No, you could not have." Unlike Samantha, who now liked to be hugged, Emily was stiff under the arm her brother wrapped around her shoulders. "The fault is hers alone, and I will not have you believing differently, Emily."

She nodded, and then stepped out of the embrace and left the room.

"I'll talk to her," Cam said.

"You'll argue with her," Dev scoffed.

"Maybe she needs that now?"

Essie watched him leave the room. "Samantha needs sleep, so we shall leave. Come, Warwick, Dorrie, and Somer." Essie gave Eden and James instructions, and advised what to watch out for with Samantha. "Perhaps you should call a doctor?"

"Why?" James questioned.

"To check her over thoroughly. After all, I am not qualified—"

"I have faith in you, so no doctor will be called," James said.

"Stay and take tea," Eden said, moving to her husband's side. He lifted an arm and she slipped under it. James kissed his wife's head. It was a gesture as natural as breathing to them now, and Essie was glad for her sister. She may not have love in her life, but two of her siblings did, and that should be enough. *Is enough,* she corrected silently.

"No, Samantha needs quiet and rest. We will come and visit tomorrow." *And I want to be alone for a while.*

The children for once did not argue, and soon she, Lilly, and Dev were leading them down the stairs.

"Where is Cam?"

"Talking with Emily, and he is being nice," Warwick said.

"All right, well he can find his own way home then." Dev ushered them to the front door.

"Max is devilishly smart, Dev."

"Is he? How did you come to meet him?" Essie said.

"He was walking along the path beside the park and Myrtle ran to greet him, and then I called out hello," Somer said.

"And then I arrived," Dorrie added, not wanting to be left out. "And we told him to ask us questions, and he did."

Essie knew he could be kind to children, as evidenced by those he looked after. But what did he now think of her, and her family?

"He ran straight to the water, and tore off his coat and jumped in," Warrick said. "He did not hesitate either, Essie."

"What if he tells other people what he saw, Dev?" Essie whispered to her brother.

He took her hand and squeezed it. "I think we shall pay him a call, and thank him for what he has done. Only then will you feel calmer."

"Oh no... I don't think that is necessary."

"No, it's a good idea really. James will likely get to it, but not for some time, so we shall thank him on his behalf," Lilly said. She then looked around her. "Where is Myrtle?"

"She is with Max. I heard her bark."

"Are you sure, Warwick?" Essie's heart sank when her little brother nodded.

Before she could stop them, her little sisters and brother had begun marching up to Max's door.

"Come back here at once! We cannot simply arrive. It is... well, it is not done."

"We have to retrieve our dog, surely, sister?" Dev placed a hand on her back, took his wife's hand, and propelled her forward. "I'm not sure what is going on between you and Huntington, but I believe there is something."

"What? No." Essie shook her head. "There is nothing. He is of course grateful, as I saved his life."

"I think you doth protest too much."

Dear God!

CHAPTER 19

Max had left the duke's house after Essie had got the child breathing. He wasn't sure what had happened, but knew he'd witnessed something... some kind of miracle. He had seen dead people before, and that child, to his mind, had been in that state. Then Essie had told her family to form a circle, and touch each other, and she had breathed life into the child.

He shook his head. Max had tried to find a rational explanation for what he had seen. He'd heard of such things, that a person could be resuscitated, but never seen it done before. But there was more to the miracle he'd witnessed than that. He'd felt something in that room, as he had stood in tense silence beside the duke and Miss Tolly. Like he, they had not joined the circle. He had felt power flow as the Sinclairs had held hands.

And you are going mad, Huntington.

The bond between those people in that room had been undeniable. The connection they shared with each other was all-encompassing, and he had for those few precious moments felt part of it.

"Will that be all, Mr. Huntington?"

"Yes, thank you, Phillip."

Moving to the windows now that he was warm and dressed in dry clothes, he looked to the street below.

Fear had dogged Max's footsteps in his youth, and he had lived a life that he'd often thought resembled hell, but pulling that young girl from the water had shaken him. She had been terrifyingly limp in his arms. Looking down into her cold, lifeless face he'd felt a helplessness that he had long ago left behind. Why had seeing her in that condition upset him more than it should? She was nothing to him, surely? He'd seen people who had died from drowning before, even pulled dead boys from the water.

Max rarely felt fear, shame, or hurt anymore, and yet these bloody Sinclairs and Ravens were wrenching it from him far too often.

"Distance, Max. From this day forth, you must keep your distance."

Essie had been magnificent. How could she believe she was not as special as her other siblings, when she was so much more than any person he had ever known?

When she had appeared, relief had made his knees weak. She would save the child, he had instantly known that. The woman could perform miracles; Max had seen them firsthand.

It was a strange thing, the bond these families shared. How was it that the elder Sinclair brothers had arrived at the Raven house at the exact time he and Essie had? Was their closeness such that they were aware when the others needed them? It did not sound feasible, and yet Max had seen much of the world, and discounted nothing without proof.

He now watched Essie, Lord and Lady Sinclair, and her siblings leave the duke's house, each adult holding a child's hand. Solemn-faced, they did not skip or smile like they had in the park, and he knew what had happened had scared them. He prayed this was the only fear they ever knew.

The children stopped outside his house and looked up to where he stood. Seconds later, the boy was walking toward it, and even three stories above them, he could see the horror on Essie's face. She was saying something to Lord Sinclair, who shook his head and then propelled her to Max's front door.

"Your family have come to retrieve you, Myrtle."

The dog was sitting at his side, leaning into him as he scratched behind her ear. It was a strangely comforting feeling, and while he should not have let her follow him home, he had, because he wanted the companionship.

"Come along, you pesky animal."

Max reached his front door at the same time as his butler.

"I have it, thank you, George." He motioned him away.

Opening it, he looked down at the little people, and not, as he wanted, at the woman lurking some distance away.

"Hello. I see three Sinclairs on my doorstep."

"Six," Somer said. "Dev, Lilly, and Essie are behind us."

Lifting his eyes, Max acknowledged them. "My lord, my lady, Miss Sinclair."

"Forgive the intrusion, Mr. Huntington, but we wished to thank you for rescuing Samantha. She is very dear to us all. And also retrieve our dog, which I believe you have stolen." Lord Sinclair was smiling, so his words had been intended as humorous.

"I'm sure if I were to steal a dog, it would be one with better manners than this one." Max looked to where Myrtle was now seated on his boots, looking at her family.

"She likes you, and I've always found Myrtle a solid judge of character."

Max wasn't sure what the look in the other man's eyes meant, so he looked at Essie, and saw the fear. Her hands were clenched at her sides, and her eyes were wide. Healing the child had shaken her, as helping Tiny and Peter had.

"How is the patient? Recovering, I hope?"

"She will b-be fine, thank you, Mr. Huntington."

Did her family not see how she suffered after doing what she did?

"Allow me to commend you. What you did saved that child's life, and while I do not understand what took place in that room, I know that she would not be alive were it not for you."

"Th-there is nothing to explain, I—"

"My sister is a very talented healer, Huntington."

"She certainly is that, my lord."

The straw bonnet framed her pretty, pale face, and the lemon satin ribbon was the same color as the flowers on her white dress. Why was it that every look this woman wore was alluring? Wearing her worn dresses and wool hair ties she'd aroused him, and the effect had not eased upon seeing her dressed as an elegant young lady.

"Will you quiz us again, Max?" Somer's voice drew his eyes away from Essie.

"Surely you have no wish for me to trounce you once more with my superior knowledge?"

"You only beat us because you cheated."

Max placed a hand on his chest. "I beg your pardon. You said ask any questions. It is hardly my fault you know nothing about steam power."

"That will change," he heard Lord Sinclair mutter.

"Pardon?"

"They will now study everything they can on the subject, so brace yourself, Huntington, you will not win so easily next time." The eldest Sinclair looked down at his siblings, and Max again saw the love this family shared.

What would it be like to be loved?

"James scolded Samantha for being reckless."

"Thank you, Warwick, Mr. Huntington does not need to know all the details," Lady Sinclair said.

"I am glad she is to suffer no ill-effects, then."

"Samantha is very important to us," Dorrie said.

"She's all right when she's not giggling and squealing," Warwick added.

"She does not squeal, Warwick."

"That will do, thank you, Somer." With ease of familiarity, Lord Sinclair stepped in to stop the argument that was about to escalate.

"We will bid you good day, Mr. Huntington. Say your goodbyes, children."

"Can we look in your house?"

"Dorrie!"

Max swallowed his smile at Essie's horror.

"Of course, come in now if you like. Besides, I have something I wish to show Miss Sinclair."

"What?" Her brows lowered.

"Come and have a look."

Her brother was looking at her, and then his eyes transferred to Max. They weren't noticeably cooler, and yet he saw the question in the green depths.

"Just a few minutes then, Huntington."

Lady Sinclair moved to follow the children, which left Essex and her brother little choice but to follow. Max was fast beginning to like Lady Sinclair.

"Of course."

He led the way, with the three little Sinclairs skipping at his side. They went down some steps and then along a hallway, and at the end he motioned Warwick to open a door.

"Oh my!"

He heard the awe in Essie's words, and couldn't help but

smile. He'd had the same feeling when he'd first seen it, but only because he knew she'd love it.

The roof was glass, as were the walls on both sides. At the end there was a door that led out to the gardens. The room was large and the air heavy with the scent of exotic flowers, fruit trees, and herbs.

"May I offer this to you if you should need anything from it, Miss Sinclair, for your supplies."

"Thank you." The fear had been replaced by wonder, and that, Max thought, was an excellent thing.

Max had often contemplated if he should tell her about this place. Self-preservation had held his tongue.

"There are so many things here I could use." Essie's eyes were going everywhere. "I have searched London for some of what I see."

Lord Sinclair moaned. His wife laughed and clapped her hands. "How wonderful, Essie dear, and so close to home. You will not need to travel hither and yon anymore for your herbs."

"Is there a problem, my lord?" Max could see that the man still looked pained, and went to stand at his side as his wife and siblings went deeper into the conservatory.

"It has things that grow, Huntington. Have mercy, I will never get my sister out of here now."

"Forgive me, my lord, but I knew of her gardens at Oak's Knoll, and thought it would be of interest to her."

The men stood and watched as she went from one side of an aisle to the other, looking everywhere. Seemingly he and her brother had been forgotten, which allowed him to observe her. When presented with such treasures, all else had paled into significance. She broke off leaves and chewed or sniffed them.

"You have twenty minutes and no longer," Lord Sinclair said to his sister. "I will still have to drag her out of here."

"Can I provide you with refreshment while you wait, my lord?"

Those green eyes turned on Max.

"No, but you can tell me what lies between you and my sister."

"She saved my life," Max said, holding his eyes. "I can never repay her for that. Without her, I would have surely died."

"And you feel gratitude?"

Max nodded. He was not about to add more to that.

"Max, Dev! There is a statue of a naked man and woman back here!"

"Christ!" Lord Sinclair ran down an aisle. Max could hear Lady Sinclair giggling. He followed more slowly, taking the route that passed Essie.

"Please use whatever you wish."

She was on her knees, uncaring that her skirts were getting dirty, grubbing about in the soil.

"Oh yes, thank you. I will, if you do not mind. There are some herbs here that I have been unable to locate."

"You did not know that Lord Alverson had this here, then?"

She frowned, looking cross, and Max thought it was a better look than the fear. "No, and that displeases me hugely, as I once spoke with him about herbs, and even gave him a tonic for an ailment he was suffering from. Beastly man, how dare he keep this from me."

"Perhaps he does not like to share?"

She was still frowning, and for once it was not because of him. In fact, Max realized that momentarily she had forgotten what lay between them. *To have such a passion as she does must be a wonderful thing.* What would it be like to be the sole focus of her passion? He'd experienced it once, and wasn't sure he'd recovered fully.

"But herbs are for healing, and eating. Both of these things are meant to be shared. Knowledge gives us strength, and whoever planted these herbs knew what they were for, as this conservatory is filled with an extensive array of vegetation."

"Not everyone is as kind and giving as you, Miss Sinclair."

And just like that she remembered. The excitement went from her eyes, and suddenly she was guarded once more. Max hated to see it.

She got to her feet, ignoring the hand he held out to her. He smelled the herbs she now clutched, and clenched his fist to stop from brushing the dirt from her skirts.

"Thank you, Mr. Huntington. Now I know you have these herbs down here, I will send a maid to retrieve any I need."

"What was that thing you did today, Essie? Breathing air into the girl's lungs?" He had thought it strange at the time, but when she had started to breathe on her own, he'd known the action had saved the child's life.

"I, ah, read a paper on it. It was first performed in 1744."

"You read a great deal?"

She nodded.

"There is an extensive library here, if you wish to take a look."

"Thank you, but I have plenty to read at the present time."

He hated that cold, composed tone she retreated behind.

"What happened in that bedroom, Essie?" He touched her cheek briefly, needing the contact.

"I— Pardon?" She tried to step back, but had nowhere to go. "I just told you what I did."

"I understand that. However, I felt something when you all touched each other. A charge of energy seemed to travel through me, and then you brought that girl back to life."

The color that had risen in her cheeks drained away before his eyes.

"Th-that's a strange th-thing to say, Mr. Huntington."

"I mean you no harm, Essie, I merely wish to understand what I saw."

Her fear confirmed his belief that what had taken place in that bedroom was not normal.

"We… we like to be close in times of trouble."

"No, there was more to it than that, because if that is indeed the truth, then why were the duke and Miss Tolly excluded?"

"I-I have to go."

He stopped her. "I saw your fear again after healing Samantha. Why do you not tell your family this happens to you?"

"I-it is nothing."

"It is not nothing, Essie. Talk to me." He tried to stop her, but she simply turned and walked through the garden, coming out the other side.

He found her family before she did, and Max knew she was taking the time to regain control of herself.

"Her breasts were bare, Dev."

"Yes, thank you, Warwick, I think we all saw that."

Max heard the strain in Lord Sinclair's voice. Lady Sinclair, however, was still laughing.

"The male was naked also, Dev."

"We saw that too, Dorrie, thank you."

"They are curious, Dev, let them look," Lady Sinclair said, to which her husband shook his head.

"No. The questions will be endless, and I am not ready for that."

"I'm ready to leave now," Essie said from behind him. Turning, he saw she was once again composed.

Max took them back to the front door and watched them walk away, and only the dog threw him a last look before she fell in behind her family.

Closing the door, he wondered what secrets that family harbored. They were unusual, he could now not doubt that. The duchess seemed to have an uncanny ability to hear things no one else could. Then there were Lord Sinclair's eyes; they were unlike any Max had seen before. And what of Cambridge Sinclair? He seemed to sniff the air a great deal.

"Hardly enough evidence to say they were strange, Max," he reminded himself.

And yet he had seen them today. Seen them touch each other, and felt the power flow through him. He hadn't felt afraid, or threatened by them; what he had felt was wonder. But now he wanted to know why.

CHAPTER 20

"The Duke of Raven and Lady Samantha have called to see you, Mr. Huntington. They are at present in the upstairs salon."

Max, who had been reading the morning paper, looked at his butler.

"You took them upstairs when I am seated downstairs?"

"It was the proper thing to do."

"I'm sure it was," Max said, rising. "You are far more proper than I, George."

His butler managed a small smile at that.

"And are they in the formal salon, or the less formal one at the rear of the house?"

"He is a duke, Mr. Huntington."

"The formal one it is then."

Max had managed to master most of the nuances of society, but there were still things that confused him. For instance, the need for formal and informal rooms, and morning calls being undertaken in the afternoon. There were any number of strange customs that he was glad he did not have to understand, as he walked on the fringes of society.

He was also in trade, and thus something of a barbarian in the eyes of many, so if he committed a faux pas, no one would be surprised, and indeed some would expect it of him.

Climbing the stairs, he guessed the duke was about to make his sister apologize.

"Good day," he said, entering the room. The Ravens were seated on a sofa, but both rose as he walked in.

"Good day, Mr. Huntington."

Max looked down into the sweet face of Lady Samantha. Her fair curls bounced as she shifted her weight between each foot, and her eyes moved from his face to his necktie and back again. She was exhibiting all signs of nervousness. Max was simply pleased to see her alive.

"Samantha," her brother said in that voice Max was sure he used to get people to do his bidding.

"I have to apologize to you, Max... Mr. Huntington."

"Max will do, Lady Samantha."

"And I am Samantha."

"And a very pretty name it is too." He looked at the duke, who nodded, which Max gathered meant it was acceptable for him to use the girl's name.

"Sorry," she said in a forlorn voice, "for making you get wet to save me, and for worrying you... and everyone else."

"Well then, I think you have thanked me enough, and as I accept, we shall let the matter rest now."

"My sister—"

"Feels bad enough, your Grace. There is no need for me to make it worse."

The duke exhaled. "Of course, and you are right, but I need her to know the consequences of her actions."

"Which I fully understand, but as she probably received the worst shock of her life that day, I believe we can leave the matter alone now."

"Oh no, I have received worse. Our father was a very bad

man, and he did things to us that shocked me worse than falling in that water." The little girl looked up at him with a sweet smile on her face, fully aware that she had just removed the attention from her with her words, and in doing so made her big brother extremely uncomfortable.

"Well then," Max said, as he could come up with nothing else. That anyone would harm this sweet child made him angry. Looking at the duke, he saw something in the depths of his eyes that confirmed his sister had spoken the truth. Discomfort, certainly, but something else, a darkness, and as Max was the master at hiding those dark places inside him, he gave the man a moment to hide his once more.

"And have you been back to the park, or has your brother forbidden you?"

Samantha smiled at him, and he found himself responding as he did with the Sinclair children.

"We went yesterday, and I had two footmen with me, plus James and Emily."

"I think you should learn to swim, Samantha, then you would always be safe around water."

"We discussed that, actually." The duke moved to stand behind his sister. "I think in light of her dunking I will make it happen."

As he would, Max thought. The mighty duke would snap his fingers, and his sister would be taught. Although, perhaps now he did not see him as quite so mighty, in light of the small insight into his childhood his sister had shared.

"You had something else to ask Mr. Huntington, Samantha."

Max looked from the duke to his sister.

"We are going to the Bartholomew Fair tomorrow, Max. Would you like to come with us?"

"My sister wanted to invite you," the duke added.

"We are all going. The Sinclairs and that pesky Warwick."

"Samantha, that will do."

"Why is he pesky?" Max said, to give himself time to think. When she'd invited him, he'd had the instant urge to agree, then his mind had cleared.

"He ties my shoes together, and he tells me to be quiet because he says I talk too much."

"And of course, you, Dorrie and Somer, never do anything to him, do you?" The duke snorted.

"He deserves it."

"The boy has my sympathy. I imagine being a minority cannot be easy."

"Exactly," the duke agreed.

Samantha's smile fooled no one.

"So will you come?"

"Ah, well as to that, I—"

"We are to take a picnic and there will be so many wonderful things, like cherry cakes, and toffee. So please do come, Max."

"Don't push, Samantha. Perhaps Mr. Huntington has something else to do tomorrow."

"Do you?"

Max looked down into her face, and couldn't find a single word except "Yes, I would love to come."

She clapped her hands, then took his and did a little jig, swinging it back and forth.

"We shall have so much fun."

"There is a seat in one of the Sinclair carriages, should you require a ride, Huntington."

"No, I will ride, thank you, your Grace."

"Very well, we shall leave at 11.00 a.m."

The duke placed a hand on his sister's shoulder.

"Good day to you, Mr. Huntington."

Max nodded. "Good day, your Grace, Samantha."

He heard them leave, and still stood staring at the wall.

What the hell had he just agreed to, and furthermore, why? Max did not do things like this. But that little girl had asked and he'd agreed, because he had found no words not to.

"I am unravelling," he said, falling into a chair. "Or ailing for something." He touched his forehead, but it was annoyingly cool.

Dear Christ, he was going to a fair with them. What the hell was he thinking?

Essie was seated inside the carriage as Max rode up on a large bay horse. He looked comfortable, his seat, unlike hers, perfect. His black hat was settled on his head, and the tawny curls beneath fluttered. His jacket was deep chocolate, and his necktie and shirt a crisp white. He wore a fawn-and-chocolate waistcoat, and fawn breeches. The sun glinted off his polished Hessians.

Oh for a slight imperfection, Essie thought. *A squint or permanent snarl.*

Had she not been seated across from Lilly and her two youngest sisters, she would have sighed. How could a man look so handsome riding a horse, seeing as she loathed horses? Which made no sense, but perfect sense to her. She was constantly confused and off-balance around this man. Even more so now he had said what he had about that day she had saved Samantha. He knew there was something different about her family.

"Mr. Huntington is a very handsome man, don't you think, Essie?"

"Pardon?" She looked at Lilly.

"Mr. Huntington. I saw you looking at him."

"No, I wasn't!"

"There is no shame in admiring a handsome man. Even my old married heart enjoys seeing such a sight."

Lord, he's beautiful, Essie thought as he drew closer. And she had touched that body, run her hands through that thick mane of hair.

"You just sighed, Essie, are you all right?"

"Yes, thank you, Somer."

Dorrie and Somer leaned out the window.

"Hello, Max!" they shrieked.

"Must you shriek out the window like two hoydens?" Dev said, entering the carriage.

"Yes!" they cried together.

At least the twins had created a diversion, Essie thought as Lilly accepted a kiss from her husband.

"How is your sickness today, Lilly?"

"Much better, after you gave me that herbal tea to drink before I get out of bed."

"I am glad."

"Of course Eden is not sick, which is unfair, don't you think?" Lilly said loud enough so that Eden would hear.

"Yes, but she is already bloated, dear, and you are not, so you see there is a fairness there after all."

Dev snorted, and Lilly winked. In the next carriage she was sure that Eden would be rolling her eyes. Of course she was not bloated, or anything but beautiful, but still, it made Lilly feel better to pretend.

"You look beautiful," Dev said to his wife. He bent to tie up Dorrie's shoe ribbon. Her brother would be a wonderful, if overprotective parent.

"Thank you, darling."

"Is Toby coming, Lilly?"

"He is, and at present is seated with Warwick, as he did not feel comfortable in here surrounded by such beauty, Dorrie."

Essie swallowed her smile as her sisters preened.

The carriages rolled out then, and they were soon travelling through London. Of Max she thankfully saw no sign, which suggested he rode with the first carriage.

"We have been blessed with the weather," Lilly said.

"Indeed we have."

She listened as Dev and Lilly conversed, and the twins chattered, excited about their outing. Essie spent the time counselling herself on her behavior toward Max. She would be calm, and treat him like she would any stranger.

But he's not a stranger, is he? He knows you intimately…. Well, her body anyway.

Did he think about what they'd done? Had it meant as much to him as it had to her?

"Are you all right, Essie? You look flushed."

"Fine, thank you, Dev."

She would be polite and yet keep her distance. She would treat Max as she did every man who was not her family. The trouble came when he was alone with her, or when he touched her, so she would ensure those situations did not arise.

"I'm surprised Huntington decided to join us. I did not think him the type to engage in family outings."

"Perhaps it is the novelty," Essie found herself saying. "I don't believe he has close family ties."

"Did he tell you that at Oak's Knoll?" Her brother's eyes held hers.

"He did. Apparently his family still live in France, where he was raised."

"I wonder why he landed in England then?" Lilly said.

"I have no idea, we never discussed the matter," Essie said. But he'd told her he had no relationship with his family, and she remembered offering her home as his, should he need it, because she felt sorry that he had no one at his back.

Distance, Essie, she reminded herself. *Put it behind you.*

CHAPTER 21

"Children will take the hand of an adult, and there will be no running off."

Max listened silently to the orders both Raven and Sinclair were firing at their families in perfect harmony. The children listened patiently. The adults rolled their eyes.

He had wanted to send word several times over the last twenty-four hours that he would not be able to attend, and yet something had always stopped him from doing so. What, he had no idea, but this morning he had convinced himself it was because he wanted to observe this unusual family, and it had nothing to do with the eldest Sinclair sister.

His eyes found Essie, standing to the rear of the group with her brother Warwick leaning on her legs. The boy did that often, Max had noted. Not quite as confident as his sisters, he was usually found with an adult. But then, having a best friend at your side since birth had to be confidence building.

She was, as usual, exquisite. Dressed in rose today, she looked so bloody beautiful it actually made his chest hurt, which couldn't be a good thing. Yet still, here he stood, with this unusual group of people he was no closer to working out than he had been yesterday. About to spend the day in her company. Why, he wondered, was he torturing himself unnecessarily.

Dragging his eyes from Essex, as she had not looked his way once and was not likely to, he focused on the other stranger in the group today, a young boy who, unlike the other children, had an air about him that was familiar to Max. His boys carried the same look. Wise beyond their years.

"He is one of my boys."

Max found Lady Sinclair at his side.

"The first child I rescued, actually. We found him beaten on the doorstep of the house I run."

"And he comes on outings with you and your family?" Max said.

"He does, because he has always been different from the others. He never wanted to leave. He now lives at Temple Street with Mr. and Mrs. Davey, who run the house."

Max nodded. He'd offered whatever support was needed to the boys he rescued, but he never gave them too much of himself. Perhaps because he did not have too much to give, or if he was honest, he did not know how to offer more than a roof, food, and financial stability to those boys. He wasn't a man who invested in emotions.

"So in brief, you will make sure you are in sight of an adult you know at all times."

"My husband had to add on the bit about the adult being someone they know, because those children are devilishly tricky, and will outsmart you in a heartbeat."

"Yes, their intellect is a terrifying thing."

Once the lecture was over, they all moved as one into the fair.

"I want to see the fire eater, Max."

He found one of the twins at his side, her hand slipping into his without asking permission.

"And then the time-telling pig."

"Pardon?" He calmed his breathing. It was a child's hand, for pity's sake, not a venomous serpent. Surely he could do this?

"It's true." She swung his hand. "There is a blindfolded pig who can tell the time down to the minute, and also pick cards from a pack."

"Oh now, you can't really expect me to believe that," he said, closing her little hand inside his. *One day*, Max thought. He would do this for a day, and after that he would move out of that bloody house and put some distance between him and these disturbing people.

"I do not tell untruths, Max, my brothers and sisters get quite angry if I do."

"Like that has ever stopped you," came the dry voice of Cambridge Sinclair, who walked ahead with Dorrie.

"I want to see the dolls." Samantha skipped at her brother's side.

"We want to see the skeleton, and the elephant that can uncork bottles," Warwick said, still holding Essie's hand. Toby walked at his side, holding no one.

"That could come in handy when one is on a bender," Cambridge drawled.

Max realized over the next two hours that he would not have enjoyed the Bartholomew Fair quite as much were it not for the company he shared.

"Well I declare, that man has a young boy on his lap… or is it a doll? Whoever he is, he speaks very well."

Max looked to where the duchess was pointing. Her eyes twinkled with laughter. It was a ventriloquist's dummy.

He didn't have to wait long for one of the children to answer.

"Eden," Warwick sighed, as if his sister's intellect disturbed him. "That is a ventriloquist"—he pointed to the man—"and that is his dummy. The dummy cannot speak."

"However, he is," the duchess pointed out.

They all surged closer, and it did indeed appear the dummy was speaking. The children gathered closer and conferred.

"The man is making him speak," Dorrie said.

"And yet I do not see his lips move," Lord Sinclair said. "Do you, Essie?"

She tilted her head slightly as if to think the matter over, and his eyes went to that place just beneath her ear that Max knew would taste so good.

"No, and surely a man that size would speak in a deeper voice?"

He'd noticed that they constantly challenged the children, questioned how and why things were as they were. Max had to admit to being impressed. He'd never had someone to guide him, but thought it would have been nice to have these people at his back.

"Perhaps there is a boy inside that doll?"

The children conferred again.

"His legs are too small," Samantha said.

"Well, your legs are small," the duke pointed out.

They discussed the dummy until all parties were satisfied, and then moved on. Much to his surprise, there was a time-telling pig, and a Red Indian up next.

"That will teach you to doubt them, Huntington."

"Had someone told you about a time-telling pig before your sisters did, you would have scoffed too, Mr. Sinclair."

"I try to be open-minded, Huntington, as life has a way of kicking you in the ass if you aren't."

"Cam said ass!"

Max laughed as Warwick went running to tell his big brother.

"They were so sweet before they could talk."

"Sinclair, had you no one to tell on you, then you would be worried. You and your family are lucky people." Max meant the words, he just hadn't meant to say them out loud with quite so much feeling.

The Sinclair green eyes focused on him.

"I know how lucky I am, thank you, Huntington."

And he did, Max realized. They all did, and showed it in small gestures, like a kiss to the head or brush of a hand. The adults had been called upon to inspect any number of things, and no one had muttered a protest. This, Max realized, was what it meant to be part of a family.

Suddenly his chest felt tight as those green eyes of Cambridge Sinclair looked pityingly at him.

"If you will excuse me, I shall return to you all shortly." He bowed and walked away.

Space, Max thought. He needed space to find the man he had always been. What had possessed him to come here today with these people? It was her, he had wanted to be near her, and the family was just part of that... her.

You are a fool, Huntington.

Walking blindly through the crowds, he kept moving until he could breathe again and the tightness in his chest eased.

"This is not for you," he rasped. He did not want this. A family, to be part of something that could hurt him.

He saw her up ahead, Essex, haggling with a man over a purchase. He found no other Sinclair, and wondered when she had broken the rules and left the group. Moving closer, he felt a shiver down his spine. Turning, he searched the crowds but saw no one looking his way, so he continued on, but Essie had gone.

Essie moved through the tent, looking at the display of scarves. She would purchase one for her aunt, and then return to the others. She had told Lilly she was going to see the herbalist, and her sister-in-law had said she would tell Dev if he asked, but made her promise to take care.

"Hello, darling."

The stench of alcohol made her nose wrinkle. Searching the face of the young man who had spoken, she did not recognize him.

"Good day."

"Are you here alone?"

"No, my family are with me."

"Well now, perhaps we could have a bit of fun before you return to them."

She tried to wrench her arm free, but the man had a fierce grip.

"Unhand me or I will scream." Essie slipped her free hand into the bag she had just purchased and gripped a handful of the ground thyme inside. Dev had made her leave her pistol behind today.

"I just want to be friendly." He moved closer. "Lovely lady like yourself must understand that."

She threw the herb into his eyes, and he released her instantly. Staggering back, he started rubbing his face.

Essie turned and ran into a hard wall of muscle.

"Is he bothering you?"

She looked up at Max. His arm was around her, holding her close to his side.

"Yes... no, I took care of him."

"With what?"

They both turned to look at the man, who was still howling and rubbing his eyes.

"He shouldn't rub it, it will make it worse," Essie said. "It's only ground thyme, but it will be extremely irritating if he keeps doing that."

"Excellent, then let's hope he continues. But first, did he touch you?"

"No."

"Tell me the truth, Essex."

She saw the anger in his tawny eyes, and shook her head.

"Honestly, he didn't."

Whatever he saw in her expression appeased him slightly. Seconds later she was being dragged outside.

"Why did you leave your family?" He led her behind the tents, where several wagons stood, and then stopped.

"I wanted to see that man's stall. The one selling things I could use to treat my patients."

He looked skyward.

"This is not a place to walk off alone, Essex. There are pickpockets and muggers here. And as evidenced by what just happened to you, men who have overindulged and would see a lush creature like you and want to take advantage."

"I-I am not a creature," Essie said, when what she really thought was that Max saw her as lush.

"No, you're a beautiful lady," he said softly. "And that alone means you should not have gone off by yourself."

"I can protect myself, and Eden would have heard me had I called." The minute she finished the words, she realized what she had said. Dear Lord, only with this man could she lose her ability to hold her tongue.

"Why would Eden hear you?"

"I... ah, pardon?"

"You heard me." He took her arms and pulled her closer as she attempted to back away. "Tell me what happened that day in Samantha's bedroom, and why your sister has hearing better than any person I know. Tell me why your brother's eyes can see what mine can't, and their color sometimes changes, and his pupils almost fill his eyes."

"No, Max, please, I don't know what you are talking about."

"Cam sniffs the air, almost like a dog catching a scent. And you," he whispered. "You have an uncanny ability to heal a person. Plus, how is it you all know when you need each other, when danger is near or someone is hurting?"

Essie had gone cold inside.

"I am an observer, Essie. Living your life on the outskirts of everything and everyone makes you do that. Now tell me what I want to know."

"No!" She wrenched free of his arms. "There is nothing to tell, and I will not let you hurt them with your lies."

She ran then, as fast as she could back toward her family and away from Max. He caught her, grabbed her arm and turned her to face him.

"I don't want to hurt you," he said. "Please, Essie, tell me you know that."

She wanted to believe it, wanted to see him as a good man, but her fears keep her silent. It was then they both heard the screams.

"Dear Lord, what has happened?"

Taking her hand, Max towed her to a barrel, then leapt on top. He scanned the scene.

"The elephant is free and stampeding, we must leave!"

"No, my family!" Essie ran from him and tried to make her way through the terrified people.

"Left!" Max caught her around the waist and settled her behind him. He then started plowing through people.

"Essie!"

"Thank God." She found herself surging forward with her family seconds later.

Warwick was on Cam's shoulders, and he held Emily's hand. Dorrie and Essie were clinging to Dev, with Lilly before him, and Samantha was on James's back, with Eden before him. Toby was struggling to stay abreast as adults buffeted him. Max grabbed him around the waist and hoisted him onto his shoulders. He held out a hand to Essie and she gripped it hard.

They heard screams and the wild cry of the elephant as panic urged it on.

"Right!" Max roared. Taller than her brothers, he could see over heads. "Ahead, a fence. Get to the other side!"

Her lungs screamed but she held on to Max and did not let go. A scream behind her made Essie look, and she saw a woman fall, her head hitting the ground hard. Her hesitation was brief, but that second was enough for people to crash into her.

"Essie!"

Max felt her fingers slip from his, and he turned but did not see her. His heart pounded with fear as he tried to stop. Hands pressed to his back, forcing him forward; seconds later he reached the fence.

"Can you see her, Toby?" Max lifted the boy down.

"She's beside a woman who has fallen, follow the same line and you will find her!"

He lowered the boy over the fence. "The others are up ahead, go to them now!" Max turned back into the fray.

Christ, let her be all right.

Fear gripped him, made his skin feel tight, and his body tense. She had to be all right. People crashed into him, but he felt nothing, intent only to reach Essie. His eyes swung from left to right.

"Move, you fool!"

He ignored everyone, and it was then he saw the elephant. It had changed course and was coming their way. Still some distance away, but definitely headed directly at Max. Desperate now, he waded through people. He felt her presence, then two men parted briefly and he found her on the ground. He had her in his arms seconds later.

"Thank God!" He lifted her high, turned, and ran. "Essie, talk to me!"

Her arms were around his neck, face pressed into his chest, but she said nothing. Reaching the fence, he found her brothers and handed her to Lord Sinclair. He climbed the fence and joined them.

"To the carriages," Cambridge roared, running ahead.

Max wanted to take Essie back into his arms; instead, he followed. They found the little Sinclairs standing outside as they approached.

"Get her inside." Max reached the carriage door and opened it. Lord Sinclair walked in with his sister in his arms, and he wanted to follow, but the duchess entered before him. Instead he had to stand in the doorway and watch on helplessly.

"Essie, talk to us, love." Her brother lowered her to the seat.

She was pale, and dirt ran in streaks down her cheeks. Max imagined her hands desperately dashing away her tears as she struggled to regain her feet. He wanted to growl, he wanted to roar; God, he just wanted to hold her.

"Essie, you are frightening us!" He heard the fear in the duchess's words.

"I-I am all right." She struggled to rise, but her brother placed a hand on her chest, holding her down.

"Easy now. Tell us where it hurts?"

"I am fine, I promise." Her voice was weak, and she winced as she struggled against her brother's hand. She was doing what she always did, being the strong, stoic one. The sibling who tended others. Well, to hell with that.

"No, you are bloody not!"

All eyes turned to Max.

"For once tell the truth! Tell them you are hurting, tell them how you feel." Rage was spiraling up inside him. Anger that he could not hold her, that he had not reached her before she was hurt, and at her insistence she was well. Something seemed to have snapped inside him. So he turned his anger on her siblings.

"She believes she is inferior to you all. Do you know that?"

"Now see here, Huntington—"

"Do you know that she does what she does because she believes herself unworthy of being a Sinclair sibling?" Max continued. "She never stops. Never gives a thought to herself, because she believes each of you is so much more than she could ever be!"

Shock etched the two faces.

"Did you know that after she tends very ill patients, her hands shake and she feels the fear she would not allow herself to feel while treating them? Fear that if she had not succeeded, they would have died."

"Stop it, Max." Her words were not loud, but he heard each clearly. They broke through his anger, and allowed reality to return. What the hell had he just done? He had no right to speak the way he had. No rights to Essex Sinclair.

"You should have known these things about her," he rasped before stalking away.

Finding his horse in the chaos, he rode as if the hounds of hell were on his heels, yet it was not hard or fast enough, because all he could see was Essie, lying broken and hurt as he tried to reach her.

CHAPTER 22

Five days after the Bartholomew Fair, Essie rose early but did not leave her room, instead taking her breakfast on a tray. Her face was still bruised, and they marred her body, dark and angry, a reminder of what could have been.

She had never really been unwell in her life. Not seriously. She'd experienced pain, but not this type. It had been agony, and she was quite sure she had no wish to endure so much of it again at any time in her future.

Essie remembered falling, and then the feel of people stomping on her in their panic to flee. She had tried to get to her feet, but had not succeeded until Max found her. When his hands reached for her, she'd known it was him, and that she was safe. The absolute belief that he would look after her was startling, as until that moment she'd only ever felt that with her siblings. Essie remembered him holding her close, sheltering her with his body, and for those brief moments the fear had subsided.

"Lord, what a mess." She sighed.

Her siblings had walked around her tentatively for five

days, but she had read the questions in Dev's, Eden's, and Cam's eyes. Max had told them things about her they had not known, and they wanted to ask her about his words. She could shake him for that. He'd had no right. Those were her thoughts to air should she wish it, not his.

Getting off the bed, Essie knew she could not stay in her room, or her brother's house, forever, so she decided to wash and dress, and then visit with Eden. Her sister would not pepper her with questions if she asked her not to. Actually, she would, but Essie could ignore Eden. Her brothers were more determined.

Leaving her room, Essie made it down the stairs and to the front entrance.

"And where do you think you are going?"

Looking up, she saw Dev leaning over the bannister, glaring down at her.

"Out. I planned to see Eden and help her with the nursery."

"You are not well enough."

"I want to go, Dev."

"I will accompany you then."

"No, you will not."

He started down the stairs, his long strides taking them two at a time. Seconds later he was before her. Even when she was angry with him she loved this man who had been the head of their family for so long. She could not fault him for his commitment to each of them, and they never doubted his love. Dev would lay down his life for any of his siblings.

"Do you know how much it hurts me to see you hurting?"

"I am hurting no more, Dev."

He lifted her chin, looking at her bruises. "These hurt you, but it is the pain inside you that worries me, and that I didn't see what Huntington, a stranger, did."

"His words were not the truth, Dev."

"Unfortunately, I fear they were."

Lying wasn't something Essie liked doing. Especially not to this man, when she owed him so much.

"Please, Dev. Can you not let this rest?"

"Why have you not told me how you felt? How could you believe yourself inferior to any of us, when the truth is so very different."

She did not speak, could not speak. How did she tell the man who had been so strong all his life that she had felt weak?

"Come, let's walk."

Morning sun greeted them as they stepped outside and started along the street. He took her hand as he had when they were children, and swung her arm as they walked.

"I spoke with Eden and Cam last night, and we talked about you. Like me, they were shocked at Huntington's words."

"Dev—"

"Shocked because it is you who keeps this family strong. When you are not here, we flounder about, at a loss, Essie. You are our backbone, and it saddens me that we have never shown you how important, how special you are to us."

They walked a few paces while Essie grappled with her brother's words.

"I will not lie to you, Dev. I have felt inferior. You are such strong people. Vibrant and commanding, and I... well, I cannot even sit a horse."

"Sitting a horse is easy. Taking out bullets and coming to the aid of young boys who have suffered unimaginable horrors, now that takes strength. Forgive us for not allowing you to see yourself as we always have, Essie."

"Oh, Dev." She hugged him right there on the street. "You and the others never made me feel that way. That was all my doing."

"I still should have known. The problem was that you always seemed so calm and strong. We never saw the fears or insecurities.

"Come." Dev released her, and took her hand again. "It is not bad enough that the other residents on this street think we are outrageous, we must add to their belief."

Essie smiled for the first time since the fair. Her family thought she was strong. It was a wonderful feeling.

"Promise that you will talk with me in the future, Essie. Come to me, or one of the others, when you heal someone and are scared for what could have been. When your hands shake. Let us care for you."

"I promise, and for the most it is wonderful, but there are times when I am scared that I cannot save or help someone."

They walked in silence along the street, both deep in thought.

"There is something between you and Huntington, and I would like you to tell me when it started."

And with those few words, her wonderful feeling fled.

"There is nothing between us," she lied. "I was aware of him when he came to Oak's Knoll, I will not deny that. He is a handsome, intriguing man, and at the time I thought him a wanderer with no possessions."

"Well, you got that wrong." Dev snorted. "But I know there is something between you, Essie. His behavior toward you is clear for anyone to see. Plus his concern, and the way he spoke after you were injured. That was not an uninterested man."

"Let it alone now, Dev. Please."

"You're asking a great deal from me, Essie. I love you, as does Cam. We know how broken Tolly made you feel, and it hurt us all, Essie, to see you in pain."

"I know, and I love you for it." She patted his arm.

"Did he compromise you?"

"Dev!" She had not expected that. "How could you think that, when I have just told you there is nothing between us!"

"Well, did he?" The words were gritted out. "Because I will tear him apart if he did."

"He had a bullet hole in his side, and I had Cam, Bertie, Josiah, and Grace to chaperone me. There is also the small matter of you believing your sister would be a trollop."

Dear Lord, I was a trollop. But Essie would never regret that.

"I know men," he gritted out. "They can be persuasive."

"Were you persuasive before you married Lilly?"

"I can't believe you just asked me that." He shot her a harried look.

"You asked me."

He swung her hand.

"That I did. I always forget how devilishly quick-witted you are."

"Even after all these years, brother, how foolish of you to underestimate any of your sisters." Essie saw the smile he was attempting to keep from his face.

"I love you, and hate that you may have been hurting and I did not know."

"Oh, Dev, you cannot fix every hurt, but in this case there is nothing to fix, I promise you." She felt bad lying to him, but it was for the best.

"And you are a prize, Essie. Never forget that."

"Thank you, Dev."

"For what?" He looked down at her.

"For being you. Fierce, loyal, and annoyingly protective. The very best big brother a sister could ever wish for."

"You're welcome, and I am not annoyingly protective."

"No, you are. I can only imagine you will be worse when the twins come of age."

He groaned loudly. "Please do not remind me of what is to come."

They had reached Eden's front door. Dev knocked.

"Now I'm here, I better see James. He has a map he wishes to show me. One only hopes he also has food."

"He is a duke. Should he require food, he need only ask," Essie assured her brother. Kissing his cheek, she left him to find his way to James, while she found her sister.

"Hello, sister dear." Eden yawned loudly. Dressed in a loose day dress with her hair bundled on her head, she looked lovely. "I felt the baby last night."

"Really!" Essie could not help the squeal of excitement. She hugged Eden close.

"Are you all right, Essie?"

She did not pretend to misunderstand. "Dev and I have just talked, and I feel better now, and I'm sorry you were hurt by Mr. Huntington's words."

"I knew some of what you were feeling, as we had that discussion in the carriage on the way to his warehouse, but not all. Forgive me for not realizing, sister."

"There is nothing to forgive, because the problem was mine, not yours. As I told Dev, I alone created those feelings inside me."

Eden gave her a steady look, but did not ask the questions that Essie knew she still harbored, and for that she was relieved. The morning had been trying enough already.

"Very well, but I hope in future you will come to me if you wish to discuss the matter further."

"I will, I promise."

"He would make you an excellent husband, sister."

"Who?" Essie lowered her brows, trying to look confused.

Eden opened her mouth and then closed it again. She pulled out an earplug.

"Why is my husband roaring?"

"Dev is with him, are they arguing?"

"No." Eden shook her head as she got to her feet. "I hear Mr. Spriggot's voice."

They ran to James's study, and opening the door without knocking, they entered.

Essie had always loved this room. Lined with shelves that reached the ceiling, it had once been the only room in the duke's house that had a soul. It had been here the Sinclair family had first told the duke of their heightened senses.

"Why are you yelling?"

James was standing behind his desk, and Mr. Spriggot, who was a private investigator, was seated across from him. Dev was prowling.

"Max Huntington is my brother!"

Essie felt her brother's eyes on her as she stumbled to a seat and fell into it. This could not be happening, surely. She must be dreaming. Pinching her arm, she felt the small sting of pain. *Apparently not.*

"And both Essie and I saved him! God's blood, will this bloody curse never end," Dev roared.

"Curse?" Mr. Spriggot questioned.

"My brother is speaking of my husband's family," Eden added quickly. "It seems they keep popping up when we least expect them to."

Mr. Spriggot nodded in understanding. "Yes, I understand how unsettling this must be for you all, especially considering Mr. Tolly and his relationship to the duke. After all, he was a brother, and his intentions were nefarious indeed."

Essie forced a smile onto her face at the mention of the man she had once believed she loved. She knew better now.

"Come, Mr. Spriggot, I shall see you out." Essie needed time to process what she had learned. *Max is a Raven. How is that possible?* She needed time to understand that yet another Sinclair had saved a Raven.

"No need, Miss Sinclair, I can see myself out." After bowing, the man left. Essie sank back into a chair and tried to grapple with what she had just learned.

"How wonderful for you, darling." Eden went around the desk to stand beside her husband. She wrapped an arm around his waist and held him. "And he is living so close, what could be better than that. You shall have plenty of time to become better acquainted."

For two heartbeats no one spoke, everyone tense and waiting, and then the duke let out a bark of laughter. He stepped away from the desk and pulled his wife into his arms, holding her close. "God, woman, I love you."

"I can't believe we saved yet another Raven." Dev sighed; his anger had slipped away. "Huntington, of all people." He shot Essie another look.

"Imagine how I feel about that fact," the duke rasped.

James had been through so much. The betrayal of his father, finding his sisters, and coming to the realization of just the man his father was. Now it seemed there was to be another chapter written to his life.

Max is a Raven. Dear Lord, is it really possible?

"I should have known something was off with him," James said. "From the start he unsettled me... us."

"We must tell him, my love. You both deserve this," Eden said.

"I know. But I'm not sure he will be happy about the fact. Or that he now has another brother, and two sisters."

Essie staggered to her feet. It was almost too much to take in. Max was to be in her life now, no matter how much she wished differently. She would have to return to Oak's Knoll. Being forced to face him constantly was more than she could bear.

"Shall we speak with him now, James?" Eden said.

"James, are.... Does this make you happy?" Essie had to ask the question. She remembered when she first met him, he had been cold and hard. The walls he had built around himself to keep him emotionally safe had been impenetrable, but of course, Eden had managed to smash through them. Now she thought about it, Max was the same.

"Strangely, it does, but perhaps that is because I need to know those that my father hurt. Know them, and make recompense. Of course, in Max Huntington's case, recompense is not necessary, but perhaps he will wish to get to know his new family, and if not...." James shrugged.

"We can be persistent, darling," Eden said, kissing his cheek.

"Well then, let us go and see how he feels about the fact he has acquired more family in his life."

Not more, Essie thought. *Some.* Max had always been alone. Now he was not. She hoped he was pleased about that fact, but had a feeling he would not be.

CHAPTER 23

Max woke late because again he had not slept. Only, last night's dream had not been pleasant like so many of the others involving Essex Sinclair. This one had featured a large rampaging beast that was determined to crush Essie under its feet. She had been begging Max to save her, but he could not reach her. He'd woken drenched in sweat.

"Good Lord, you look like hell."

"I usually start the day with good morning," Max growled at Edward as he lowered himself into a seat in his breakfast parlor.

"Good morning, what happened?"

"I slept badly, end of story."

"If I may suggest a warmed brandy in milk, and if that does not work, then a woman."

"My mood is not what I would term sunny this day, Edward, so bait me at your peril."

"I shall discuss business then."

"Good idea."

And they did, for an hour, and after his second cup of

coffee Max started to feel more like himself, whoever the hell that may be.

"Start the process for buying the Melton mill first, Edward."

"Of course, I shall get on it today." Edward got to his feet.

"The Duke and Duchess of Raven have called, Mr. Huntington, and request a meeting with you."

"Well now, that is a surprise," Edward said. "I shall leave you to your illustrious company. Send word if you need me."

"I will, and thank you."

Max got out of his chair. He could honestly find no reason for the duke and duchess to visit him.

"Where in this monstrosity have you put them, George?"

"The front salon again, Mr. Huntington."

He grunted something and followed his butler up the stairs.

"Mr. Huntington," George said after opening the door to the salon, "I shall bring a tray."

Did they need a tray? Looking at the solemn faces of the duke and duchess, he hoped like hell it had something stronger than tea on it, even if the sun had not risen high in the sky as yet. He had a sudden feeling of impending doom.

"Please take a seat." He waved them into chairs.

"Thank you," the duchess said. Her husband said nothing.

"To what do I owe the pleasure of your company?" Max decided to get to the point. He was not one for polite chat.

"Mr. Spriggot has just apprised me of some news that I have been awaiting for some time, Max. I came to share it with you."

Max frowned. The duke had called him by his first name, when he could not remember him doing so before.

"Mr. Spriggot came to you with news for me?"

"Not exactly." The duke got to his feet, and Max could see he was agitated.

TOUCHED BY DANGER

"I have employed Mr. Spriggot to look into a matter for me, your Grace. I am not sure why he would discuss that matter with you?"

"He did not. And there is no easy or gentle way to say this, so I will simply do so."

Max wasn't sure why he felt tense, but he was, his muscles clenched in anticipation.

"My father sired many children, Max. And I have been looking for them since I knew."

"No!" The whisper was torn from Max.

"Yes, you are my brother."

He'd had moments in his life before when shock had robbed him of speech and caused his body to shake. The night he'd learned his mother had apprenticed him on a ship at a young age had been one. When he'd received his first beating, one night later, had been another.

"Max?"

He looked up as Eden approached.

"Can I call you Max?"

He nodded, numb. Disbelieving over what he had learned.

"This is a shock for you, as it was for James."

"I-it is," he admitted. Over her shoulder, he looked at the duke... *dear God*, his brother.

"We are not a comfortable family, it is fair to say, Max. But a wonderful one to be part of. We are very happy to have you join us."

"I-I'm not sure that I can do that. I've been alone for so long, and—"

"I understand this news is overwhelming, and that is to be expected, Max. And now I am going to leave you alone with your brother, and there is one thing I can promise you."

"What?" Her eyes held his, and he saw so much compassion in the gray depths he had to swallow quickly, as his throat felt tight.

"Your brother is the very best of men."

She rose then, and kissed his cheek before going to her husband to do the same. Max watched the duke's eyes close briefly as he mouthed the words *I love you* to his wife, and then she left, closing the door softly behind her.

He'd heard the term deafening silence, but never really understood it until that moment. He had a duke for a brother. Max could not take it in.

"You also have two sisters, and I suspect I have another brother and sister somewhere out in the world."

"Are you sure about this?" His words were urgent as Max looked at the man now standing before him.

"Very."

"Christ."

"My words were more colorful, but yes, it is a shock. It seems your mother worked for my father at Raven Castle for many years. After you were born, he moved you both into a house an hour away, and then proceeded to visit her often. When you were young, he withdrew his support, and your mother took you to France."

"Your sisters—"

"Samantha was born to my father's second wife. Emily was born out of wedlock to another mistress. My father treated her unfairly, and she died, as did Emily's brother. There is a great deal more to that story, however, I think that is for another day."

"And yet you claim Emily as your own. She lives in your house."

"She is my sister, and I love her. I would never turn her away because the circumstances of her birth differ from mine."

He meant it, Max realized. Every word the duke spoke was true.

"As I will never turn from you now I know you are my brother. No matter how you feel about me."

"I don't know how I feel about it," Max rasped. "How could I? For years I believed…. God, I don't know what I believed."

"I understand." The duke's words were solemn.

"No. You cannot understand." Max's head was pounding and he could feel his control slipping. "I have been beaten, whipped, and those are just a few of the things I experienced. How the hell can you expect to understand?"

"I may be a duke, but my life has not been as you would expect either. My birthright did not ensure I lived a cosseted life."

Max snorted. "Your sister said something about that. But your worst days would be my best, your Grace," Max said. He felt odd, his body suddenly cold. Shock, he realized, it had to be shock.

"I am not here to trade insults with you, Max. This news has been a shock, and if I stay we will end up arguing. Therefore, I shall leave you alone, but understand one thing. I am now, and always will be, your brother from this day forth. Whether you wish it or not."

Max heard the door close once more. Suddenly he needed air. Need to be outside and feel the sun on his face. Walking out the door, he found George.

"Hat now!"

His butler made it down the stairs before him and handed him his hat. Max slapped it on his head and walked out the front door. He threw a dark look at the house that he now knew housed his brother, as he started down the road to the park.

. . .

Essie sat on the blanket as her three siblings ran about the place chasing the kite Warwick flew. She had walked home with Dev, both silent as they processed the information that Max was James's brother. She had then gathered up Dorrie, Somer, and Warwick, and made for the park with her maid.

Max is a Raven.

There had been something about him from the very start, but she had not known what that something was until now. Their connection dated back many years, it seemed, whether they wished it or not.

Something made her look to the left, a sensation that she could not ignore, and there he was. Max, walking with his head down, deep in thought. He now knew he was James's brother, and part of her ached for the turmoil that must be inside him. He did not look up until he was nearly upon her, and then he stopped, his eyes focused on her. So much emotion blazed from the tawny depths.

"Hello."

"Hello," he replied, but still he had not moved. "How do you feel?"

"Better, thank you."

"Your face—"

"I'm all right, Max."

"Max!" Somer's shriek drew their eyes as the little girl came barreling forward with her siblings on her heels.

"Hello, Miss Somerset."

She giggled. "Silly, I am just Somer to you."

"Hello, Somer then. And Dorrie and Warwick."

He had received a shock this morning that had very likely rocked the foundations of what he had always believed his life to be, and yet he still took the time to be nice to her siblings.

This, Essie knew, was a good man.

"Will you sit with Essie so we can show you what excellent kite flyers we all are?"

"And so humble also."

Somer poked her tongue out at Essie, then ran away squealing loudly.

"I'm sure that sound could break glass." She winced. "Would you care to sit, Mr. Huntington?"

He hesitated.

"I know, Max."

He exhaled loudly, the sound deflating him. His shoulders slumped, and suddenly she saw vulnerability. The man she'd believed indomitable was now not. He had no doubt seen and experienced more than she could ever imagine, but this... the knowledge that James was his brother, had, simply put, shaken his foundations.

"I-I…. It is almost more than I can take in."

His hands were thrust into his pockets, his eyes on her siblings, who were now all squealing and running about the place with not a care in the world. They were safe in the knowledge they were loved by many, and their futures, for now, secure. Fate would play a hand, but as yet, none of them knew in what way.

"Max, sit." Essie got to her knees and touched his hand. He jerked back at her touch, as if she repelled him... and yet the tortured look he settled on her told her differently.

"I-I need to walk," he said. "I do not want to stay here and hurt you again."

"How will you hurt me again, if we are just talking?"

He did not reply. Instead, he bowed deeply and walked away, body rigid, heart in turmoil, and Essie could do nothing for him.

She sat with her siblings until they tired, and only then did she gather everything and head for home. It was as she drew closer to Max's house that a thought entered her head.

"Take the children home, Grace. I will gather a few herbs from Mr. Huntington's garden while he is out, and return shortly."

"Can we not come with you, Essie?"

"No, I will visit Eden after, and we will return home to take tea with you. Go on now, as it is time for your lessons."

They grumbled, but did as she asked, leaving her alone on the road in front of Max's house. He had gone out, and she had not seen him return. Now was the time to gather the herbs she wanted to make Silver more tonic for his headaches.

She knocked, and smiled at the butler as he opened the door.

"Good day, I am Miss Sinclair. Mr. Huntington told me I could visit his conservatory when required and collect some herbs. Is this a good time?"

"I'm afraid he's from home at the moment, Miss Sinclair."

"Yes, I know, I saw him as he left, and he told me to come gather what I required."

Essie kept smiling as the butler's eyes passed over her bruises.

"Of course. If you will follow me, I will take you through."

"I know the way," Essie said. "Please don't bother yourself."

She hurried through the house and down the stairs. Entering the conservatory, she inhaled, feeling instantly calmer surrounded by nature... but not just any nature, the things she loved.

CHAPTER 24

Max had walked and walked, and felt no calmer. His brother was a duke. He could still not take it in. Entering his house, he found George hovering in the entrance.

"Good afternoon, George, my apologies for my curt behavior earlier."

"No apology is necessary, Mr. Huntington."

He shrugged out of his coat and handed it to his butler. He always felt calmer in his shirtsleeves.

"Tell me you have not been standing here since my departure?"

"No indeed, but I wanted to advise you that Miss Sinclair is in the conservatory. She said you had given your permission for her to visit there when she wished."

Essie was here, inside his house. Suddenly his head felt clearer, and he wanted to see her with a desperation that took his breath away.

"Just Miss Sinclair, George?"

His butler nodded.

"Excellent. See that no one disturbs us, please. Miss Essex and I have some procedures to discuss for the boys."

It was true, Max convinced himself as he walked rapidly to the stairs. Whatever Essie had given Silver had eased his headaches, and Peter was much better, and his breathing seemed calmer. In fact, Max had wondered if Essie would consider running a clinic from his warehouse while she was in London. This was a great time to discuss it. The fact that his life had just turned on its head did not matter. What mattered was that she was here, alone, in his house.

Max ran down the stairs so fast he tripped on the last, and only just managed to stop himself falling on his face.

When he'd seen her at the park, the need to take her in his arms had consumed him... she consumed him. He'd seen her bruises and wanted to kiss each one. How could one woman have created so much havoc inside him? He had just found out he was the bastard son of a duke, and right here and now, that took second place to the woman he knew was on the other side of that door.

Clenching the handle, he turned it, and walked inside the conservatory. Sun showered through the glass, creating shadows and burnishing plants. Looking around, he could not see Essie, but he could hear her. She was humming. Soft and off-key, it made him smile. Walking down the first row, he looked for her in the foliage, but when that failed he headed up the second row, and then down the third. He found her on her knees grubbing about in the dirt.

Why did he feel suddenly like smiling when his life was in turmoil? He had no rights to this woman, she could never be his, but he wanted her with everything inside him. Ached for her.

"Essie." Her name came out as a plea.

She turned, eyes wide. "Max." He watched her lips

whisper his name. "I'm sorry, I had thought to be gone before you returned, I—"

"No." He reached her in two strides. "I don't want you to go." He lifted her to her feet and settled her before him, close enough that he could smell her. Herbs, perfume, and Essie, the woman who intoxicated him.

"Max, are you all right?"

His hands held her hips, and slowly he pulled her closer until her breasts touched his chest, until he could see that her breathing was suddenly as rapid as his.

"Essie." He cupped her bruised cheek gently. "I can't stay away from you."

She closed her eyes, and he leaned in to kiss the damaged skin on her face. "I feared for you that day," he whispered. "When your hand slipped from mine, I have never known such terror."

"For me also."

Max saw the truth in her eyes. Closing his briefly, he gave up the fight. When he opened them, he took her lips in a deep kiss. Where he had touched her face with reverence, this was fierce. The need inside him demanded it, no matter that she was a lady, a sweet, gentle lady.

"I'm sorry," he whispered against her lips. "You are hurting, I had no right—"

"No." Her hands were in his hair, and he felt a tug of pain as she pulled. "Don't be gentle, I won't break. I need this." She rose to her toes and kissed him. "Have ached for this since that night at Oak's Knoll."

He kissed her again, drugging kisses that had no end or beginning. His hand moved down her back, tracing the knuckles of her spine to the lovely curves beneath. He cupped the swells, caressing and mapping the woman who had driven him insensible with need since that night he had taken her innocence.

"Essie." He breathed her name into the sweet skin of her neck. She arched, and he took what she offered. He unbuttoned her spencer and pushed it from her shoulders.

"Every time I got close enough to breathe in your scent, I was reminded of that night we made love. I smelled your gardens on you, the heat of your skin, the taste of nature. You intoxicated me."

She moaned as he kissed the tops of her breasts above her bodice. *How could something so right, be wrong*, Max reasoned as he searched for the buttons of her dress. Finding them marching down her spine, he released them, and then kissed each exposed piece of skin as he eased the garment from her body.

"I-I tried to push this aside, tried to forget what you made me feel, Max."

Max gripped the edges of her chemise and lifted it up her body and over her head.

"But like me, you couldn't." He cupped her cheeks, looking deep into her lovely eyes. "And every time we saw each other, the tension grew."

"Yes."

He let his eyes trail over every lush inch of her, stopping when he saw the bruises.

"I'm sorry I could not have stopped this happening."

"I am well, Max. Nothing is broken, the bruises will fade." She cupped his cheek and he felt himself leaning into her hand.

"Seeing you in pain was almost more than I could bear, Essie."

"But the pain was less, because you rescued me, as I knew you would."

He lost himself in her eyes. "You knew I would come for you?"

"Oh yes, that I never doubted."

He kissed her, and it was steeped with emotion. Emotion so foreign to him he struggled to identify it. Her hands worked his buttons free, and then she was pushing his shirt from his shoulders. He tried to stop her; knew in what was left of his resistance that he had to try.

"Your back is part of you and what you endured to become the man who stands before me today, Max. When I look at it, I see survival and strength. I hate that you suffered at the hands of some monster, but it does not change the way I feel about you. The way my heart beats harder when you are near, or how I find myself smiling when I think of what we have shared."

"I-I don't like people to see it." He felt vulnerable suddenly, as if she had stripped away his defenses and exposed emotions he had believed himself incapable of feeling.

She moved around him. "Let me touch you, Max."

He tensed as her lips touched his abused skin. He was sensitive there; each brush of her lips made him shudder, each soft touch of her fingers had the breath hissing from his lips.

"Essie."

"It's all right, Max." She reached around him and rested a hand on his heart. The gesture shocked him because it felt so right.

She kissed every inch of his tortured skin. Explored every welt until he no longer felt horror at what she saw, but was consumed with hunger for this woman. His body was aroused to the point of pain. Lust pumped through him.

"I cannot wait." His words were ragged.

"Then don't."

. . .

Essie was on fire, her body ignited by the man who held her. When he swung her up and into his arms, she wrapped hers around his neck and pressed kisses to his shoulders. She would not think of after, or even before. This was for now, for her and Max and the need that burned inside them.

She yelped as he lowered her onto the stone ledge. "It's cold."

He swallowed her words with another savage kiss, and then her breasts were in his hands, his thumbs strumming her nipples until her thoughts once again centered only on him. She slipped her fingers into his hair and held on as he drew a nipple deep into his mouth.

"Lord, Max," she moaned at the wonderful sensations.

He kissed each breast, tortured each nipple until she was panting. Only then did he moved lower and kiss the dew-drenched petals between her thighs. She felt the pressure inside her build until she was begging him for release. He rose and unbuttoned his trousers. She shivered in anticipation as he stepped between her thighs. Slowly he eased inside her, stretching the silken tissues until he filled her completely.

"Look at me."

She opened her eyes and saw the fire blazing in the tawny depths. Fire that she had lit.

"I have never felt this way before," he whispered. "Never needed someone as I do you."

Her lashes fluttered as he withdrew and thrust back inside.

"See what I feel for you, Essie."

"I see it."

He shuddered as she wrapped her legs around him, holding him deep inside her.

"I feel it too, Max. I have tried to fight it, but it consumes me." She touched his lips, let him take a finger into his mouth as he started to move his hips in and out of her. "I love you," she breathed, arching into him. The words ignited him as he drove into her again and again.

"Tell me again," he demanded.

"I love you!" she cried as she reached the pinnacle. Seconds later he joined her. They crested together as she held him close, both shuddering with the power of their release.

Breathless, Essie rested her head on his shoulder, and he hers. They sucked in mouthfuls of air until finally they calmed. Only then did he lift her back into his arms and move to the bench seat, where he lowered her onto his lap.

"I have never been loved before."

Her heart ached at the words.

"Will you accept it from me?" Essie looked at him, tried to read his thoughts.

"I will, if you will accept mine in return."

"Oh, Max, how could I not." She smiled up at him and wondered if there had ever before been a time in her life when she felt complete, as if all the pieces of her life had finally fallen in place.

"I was apprenticed on a ship at ten. The captain was a violent man. He beat me the very first night, and many thereafter."

"You must have been so scared." Essie rested her hand on his heart as she felt the sting of anger. "I hope this man has paid for his actions in many different ways." He had been so young to have his innocence ripped away.

Her words surprised a snort from him.

"What?"

"I thought you would weep for me, but I much prefer your anger, my sweet."

"I don't weep a great deal, unless it can't be helped."

He touched her lips, tracing each with a finger and his eyes.

"He thought to break me, but I would not be broken."

"I have heard of men like this... men who would hurt boys."

"No, love, he did not do that to me, and he told me the reason was because I was ugly. So my face saved me. But he did that to other boys, and I could do nothing to stop him until I was older and stronger."

"Tell me you hurt him as he did you and the other boys. Tell me you made him pay, Max."

"Bloodthirsty wench, aren't you?" He kissed her again.

"Tell me what you did to him when you were stronger?" Essie urged him.

"I saw him drag Edward into his cabin, and unlike me, Edward was a small, weak boy with a pretty face. He was an easy target for such a man. So I broke his door down and fought him. I then dragged him up on deck and threw him overboard in front of the crew. We were miles from land, and I knew he would be eaten by sharks or drowned."

"A fitting end, then."

"I thought so, but now I wonder if it is not he who is attempting to kill me."

CHAPTER 25

Max looked down at the woman in his arms. He saw only anger on his behalf, no pity. She looked tousled and thoroughly loved. Loved by him. He tested the words and found he liked them. She was his now, and he was never letting her go.

"What is this man's name?"

"Captain Rutley, and I have told Mr. Spriggot to locate him, so if he is alive, he will find him. I'm sure of that."

She nodded, and a long curl fell over her bare breasts. Max picked it up and tested the texture, running the strand between his fingers.

"He was very good at tracking down Mr. Tolly."

"Miss Tolly's brother?"

"Yes, the man I once believed I loved."

"Tell me what happened?"

She did, and he hated that another had held her heart, even briefly.

"So your sister nearly died, but you and your family saved her, as you did Samantha?"

She looked away, but Max wasn't having that, and pushed

her chin up so their eyes met.

"What are you hiding from me?"

"I'm scared to tell you," she whispered.

"Nothing you can tell me will make me feel any differently about you, Essex. Surely you know that now. Surely you know I love you."

"The secret is not just mine to tell you, Max."

"It is a family secret?"

She nodded. "I-I need to ask permission to tell you."

"Very well. Tomorrow I will call on your brother and ask for your hand in marriage, and I would like you to tell me then."

"Shouldn't you ask me before my brother?"

He looked down at her, this woman who entranced him. "Will you marry me, my love? Will you teach me about this love I feel for you? Teach me how to share my life with another?"

"Yes, oh, Max. Yes, I will marry you."

"Excellent, then I shall call on your brother tomorrow and then we shall talk, you and I."

"Max—"

He touched her lips with a finger. "I love you, never forget that. Whatever this is, it will not change that."

She nodded, and he lost himself in her lips and body once more.

"Tomorrow, my love. I will call, and then we will talk."

"You could come with me now. Dev will likely be home."

"No, I want to plan some things. I need to have everything in order when I call."

She nodded.

"I love you, Max."

"I have no right to love you, or expect you to spend your life with me, but I do... and we will." He whispered the words against her lips. "You are now mine, as I am yours."

"Yes."

They dressed, and then he walked her to his front door.

"George!"

"Why are you calling your butler?"

"He will walk you home, as if I did, your brothers would have questions, and I am not ready to speak with them until tomorrow."

"But I can walk on my own."

"But you will not. I will not be an easy husband, love, but I will be a constant one. Never doubt my love for you."

Her smile was blinding.

"My brothers are not easy men, so you shall not present too much of a challenge." She then gave him a cheeky smile and stepped outside. He stood and watched her until she reached her house. Only then did he go inside, with a ridiculously wide smile on his face.

Max retired early that night, eager to rise and go to Essie. He was not sure how he would be received by her brother, but he supposed at least now he had a duke on his side, and yes, in his lineage. A bastard, yes, but a noble one. He could still not take the news in.

Lying in the dark, he let thoughts come and go of the future that now seemed suddenly bright.

He woke to darkness, and the feel of a blade pressed to his throat.

"Hello, Max."

The guttural words could be from no other man.

"Rutley."

Max sat up as the pressure on his throat eased.

"You've done well for yourself, boy. It seemed everything I taught you, you have benefitted from."

"You taught me nothing." Max controlled the anger inside

him. The childhood fear was there too, but he was a man now, and this beast could no longer hurt him.

Behind Rutley, two men stepped forward. One held a candle, the other a pistol.

"Hand him the paper and ink."

"It's really not the time for letter writing, Rutley. If you are struggling, may I suggest another person could help you."

He took a moment, but eventually the insult was understood.

"I can read and write, you bastard!"

"Indeed I am, and not just any bastard, but the son of a duke, it seems."

"So you found that out, did you? I wondered how long it would take you." Rutley had lost what little hair he had, and several more teeth. He looked old and pathetic. Max wondered how he had allowed fear of the man to reign over him for so long.

"I wrote to him that I had his bastard son, and if he wanted to see you again, he'd better pay. The duke never replied."

"And that was why you tormented me. Because I was the son of a duke," Max realized.

"You were a sniveling rodent, and deserved a heavy hand. A whelp, raised at your mother's side!"

"Hardly that," Max said. "My mother loathed the sight of me, which is why she sold me to you."

Rutley stepped forward, waving the blade in front of Max's face. "Yes, she told me that when I bedded her for your fare on my boat."

"So it was she who told you I was the duke's son?" He was sure that should have hurt him more, but as he cared little for his mother, it did not.

"And now I'm making you pay for what you did to me!" Rutley hissed.

Max yawned. "I do not fear death, so have done with it."
But he did fear it now, desperately. He had Essie and a future for the first time in his life. A future he wanted with every part of his being.

"I want some money. Where is it kept?"

Max pointed to a desk in the corner of his room. "There is plenty in there. Take it and leave before I kill you... again."

"Not this time," Rutley said. "Now write down what I tell you."

"I think not." Max rested his hands behind his head, but tensed as a cunning look came into Rutley's eyes.

"Write what I tell you or, I will go through this house and gut every servant in the place."

Tamping down his rage, he did as he was asked.

"Time for a sleep."

He fought the hands that pressed the cloth to his face, but there were too many. His last thoughts were for the woman he loved.

"How is Bids' family, Essie?"

"Mother and baby are doing well," Essie said in answer to Dev's question. The toast she was nibbling on tasted like ashes in her mouth. "The father, however, is still a little shaky."

Last night Essie had delivered Bids' baby boy, and while the moment had been joyful, as it always was, she had found little joy in anything since.

Two days had passed, and still Max had not called. Essie tried not to let her family see that her heart was breaking. Tried to smile and converse when required, but inside she was crumbling all over again, only this time it was worse, and far more painful than the last.

In desperation, she had called upon Max early this

morning to ensure he was not sick. His butler had simply said that Mr. Huntington had left town for an extended visit to a property he owned, and he was unsure when he would return. When Essie had questioned as to where, the butler had said he did not know.

And that, she had realized, told her exactly how he felt about her. His declarations of love and intention to speak to Dev had been empty lies, and now she was left to pick up the shattered pieces of her heart once again. She had been a fool for the second time over that man.

But he seemed so sincere, a voice inside her head cried. Was she such a fool to believe he really did care? Had the magic they shared in his conservatory meant nothing? Was he so good at his lies that she had fallen again for a man who could not love her in return?

I love you, never forget that. Surely there was a reason he had not called? Surely he would return and tell her why he had left without word? *Please, come back to me.*

"What is wrong with you?"

Cam thumped the breakfast table with his fist, and the three Sinclairs present all jumped out of their seats.

"Wh-what did you do that for?" Essie pressed a hand to her chest, where her heart was thumping hard.

"For two days you have had a brittle smile on your face, and answered everything directed at you with a polite sweetness that is making my teeth hurt."

"Cam, we discussed this, and decided we would wait for her to tell us," Dev said softly.

"Yes, because we need to respect her wishes." Cam waved a hand at his brother. "To hell with that. I no longer wish to wait. She is hurting again." Cam's anger faded away on the last word. "I cannot stand to see it."

"There is nothing wrong. For heaven's sake, Cam, stop being dramatic."

He stared at her hard, as did Dev, and it took all her willpower not to look away.

"Your color is lighter," her eldest brother said. "Weaker, as if you are suffering in some way."

"I have no idea what you are talking about." She tried to appear confused.

"Can you not tell us what has upset you, Essie?" Lilly got out of her seat and came to wrap an arm around her. "Please, dear. Tell us what is wrong."

She felt the pressure of tears behind her eyes but refused to let them fall. Never again would she cry because a man did not love her.

"I will return in time for the births, but I want to go to Oak's Knoll, now, today." Desperation had her rising from the table. Now she had made up her mind, she wanted to leave London at once.

"Will you not tell us what has happened?" Dev's concern was written all over his face. "Who has hurt you?"

Essie shook her head.

"I cannot let you leave London in this condition, Essex, and you cannot ask that of me."

"It's Huntington, I know it is!" Cam hissed, getting to his feet. "I'm going to confront him, and I don't care if he is James's brother!"

"No, Cam!" Essie cried, but he had stormed from the room before she could do so.

"He is not there. Dev, you must go after him."

"How do you know he is not there?"

"I-I paid him a call this morning, to get some herbs."

Essie held her breath as Dev looked at her. He then shook his head, and walked from the room, leaving her to exhale... loudly.

CHAPTER 26

"Do you know, Essie, I am usually an astute judge of character, and I'm of the opinion that Max Huntington is a good man. I even would go so far as saying he would rather hurt himself than you."

Lilly had taken the seat beside hers. One of her gloved hands touched Essie's arm.

"Now that your silly brothers have gone, we can talk, just the two of us. Come now, tell me what is going on inside you, please."

"He said he loved me, Lilly." Essie could hold back no longer. It felt good to say the words after holding them inside for two days. Lilly would not judge her, nor would she track down Max and beat him senseless, as her brothers would.

"Then he does, Essie."

"But he promised to come here and speak with Dev two days ago, and yet did not. And when I went to his house this morning, I was told by his butler that he had left word he was leaving town, and did not know when he would return."

Lilly made a humming sound. "You of all people know that what we see or hear is not always the truth, Essie."

Essie thought about Max. About the moments in his conservatory when he had made love to her, when they had shared what they held in their hearts, and the secrets he had kept inside him for so long. *His words were the truth.*

"Dear Lord, Lilly," Essie said as she realized how wrong she had been to doubt him. "I have allowed my fear to cloud my thoughts. I was so afraid he had turned from me, deceived me as Tolly did, that I did not allow myself to see that he would never do that. Not Max."

"Max is not Tolly, is he, Essie?"

"No!" She surged to her feet. "He would not hurt me, Lilly. He loves me."

"Yes he does, so what do you wish to do about that?"

"We need to go to Max's house, Lilly. Will you accompany me, and help me convince my brothers not to murder the man I love... when we locate him, that is?"

Her sister-in-law smiled.

"Of course I will. Do you think I would miss this?"

When they arrived at Max's house, it was to find her brothers, James, and another man, whom Essie recognized as one of Max's employees, Edward.

"I tell you he would not simply have left without telling me," Edward was saying, and his tone told Essie he was worried about his employer.

"So you have said, but as my sister is upset, and I hold Huntington responsible—"

"No!" Essie stepped up behind her brothers. "Max is not responsible for my pain. He loves me, as I love him, and he would not have left if he had not been forced to."

She wasn't sure why she believed this now, but she did... vehemently. Max loved her.

"You love him?" Dev looked horrified. "You don't know this man, Essex."

"I do know him, and he would not have willingly left London and me. He was to come to speak with you just two days ago and ask for my hand in marriage."

"I beg your pardon?" Dev glared at her.

"I love him, and we are to marry."

"You don't even know him!" Cam roared. "His past could be littered with brutal acts and fiendish endeavors—"

"It's not. He has told me some of it, and I care nothing for that, only him." Essie knew she was right. Knew that Max was a good man.

"When have you spent time together to come to this conclusion?" Dev's words were a low growl. "If he touched you, he is a dead man."

"That's my brother you speak of, Sinclair. Have a care."

Her brothers spun to face James as he entered the fray.

"You know nothing of him, and yet you will stand at his back?" Cam looked horrified.

"He is a good man, Cam, and you said so yourself. He saved my sister, and rescues boys being mistreated on ships. He runs a house for them, for heaven's sake. Don't jump to conclusions simply because you believe he has hurt Essie. Especially when she has declared otherwise."

Cam and Dev exhaled in unison.

"Hello, family, have I missed the fun?" Eden arrived.

"You no doubt heard it all, my love." James took her hand in his. "But in short, I am attempting to stop your brothers from beating mine to a pulp when we locate him."

"I did hear it all, and have to say I side with James and Essie in this. Max is a good man. Anyone who treats our little ones with the respect and kindness he does, could not have hurt Essie, or left her after declaring his love."

"Essie does not know her mind!" Dev snapped. "She has been hurt before, and was lured by Huntington."

"That will do, husband," Lilly said calmly. "Your sister is no simpleton. She knows her own mind. And Max is not Tolly."

"Exactly, thank you, Lilly. Now stop behaving like a caveman, and let us work out where the man I love has gone!" Essie snapped.

"If I may interject?"

Essie had forgotten Edward was still standing in the doorway to Max's house, overhearing the entire discussion.

"What?" Dev rounded on him, forcing Edward to take a step back.

"I would like to say something."

Essie grabbed her brothers' arms and forced them to retreat and give the man some room.

"Let him speak."

Edward cleared his throat and adjusted his tie.

"Well, speak!" Cam demanded.

"Pay them no mind." James stepped forward and held out his hand to Edward. "I am the Duke of Raven, and Mr. Huntington is my brother."

"Ah… Max is your brother, your Grace?"

James smiled. "Indeed he is, and I find I like the idea hugely."

Edward stuttered out his name as he bowed and then took the hand.

"My name is James, Edward. If I may call you that?"

Edward nodded.

"Please ignore the two Neanderthals at my back and tell me what you wish to say?"

"Max would not leave London without telling me first. He would also not leave Miss Sinclair, if he has vowed to wed her. He is the most honest, loyal man I know."

"In what capacity do you work for him, Edward?"

"I am his steward, but we are friends. You see, it was Max that saved me when we were crew on a ship. The captain would have killed me, but Max intervened. He then threw the man overboard, and we believed he would drown."

"Surely that is not the act of a rational man?" Cam exploded.

"Captain Rutley had been whipping and beating his crew and most especially his cabin boys for years... among other things. He deserved his fate and a great deal worse," Edward said softly.

"Dear God, was it he who did that to Huntington?"

"It was, Cam," Essie said. "Max told me about it."

"Christ." Cam lowered his head. "I'm sorry, Edward, I had no right to judge him in light of what I have learned."

Edward pulled a letter from his pocket and held it out to James.

"It is written in Max's handwriting, but signed from M.C.R. Huntington. Max would never sign anything but Max in a missive to staff or me. It is his way, and always has been. He will not stand on ceremony with those who he believes are his equals."

"C. R. Do you believe he was trying to tell you something?" James said, and Essie prayed he was. Prayed it would lead them to Max, because the panic inside her was growing.

"I do. I believe that he was taken by Captain Rutley."

"And you believe he has had him for two days?" Dev questioned in a surprisingly calm voice.

"Yes."

"We will help you look for him. That will be the only way we can ascertain whether you are right, and whether he has mistreated my sister. But if he has, even his lofty brother will not be able to save him."

. . .

Max had lost count of how long he had been chained to the wooden pile. His hands were bound around the wood, and his feet shackled together. High tides had reached his neck, and he'd managed to stay upright, but he feared his strength was waning, and the next one would drown him because his legs were threatening to give out. Cold had seeped into his bones, and shivers wracked his body. His eyes kept closing. In short, he was running out of time.

He'd yelled so much his voice was hoarse, and still no one came. Only Rutley, every few hours to look down on him and laugh.

"Essie," he whispered. He focused on the vision of her in his arms that night in his conservatory.

"I love you, Max."

Did she believe he had deserted her? Did she believe he had run from her love? Surely she knew he would not do that. But then, someone had hurt her before; why would she believe his words now, so many days after he had promised to call on her brother? His disappearance would be seen as a sign of his perfidy in her eyes.

Thirst clawed at his throat, hunger gnawed at his insides, but still he felt hope. He could not have found his first and only love just to have his life snuffed out, not now.

"Help me!" He roared the words with the last of his strength. "Dear God, help me, please," he whispered, slumping against the wood.

The aches in his body were nothing compared to the pain in his heart. He felt the muscles in his legs quiver, and then suddenly they gave out, and he was sliding down the pole and into the water below. It enveloped him as he struggled to keep his head above.

"Essie," Max whispered.

"It came from over there, I tell you."

Max heard the words, and struggled to speak. "Help." It was a pitiful rasp.

"Over there!"

The sound of running feet made him fight to stay upright. Looking up, he searched the wharf above.

"Help!" he managed again, and seconds later he was rewarded with a face appearing, and then several more. He tried to focus, but could not make out the features.

"Down here," he rasped.

"Christ!"

"Max!"

It couldn't be. "Essie!" Please God, let him not be dreaming.

"Hold on, Max, we're coming!"

He struggled to his feet, using his arms to work his way back up the pole. Essie was here. Dear God, he was weeping like a babe.

He saw a pair of legs dangling over the platform above him, and then they were followed by a body, and he saw it was the duke, his brother, being lowered into the water.

"It's all right now, Max, I have you."

A jacket was lowered around his shoulders, and the warmth was bliss.

"Drink this. Just a sip."

Max allowed James to drizzle some brandy into his mouth, and it burned down his throat, but the warmth was bliss.

"Shackles," Max whispered. "Keys."

"We will get you out, no matter what it takes."

He squinted through gritty eyes into his brother's face.

"D-don't want to d-die."

"You're not dying when I've just found you," the duke snapped.

"Essie."

"Yes, and she loves you, so focus on that while I work out what we're going to do. Also on the fact that you have to convince those two idiots she's related to, to agree to letting you marry her."

He couldn't focus, and he struggled not to let the darkness consume him. He had to stay strong for her.

"Focus on my voice now, brother."

The duke was looking at the shackles on his hands.

"He's shackled!"

Several curses rained down on them from above.

"Let me down there now!"

Max heard Essie's cry, and the sound of her distress had him struggling.

"No!" He managed to put some force into the word.

"Yes, or I'll jump in!"

"God save me from hardheaded Sinclair women," the duke said.

Several more curses were heard, and Max slumped back against his brother as his legs gave out again.

"Get down here, Sinclair, I need your help!"

Max heard another splash, and suddenly Lord Sinclair had arrived.

"My sister is being restrained," he gritted out. "By Edward."

"How are we to get him out, Sinclair?"

Max slumped against his brother; even talking was beyond him now.

"The pole is too high to lift him over, and we could hurt him if we tried to break the shackles. I don't suppose any of you Sinclairs can pick a lock?"

Sinclair cursed.

"What?" the duke said.

"Send her down, Cam, we need locks picked!"

"No!" Max tried to lift his head.

Lord Sinclair bent so his face was level with Max's.

"Your beloved is a master lock picker, Huntington, so be on your guard, and don't bother locking drawers with things you don't want her to see."

"Essie?" James questioned.

"Hard to believe, isn't it. The gentlest among us could have a career as a criminal. She learnt from a man in Crunston Cliff. He made a living out of stealing, but when she saved his dog from an infection, he was devoted to her."

Max couldn't believe they were standing waist deep in water discussing this. "Do something," he whispered as Essie's legs appeared above him. "St-top her."

"Lower her," Sinclair said, ignoring him. "One thing you need to learn very quickly, Huntington, is that you can't stop my sisters from doing anything."

"I— Please sh-she should n-not be here. S-see me like this."

"Be still, brother, this is the only way." James said the words into his ear.

Max watched Essie fall into her brother's arms. Felt his heart leap that she was so close.

"Essie." Her name was barely a whisper now.

"Max." His name was torn from her, and he could do nothing to hold her, nothing to ease her fears. She moved as close to him as she could, and pressed her face into his neck. Max closed his eyes and inhaled.

"Essie, I-I love you." Through the long hours alone, he had thought only of her. His fight had been for her, them, and the life they would have together.

"I love you too."

Her lips touched his cheek, and then she pulled away, and he bit back the words to make her stay. He felt her hands on his face. "B-be strong for a little longer."

"Pick the locks on his hands, Essie, and then we can lift

him out, and you can do the ankles later. He is cold, and needs attention quickly," James said.

Max focused on her, saw the worry in her sweet face. His woman, he thought as she pulled a pin from her hair. He concentrated on that thought alone.

"Sh-she... c-cold," Max stuttered out.

"She's a Sinclair, they have nine lives, brother. Don't worry."

He felt the shackles give, and suddenly he was free and Essie was in his arms. He pressed his cheek to hers, listening as she soothed him.

"Come, now we will get you up and out of this place," James said.

It was not an easy task, as he was a big man, but eventually they managed to get everyone back on the wharf and Max was soon wrapped in several coats.

"Someone's coming!"

The duchess said the words, even though Max heard no voices.

"Everyone behind that wall," Devon said, and they hurried to do as he said. In Max's case, it was more a stumble, with James on one side and Essie on the other, tucked beneath his arm.

"Rutley," he managed to say as he heard someone speaking.

"Essie, Eden, you two stay here with Max."

The sisters did not argue, he was pleased to note. However, it did not sit well with Max that he was unable to help. He watched, helpless, as the other men drew their pistols and stepped from behind the wall.

"L-let me see," he said.

They helped him move around the wall, and it was in time to see Rutley raise his pistol. Max's heart kicked as he saw it was pointed at James.

"No!"

Rutley turned at his hoarse cry, and the distraction allowed Edward to fire. Seconds later, Captain Rutley was staggering backward, clutching his chest. He fell into the water below, and his men fled.

"Ch-check he is dead," Max said, just before his legs gave out and darkness followed.

CHAPTER 27

He woke slowly, rolling to his side. Moaning as his tortured muscles protested, Max managed to lever himself upright and swing his legs over the edge of the bed. His first and only thought was for Essie. Where was she? He ached everywhere, but the need to see her surpassed that.

Enough light filtered into the room to tell him he was not in his own bed. Where was she? As if she'd sensed his thoughts, the door opened and she walked in with a tray in her hands, and Max fought the urge to weep again. His emotions were raw and near the surface, making him vulnerable, but he cared nothing about that, only her.

"You are awake." She hurried to place the tray on a small table.

"Essie." His voice was weak. "Come here."

She did, her steps tentative as she approached him.

"Are.... Do you hurt, Max?"

"I ache for you." He took her hand and pulled her between his legs. Slipping his fingers beneath her hair, he kissed her.

Max drank from her lips. He wanted to consume her. She was like a fever in his blood.

"For so long I needed no one." He pressed his face into her neck. "But from the first night, you filled my head and heart."

"Oh, Max." Essie cupped his face, kissed every inch. "I was so scared when I realized you had been taken by that man. I love you so much."

He took her hips and pulled her closer, needing to feel her body pressed to his.

"Did you doubt me?"

He read her guilt, but she did not look away.

"I did, especially after being betrayed by Tolly. But then, when I allowed myself to think clearly, I knew that you would never leave me. That you were loyal and true, and that I had been wrong to ever doubt you."

He sighed as she gently raked her fingers through his hair.

"I knew then that you had been taken against your will."

"I would never leave you."

"I know that now. Forgive me for ever doubting you, my love."

He didn't want to let her go, but she insisted he do so.

"You need to eat now, Max, and let me rub some ointment into your sore muscles."

He watched as she walked to the tray, and then back to him. This would be his life now. She would care for him as she did others. The thought was humbling.

"You kept me alive, Essie. Thinking of you gave me the strength to stand in that water. Had it not been for you, I don't think I would have cared."

She urged him back against the pillows.

"Death has never worried me before now. But knowing that I could have a life with you urged me to stay alive."

"I believe differently, and think you would have fought death, Max. You would not have left those boys, and Edward, and all the people who rely on you."

"I-I have done things, Essie."

"As have I."

"Bad things," he pressed on, ignoring her words. "My life has been vastly different from yours, and this will make me possessive. I have never had or wanted a home, but now that I do, with you, I will not be an easy husband."

"And I would have you no other way, Max. I want you just as you are."

He let her settle the tray on his lap.

"My brothers are men like you. Strong, honorable men."

"I am not honorable." Max needed her to see that.

"You are!"

He looked from the tray to her as she snapped at him. Her mouth had firmed and she wasn't exactly glaring, but it was close. Suddenly he wanted to smile at her ferocity in believing him honorable.

"You are more honorable than many who bear that title, so I do not want to hear you say another word on the matter."

Max wasn't used to people defending him... even from himself. He found he liked it.

"Now eat, please."

She made him eat coddled eggs, cheese, and lastly a wedge of fruitcake. He chased it all down with tea, and then she removed the tray.

"Are you up to leaving the bed? James would like to see you, as he has been very worried."

"Is that where I am?"

She nodded. Max needed to touch her, so he took her hand in his.

"I remember snatches of last night. Him jumping into the

water, and then your brother. I remember Rutley. He fell into the water—"

"My brothers checked. He is now dead, Max. That man will cause you no more pain."

He nodded, relieved.

"I want to stay in this room with you, my love."

"As do I, but my brothers will soon appear and track me down if I am not where they can see me."

"They have a right to be worried, as all I can think about is ravishing you."

She snorted. "You do not have the strength."

"I'll always have the strength for that." He made to grab her, but she stepped out of his reach. "Up now, and here is a robe, as you are not up to dressing yet."

"Surely I can manage my breeches?"

She held out the robe.

"Are you to be the tyrant in our marriage then, love?" Max stepped into the robe. "Not that I mind. I have never had another watch over me."

"I had to be forceful, surely you see that, considering who I was raised with."

He snorted. "Yes, I can see it would be sink or swim in your family."

"You shall fare well." She tied the belt for him. "You are made the same way as us."

He wrapped his arms around her, ignoring the pain in his shoulders in favor of holding her. Resting his head on hers, he pressed her to his chest.

"I can't believe you picked those locks to free me."

"There is a great deal you do not yet know about me." Her words were muffled.

"Will you tell me then?"

She pulled away, suddenly nervous.

"Come, they are waiting for us."

"Essie." He tried to stop her, but she simply kept walking out the door. He followed more slowly; his legs were stiff and sore. She entered another room, and he followed, this time into the duke's study.

The ceiling was high, with the farthest wall holding floor-to-ceiling windows that made it seem as if she were stepping into the sunlight. Books lined two walls, high enough that a ladder would be needed to reach the top ones. The furnishings were of rich, deep reds and blues with woven patterned rugs scattered on the polished wooden floors. It was alive with a feast of color and light, and he had a feeling the duke spent a great deal of time here.

Standing behind his desk, his brother was watching him. Brother. The word felt easier inside his head. Essie had done this to him with her love. She'd made him more accepting.

"Thank you for rescuing me."

"It was my wife who actually located you. Will you sit, and I will tell you what happened."

He took the chair in front of the desk, beside Essie.

"How do you feel?"

"Stiff and sore, but surprisingly better than I thought," Max said honestly.

"Do you remember anything about what happened?"

Max nodded. "Most of it, the end is a bit hazy however. But Essie assures me Rutley is dead."

She gave him a gentle smile, and Max felt the ridiculous urge to sigh. What the hell was happening to him? First he'd wept, and now sighing. Love, he realized, was a wonderful thing.

"Dev and Cam went to your house to tear you apart, as they rightfully believed you had hurt their sister."

"But he did not, I was wrong," Essie quickly said.

"Reasoning is not a Sinclair strength," the duke drawled.

"No." Essie shook her head. "We're not entirely rational when it comes to people we love."

"Edward was at your house when the Sinclair brothers arrived. They demanded to know where you were, and he produced the note you'd left. He also said he believed you had met with trouble, because you had finished the note with M. C. R. Huntington."

Edward had picked up his clue.

"To Edward, this was a strange way for you to sign the note. It did not take him long to work out what the C. R. meant."

"He is a very smart man," Max rasped.

"Call for tea, James, his throat is very sore."

"I'm all right, love." He reached into Essie's lap and took her hand in his.

James smiled at the gesture, and Max was pleased to see it was genuine.

"The Sinclair brothers then calmed down enough to allow Edward to speak. Essie, Eden, and Lilly arrived, and the rest is history. It was my wife who heard you calling."

"Care to tell me how she heard?"

"And that is my cue."

Max turned to watch Devon and Cam Sinclair walk into the room with Eden.

"You're holding my sister's hand, Huntington."

"Yes," Max said, tightening the grip on her slender fingers.

The eldest Sinclair looked like an avenging angel as he glared down at Max, but he wasn't intimidated easily, having lived the life he had, so he simply glared back.

"You will call upon me tomorrow, Huntington."

"I will."

"Do you love her?"

"Eden!" Essie sounded horrified.

"More than I can ever say," Max said without hesitation.

"And will you marry her?"

"Is today too soon?"

Several Sinclairs huffed; the elder one sighed.

"Very well, but you hurt her and we'll kill you."

"Eden!" Essie looked outraged.

"No, love, she's right." Max looked at her. "If I ever hurt you, I will deserve whatever punishment your brothers mete out."

Max heard groans from the men and sighs from the women.

"Cut that out right now, Huntington. You'll make us look bad," Sinclair snapped. Stepping forward, he held out his hand, and Max took it. "Welcome to the family."

"Just like that?"

"Oh, you and I will have a talk tomorrow, but my sister will likely not speak to me again if I don't let her marry you. We are unorthodox, perhaps we should have told you that first."

Max shook his head. "Nothing would change my mind about marrying your sister, Sinclair."

"Hold that thought," Cambridge Sinclair said.

"We are different, Max."

"That I already knew." He smiled at Essie.

"Listen now, Huntington, and don't interrupt," Cambridge said. "This is a story that takes some believing."

Essie tried to ease her fingers from Max's. Fear that he would turn from her when he learned what the Sinclairs were capable of had her withdrawing. Max had other ideas. He tightened his grip.

"We have heightened senses. Mine is sight, Eden's is hearing, Cam's is smell, and Essie's is taste. Warwick, Somer, and Dorrie also have them."

Essie could not make herself look at Max as Dev continued to speak. Would his eyes be filled with horror?

"I'm not sure I understand?"

"And likely you never will. Even we still struggle to grasp it," Cam drawled.

"In 1335, Baron Sinclair saved the powerful Duke of Raven from death, and from that day onward, we, the Sinclairs have been protectors of the Raven family. Our heightened senses are, we believe, a result of that day." Eden spoke now.

Essie made herself look at Max. His eyes met hers, but she saw no disbelief, only curiosity.

"He, our ancestor, was given the title, and land at the base of Raven Mountain so the Sinclairs could watch over the Ravens," Dev continued. "You see, Huntington, your family are notoriously reckless with their lives, and needed us to ensure their line did not become extinct."

"Which they will never fail to remind you of."

Max's eyes swung to James after these words.

"They saved you?"

"Yes, Eden rescued me from drowning, and Dev when we were away fighting for our country. He then saved Lilly, who is my cousin, but also has a connection to the Sinclairs from many centuries back. Hence she has a heightened sense of touch."

"She does?" Max spun back to look at her.

"It is a lot to take in," Dev said.

Essie nodded. The breath seemed to have lodged in her throat. "D-do you believe us?" She had to ask.

"Of course. I know you would not lie to me, and yet it seems almost too much to believe."

"It takes some time to understand, brother, but you will,"

James said. "And there is no family I would rather be aligned with than this one."

"So I have a duke for a brother, and now a betrothed with heightened senses? I wonder what next week will bring?"

Essie felt the tension inside her slip away as Max gave her a gentle smile.

"Nothing would change the way I feel about you, my love. This only makes you even more special."

"Huntington, you will need to stop this right now. You are making us look bad in front of our wives."

Max ignored Dev's words, and simply looked at Essie. She saw the love he felt for her, and knew it was matched in her own eyes.

"James, can we come in now?"

Everyone turned as Samantha and Emily entered the room. The little girl looked excited, the elder nervous. Essie watched as Max got to his feet to greet them.

"Hello, Max."

"Hello, Samantha."

He held a hand out to her, and she ran across the room to wrap her arms around his waist. Essie could not stop the tears falling as Max bent to put his arms around her.

"You're my brother now."

"I know, are you happy about that?"

"I am. Big brothers are wonderful." She sighed.

"Then I shall try to live up to expectation."

Essie watched as he kissed the top of her head before straightening. His body must be sore, muscles pulling, and yet he showed no sign of it. He held a hand on Samantha's shoulder as he looked at Emily.

"Hello, Emily. Do you mind very much if I share you with James?"

The words were perfect, as Emily's shoulders relaxed slightly, and she walked forward.

"I don't mind. We're glad to have you in our family, aren't we, James?"

Max leaned forward to kiss Emily's cheek.

"We are indeed," James said, coming to join the group. "We are now four Raven siblings. We only need to find three more, and we shall rival these bloody Sinclairs."

CHAPTER 28

The Sinclair and Raven families had retired to Crunston Cliff for the births of Eden's and Lilly's babies. Everyone was staying at Raven Castle, except for Max and Essie, who were at Oak's Knoll.

Their marriage had been a quiet one in the church on Raven Mountain, with only family and a few of Max's employees to attend.

The days since had been spent getting to know this wonderful and complex man she was now married to. He had the energy of ten men, and worked tirelessly on his interests. Except now, when she was settled in his lap in the room he had set up as his office that overlooked her garden.

"You are a distraction, Mrs. Huntington."

"You need distracting." She kissed his chin and then her mouth found his lips, and it was several heated minutes later that they broke apart.

"I never thought I would want to be part of a marriage or family, but I find myself wondering how I survived so long alone, my love."

His kiss was gentle, and left her head reeling.

"Someone has arrived."

"Ignore them." He ran a finger around the edge of her bodice, but she slapped his hands aside.

"Someone could be hurt."

"I'm hurting," Max muttered, but he stood her gently on her feet.

Essie opened the door to Bertie's knock.

"A note has arrived from the castle."

She read it quickly. "Dear Lord, the babies are coming."

"What, both of them?" Max came to her side, his hand settling on her shoulder, calming her.

"W-we must go, Max. I—"

"It will be all right, my love. Take a deep breath now, and we shall gather what you need and go to the castle."

They left ten minutes later, she sitting before Max on his horse.

"What if something goes wrong?" She said the words that had been riding her since she had read that note.

"It won't."

"But how do you know? How can you be so calm?"

His arms held her tight, pressed into the hard planes of his chest.

"Essie, you will do what must be done with your usual competency, and these children, our nieces or nephews, will arrive on this earth healthy and strong."

"I'm scared, Max."

"Which is entirely natural," he assured her. "But I am here with you, so you have no need to fear."

And it was true. She was stronger when he was near. He was so much a part of her now, she could not imagine life without this man she had married.

The castle was in mayhem when they arrived. The mothers, thankfully, had been placed in rooms adjacent to each other. The fathers were pacing the hall between. Cam looked harassed.

"About bloody time you got here!" Dev roared at her, and she knew it was worry speaking.

"That will do, Dev. Essie is here now, and all will go well. But it will be even better if you stop roaring loud enough that Lilly and Eden can hear," Max said calmly. "Now go and see to the mothers, my love, and I will tend these idiots."

"I am to be a father, Max."

"I know you are, brother, but not for a few hours, I think."

She opened the door to the first bedroom on Max's words, a small smile on her face.

Many hours later, as the sun rose on Raven Mountain to mark the dawn of a new day, Max gathered his tired wife in his arms and carried her to the room the butler had made up for him.

"A niece and a nephew. But you knew that, didn't you, Mrs. Huntington?"

"Yes, and they are adorable, Max."

He privately thought they looked like wrinkled prunes, but he had not been able to mistake the jolt of delight that they would now be part of his life, and this wonderful family he had married into, as he had caught his first look at the babies.

"Isabella was my mother's name. Eden has always wanted her daughter to be named after her."

"And Lilly named her son, Mathew, after her father."

Max could hear the tiredness in Essie's words. Dark smudges marked her skin beneath bloodshot eyes. She was exhausted. Lowering her to her feet, he stripped off her clothes and pulled back the blankets.

"I need to wash."

"Tomorrow is soon enough." He urged her onto the bed.

Removing his clothes, he soon followed. Wrapping an arm around her waist, he pulled her tight into his chest. "I'm so proud of you, wife."

"Eden and Lilly did the work, I merely assisted."

She never took compliments well, but Max was working on that. Just as she was working on him.

"Max?"

"Hmmm?" Sleep was pulling him under.

"I want a baby."

He smiled into her hair as his hand moved to her stomach.

"Me too."

"Thank you for your strength," she whispered. "I love you."

"I love you too."

Closing his eyes, Max fell asleep as he did every night, with everything he wanted and needed in his arms.

THE END

TOUCHED BY DANGER

⌘

*T*hank you for reading TOUCHED BY DANGER! I hope you enjoyed Essie and Max's story. Book 4 in the Sinclair and Raven series SCENT OF DANGER is available now!

As the illegitimate sister of the Duke of Raven, Emily knows only too well how society judges a woman like her, and what a debt of gratitude she owes her family. She also knows the vital importance of maintaining independence, and how cruel fate can eclipse good intentions anytime. Certainly she's not going to let her head or heart get fooled by the devilishly annoying Cambridge Sinclair, her family's protector, and London's notorious rake... who also happened to save her life... more than once.

Cam has been intrigued by the mysterious Miss Emily Tolly for years, even though theirs is a turbulent relationship. With her family and others, she's shy and timid, but with him, she's anything but. He knows this kitten has claws beneath the quiet exterior and a whole lot of other secrets she's hiding. But her passion and intelligence draw him irresistibly to her, so when he's given the opportunity to rescue her once again, he grabs it with both hands. This rescue, though, takes the form of a hastily arranged marriage, which Cam enters into willingly for her sake and her family's. What he doesn't count on is the closer he and Emily get, the stronger their passion burns, and Cam finds himself wanting not just her body, but her heart too.

It was meant to be a dutiful betrothal from the start, but it soon becomes something more. As Emily sees the real man beneath the roguish reputation, her carefully guarded heart begins to believe and hope. Dare she trust the one man who could destroy her?

LADY IN DISGUISE

Be swept away by the romance, intrigue, unconventional heroines, and dashing heroes, by USA Today Bestselling Author Wendy Vella's regency romance series.
The Langley Sisters Series

LADY IN DISGUISE

Will her secret bring her ruin or love?

Desperate and penniless, Miss Olivia Langley is out of options. To ensure her family's survival she and her sister decide to take a drastic step - they don masks and take to the road as highwaymen. Disaster strikes when, inside the first carriage they rob, they find the one man Olivia had hoped never to see again. Five years ago Lord William Ryder had broken Livvy's heart. Now he has returned and she has a bad feeling that if anyone can succeed at unmasking her deepest secrets, it will be him.

Can a rake reform?

Will knew his return would be greeted with both joy and resentment, but after five years of hard living he was ready to come home and take his place in society. He had never forgotten Olivia no matter how hard he'd tried, and whilst he hadn't imagined she would welcome him with open arms, the hostility and anger she displays are at odds with the woman he once knew. Will is horrified to find she's living a dangerous lie and refuses his help. But now that he's back, Will is determined to do whatever it takes to protect her, and finally claim her for his own.

BOOKS IN THE LANGLEY SISTERS SERIES
Lady In Disguise
Lady In Demand
Lady In Distress
The Lady Plays Her Ace
The Lady Seals Her Fate
The Lady's Dangerous Love
The Lady's Forbidden Love

ABOUT THE AUTHOR

Wendy Vella is a bestselling author of historical and contemporary romances
such as the Langley Sisters and Sinclair and Raven series, with over a million copies of her books sold worldwide.

Born and raised in a rural area in the North Island of New Zealand, she shares her life with one adorable husband, two delightful adult children and their partners, four delicious grandchildren, and too many cantankerous farm animals.

Wendy also writes contemporary romance under the name Lani Blake.

Sign up for Wendy's newsletter
www.wendyvella.com/newsletter

Printed in Great Britain
by Amazon